THE OBEDIENT ALICE

'Bind tight a pretty girling toy,
And flog her soundly for good measure:
Submissives give the greatest joy,
For in pain they find their pleasure.'

GW00470310

THE OBEDIENT ALICE

Adriana Arden

This book is a work of fiction.
In real life, make sure you practise safe, sane and
consensual sex.

First published in 2003 by
Nexus
Thames Wharf Studios
Rainville Road
London W6 9HA

www.nexus-books.co.uk

Typeset by TW Typesetting, Plymouth, Devon

Printed and bound by
Clays Ltd, St Ives PLC

ISBN 0 352 33826 1

One

Alice Brown dropped her blazer and textbook-laden satchel and gratefully flopped down into the shade of a gnarled oak. In the distance traffic droned along the bypass, but here on the edge of Shifley Woods was a small, if slightly scruffy, oasis of calm.

The day was hot and the walk home from Wellstone High School seemed longer than usual, even with the short cut her parents did not like her taking. Still, there was no hurry. Her mother would not be home from work for a couple of hours yet.

Alice rolled over onto her back, her collar-length bob of blonde hair spilling onto the cool grass. Hitching up her skirt, she bent her knees and splayed her bare legs, opening the sweat-damp crotch of her panties to the air. Undoing the top buttons of her shirt, she eased the tension on the fabric and exposed the glistening valley of her cleavage. For a few minutes she enjoyed the cooling air playing across her skin, then her normally bright face clouded and a frown creased her brow.

Alice had just turned eighteen and was in the last few months of her A level studies. If things went as expected, she had a good chance of going on to university. It was what her parents wanted, but she was not sure it was right for her. Some of her friends had already left school and a couple had even found steady partners. Of course, she did not want to wind up in some boring dead-end job, or get pregnant by some bloke who then abandoned her, but at least her friends had made the transition to the adult world.

Alice idly caressed her body. The puppy fat of adolescence had turned into mature curves, especially her breasts, which had drawn comments in the school changing rooms. She really wanted to be treated as an adult now, but university would mean being a student for another three years. And what would she have at the end of it? A degree in English. It was the subject for people who could not think of anything more interesting. What would it get her? Surely there was something better out there?

Unthinkingly, she slid her hand under her skirt and the waistband of her panties and tickled her tight, pouting lips. In seconds warm slick fluid filled the fleshy cleft. With youthful eagerness her nipples perked up hard against the fabric of her bra.

Of course, she thought with a smile as she rubbed harder, there was always this pleasurable adult diversion she had recently discovered. But she knew there was more to life than just playing with herself. Something bold and different. A real adventure!

The moment passed, reality returned and Alice withdrew her sticky fingers from her groin.

The trouble was nothing exciting ever happened in Wellstone. It was respectably boring and terminally dull; rather like her parents. Of course, she was grateful for what they had done for her, but sometimes she just wanted to find the courage to escape from everything safe and conventional and do something really wild.

Perhaps what followed was just a coincidence from the far end of the probability curve. Perhaps someone, or something, overheard Alice's wish. Hopes and dreams can be dangerous things. There are places where a million idle thoughts and fancies gather and crystallise into something tangible, warping the fragile interplay of forces that we think of as reality and taking on a life of their own. Those who stumble upon such divergent realities learn that getting what you wished for is not necessarily the same as getting what you need.

Alice sat up with a start, pulling her shirt front closed and smoothing down her skirt.

She had glimpsed a small figure moving through the trees deeper into the wood from where she lay. Had someone been watching her fingering herself? Was it a child? Then she caught a clear view through a gap in the intervening foliage. It was only for a second, but what she saw made her jaw drop.

'Oh, jeez-us!' she exclaimed.

Momentarily she was paralysed with surprise, gaping incredulously as the figure flitted away. Then a sense of purpose returned and she scrambled to her feet and dashed after the incredible 'thing'. As she ran she thought wildly: it's not what it seems. It can't be! But she kept running because she would never be able to live with herself if she did not discover the truth.

She gained on the figure, silently thankful for all those PE classes she had reluctantly attended over the years. It looked back over its shoulder at her in alarm and she saw its face quite plainly. There was no mistake. It was what she thought it was. But that was impossible.

She called out, 'It's all right . . . I won't hurt you!'

As the figure hesitated, Alice closed the gap and suddenly she was standing right in front of it.

The tips of its ears just reached to Alice's shoulder. It wore a check jacket over a mustard-coloured

3

waistcoat. A small rolled umbrella was tucked under one arm. Old fashioned stiff white collars framed its small face. Whiskers twitched nervously. A watch-chain was slung across its chest. Its fur was white. It walked on its hind legs.

'No, no! I'm late,' the White Rabbit exclaimed, in a petulant, anxious voice.

Alice gulped as she felt the world spin around her. She pinched her eyes shut. It had to be a dream! But when she opened them again the creature was still there, larger than life, even as common sense insisted it could not be what it seemed. She half turned, looking for the hidden cameras and the people ready to shout: 'Got you!' when she would find out it was all a joke. But she and the impossible thing were quite alone. She looked back at the Rabbit, which was blinking uncertainly at her. Was it an animatronic runaway from the latest fantasy epic that somebody was filming . . . in boring Wellstone?

Alice realised she had run out of rational explanations. She could see it was not a dummy or a little person in a suit. No make-up could be that perfect, and in any case the proportions were all wrong. It was a real living, breathing impossibility straight out of the book Aunt Louisa had given her when she was eight. The book Alice had thought grotesque and rather tedious, with its silly heroine whose name she bore.

With a front paw like a small but perfectly formed hand, the Rabbit drew out a gold pocket watch and examined the dial closely. The watch face seemed to be set out rather oddly.

'I must be going,' he protested. 'I only took this short cut because I was in a hurry. I have a most important date.'

'Down a rabbit hole,' Alice mumbled automatically, even as she thought: OK, I'm talking to a fairytale rabbit, but I can handle it.

The Rabbit started. His ears twitched and he looked around anxiously, as though worried that they might be overheard. 'How did you know we call the portals rabbit holes?' he asked.

Alice blinked. 'Portals?'

'The transdimensional portals, of course,' he said, suddenly impatient. 'Now detain me no more, child.'

He turned away but Alice caught his shoulder (it felt warm and perfectly solid) and said, 'You're really going to –' she nearly choked on the name, '– Wonderland?'

'Not Wonderland but Underland!' the Rabbit snapped. 'There is no wonder, but it does lie under.'

'Wherever. This . . . Underland really exists?'

'I would hardly be going to a place that did not exist,' the Rabbit replied haughtily. 'That would be very foolish.'

'Yeah,' Alice agreed. 'Really dumb.'

Slowly the realisation penetrated her numbed mind that this was the moment she had wished for. If the White Rabbit existed then anything was possible, even Wonderland. She wanted an adventure and here was the ultimate opportunity. The notion that her parents might worry if she suddenly disappeared crossed her mind, as did the recollection that she had left her blazer and satchel behind. But those details seemed to shrink into insignificance as she was suffused by a growing sense of her own purpose. This was the moment when she would take charge of her life. To do otherwise was simply not an option. How could she ever tell anybody: *Guess what, I met a talking rabbit the other day right out of Alice in Wonderland. Where did he go? Oh, I couldn't be bothered to find out.* Of course she had to do it!

She took a deep breath. 'I want to go to Underland as well. Please.'

The Rabbit shook his head. 'That's quite impossible. Times change, you know. Underland is no place for children.'

'So what, I'm not a child!' Alice said. Even as she spoke she realised how much cleavage was showing through her half-open shirt front. Boldly she put her hands on her hips and pushed her chest out further. 'See?'

'Just because your mammary glands have filled out doesn't mean your head's full of sense as well,' the Rabbit retorted. 'Are these as soft as your brain, I wonder?' Experimentally he prodded her right breast with the tip of his umbrella.

'Hey!' Alice exclaimed, flinching away. 'Stop that!'

'So you want to jump into the unknown but you can't take a mere ferrule of discomfort?' the Rabbit said with a sneer. 'Hardly a suitable candidate for Underland. Oh, dear me, no!'

'But I am,' Alice protested. 'I'm old enough to do what I like!'

The Rabbit sniffed in disbelief. 'And take the consequences?'

'Yes!'

'Yet you are still in school dress and hardly full grown.'

'But I am. Can't you see?'

'Appearances can deceive,' the Rabbit said, waving his umbrella at her breasts. 'Perhaps these are only vanity padding.'

'They're real!' Alice insisted.

'Then show me.'

'What?' Alice said, aghast. 'Are you a perv or something!'

'As I thought, your bold words exceed your resolve. You are but a child and unfit for Underland.'

6

The Rabbit consulted his watch again. 'Now, I must be going . . .'

'No, wait!'

She realised the Rabbit was challenging her, or perhaps trying to frighten her off going to Underland for some reason. He said things had changed there, and he was certainly behaving, well, oddly. But she would not be dissuaded so easily.

Glancing around to make sure they were still alone, Alice gritted her teeth and unbuttoned her shirt the rest of the way. Heart thudding, she reached behind her and unhooked her bra, then slid the straps off under her sleeves and over her arms and let it drop to the ground. Taking a deep breath, feeling as though she was entering her own fantasy world, Alice held her shirt open wide for the Rabbit to see her naked breasts.

'There!' she said, feeling embarrassed yet strangely elated at her exposure.

Her breasts really had filled out in the last year, so that the phrase 'a pair of melons' was a crude but only slightly exaggerated description of the milk glands that rose from her slender chest. They were creamy-smooth, the upper slopes displaying a pneumatic convexity that tapered to the cones of prominent pink nipples. Unconstrained they trembled in rhythm with her excited breathing.

The Rabbit considered the pale mounds thoughtfully for a moment, then very deliberately brushed the tip of his umbrella across her left nipple, then her right. The rubbery nubs of flesh folded under the passing pressure of the metal cap, then popped up alertly again. The Rabbit teased her nipples with greater firmness, setting her breasts swaying. To Alice's dismay, her nipples began to swell and harden. There was something perversely arousing about being

7

examined like this. She bit her lip but held still. If this was a test she was not going to fail it.

'Well, these seem adequately developed,' the Rabbit conceded. 'Now, what about down here?' He began to lift the hem of her skirt with his umbrella.

'Stop that!' Alice exclaimed, stepping back quickly and pulling her shirt closed again. 'You've had your eyeful. Now let's go.'

'Patience, girl,' the Rabbit said. 'If you wish to enter Underland, you must demonstrate you are full grown as you claim. I need to test your bodily responses:

"To investigate and stimulate,
confirming you are,
in every sense appropriate." '

She blinked at the little rhyme. 'You want to touch me up? You're sick!'

'It matters not what you think of me,' he said with a shrug.

'But you can't expect me to let you . . . No way! This is crazy. It doesn't make sense!'

'Maybe it is without rhyme or reason, or perhaps cunning is in season,' the Rabbit quipped. 'Do you expect less? Underland is a mad place, as well you should know. Its laws are not your laws. To enter you must obey them, unless you are clever enough to find your own way there, as some do. The choice is yours alone.' He looked at his watch again.

Alice chewed her lip but knew she was committed. It had become a matter of pride and nerve to see it through.

Swallowing hard, she gathered her skirt up over her hips, revealing her white cotton panties. At least she was not wearing tights in the warm weather. Hooking a thumb under the waistband, she wriggled them over her hips until they fluttered round her ankles.

She stood naked from the waist down.

The Rabbit walked round Alice, peering at her closely. Her legs were shapely, with strong calves and thighs. Her hips were on the slim side, emphasising the weight of her breasts. Her buttocks, however, were well-rounded hemispheres of pale flesh, divided by a deep cleft. The Rabbit prodded both with his umbrella, testing their resilience, driving the ferrule in deep, making Alice bite her lip.

'Legs spread a little more,' the Rabbit commanded. Alice shuffled her feet wider until her panties were taut about her ankles.

'Now bend forward and hold your posterior cheeks apart,' he said.

Alice stifled her instinctive response and mutely obeyed. It seemed impossible to say no now she had gone this far. As though in a dream she bent over, reached behind her and pulled her buttocks apart, surrendering another private part of herself as she exposed the dark, crinkled pit of her anus and the pouch of her sex that swelled below it.

The Rabbit considered the new aspect of her for a moment, then pressed his nose into the humid valley of flesh and sniffed several times. Alice gave a little gasp and then, despite herself, a giggle. His whiskers tickled! The intimacy shocked yet also excited her.

The Rabbit lifted his head. 'A presentable rear aspect, I suppose,' he muttered, half to himself, 'and a not unpleasing scent. Now what about her pudendal puss? Will it purr or will it stay mute, I wonder? Let us view it from the front.'

Alice gulped but said nothing as she straightened herself up.

9

The white triangle of a bikini silhouette made Alice's loins look even more naked and exposed. Her pubic lips pouted from under a small delta of fine fluffy hair, slightly darker than that on her head, which left the delicate pink-flushed labia themselves quite bare.

'Hardly a mature growth of pelt,' the Rabbit said. He reached out a small hand and pinched a tuft, rolling it between his fingers. 'Still, it is not coarse. Are you a virgin, girl?'

Alice said faintly: 'No . . .'

'Good. Hold your lips apart.'

As though somebody else was working her hands, Alice felt them go to her cleft and pull the elastic petals of flesh open, revealing the intricate and glistening pink folds of her interior anatomy. There was the bud of her clitoris, her tiny pee hole and the tight ripple-edging about the dark cavity of her vagina.

The Rabbit rubbed his umbrella handle against the soft, warm wetness of her gaping nether mouth. Alice shuddered and closed her eyes. Blood was pulsing in her loins as instinct took over. An unexpected fluttering of pleasure made itself known and grew steadily stronger. She swayed, trying not to fall over.

Gradually the angle of the umbrella became steeper. The small knob at its tip teased her hole, nuzzling it a little wider. Then, without any fuss, it slid upwards all the way. The handle had become a dildo. Its full length was inside her. She had been penetrated.

Alice made no sound. As though in a trance she held her posture and just let it happen. Watching her closely, the Rabbit continued to work the umbrella steadily up and down.

All sense of convention and propriety forgotten, Alice only knew that it felt perversely exciting to be used like this. She was getting hotter and wetter. Her erect nipples were tingly hard. Her vulva felt swollen, her juices dripping onto the shaft of the umbrella as it pumped up and down. God, what a display she was putting on! How could she . . . how *couldn't* she? This was even better than playing with herself, or what she and Simon Gately had clumsily done that Saturday afternoon alone in his house.

The handle was working faster. She was going to come . . .

Suddenly the umbrella was withdrawn with a liquid pop. Alice blinked and gasped, feeling weak at the knees and horribly empty and cheated. 'No, please don't stop . . .' she choked out, amazed at how pitiful she sounded.

The Rabbit appeared unmoved. He wiped his umbrella across the grass to remove her juices from the handle, then regarded her with a look of reluctant approval.

'Your response was . . . satisfactory,' he said. 'You may enter Underland.' Then his nose twitched. 'But you'll have to catch me first!' he added. Then he turned and scampered away into the woods.

'Hey!' Alice exclaimed, lunging after him, only to trip over her panties and fall flat on her face.

Swearing, she pulled them back on, got to her feet and sprinted off after the Rabbit. Her shirt flapped open and her unconfined breasts bounced and bobbed freely, but she did not care. After the humiliating examination she had just endured, she had won the right to an adventure.

As Alice gained on the Rabbit, she saw he was twisting the winder of his watch as though adjusting the position of the hands. Ahead was a bank of earth pocked by rabbit holes. As the Rabbit darted towards it, one of them seemed to expand, blurring at the edges until it was a good metre across. Ducking his head, the rabbit vanished into the darkness within and the hole began to shrink once more. With a wild yell, Alice threw herself forward and plunged after him.

The rabbit hole closed behind her and all was still in Shifley Woods once more.

Alice felt a wrenching, churning sensation in her stomach as she tumbled into darkness. She was falling but there was no rush of air past her.

Confused thoughts spun through her mind.

This is crazy, what have I done? Maybe it's all a dream. I fell asleep under the tree just like Alice. That story was a dream and so is this. No, the Rabbit was real, I know he was. And all this is real too. He talked of transdimensional portals. Yes, that's what I'm in now. Simon reads science fiction and he goes on about that sort of thing. Endless universes where every sort of world exists somewhere. He said even serious scientists agreed it might be possible. But how did Wonderland become a children's story? Perhaps you can pick up impressions of other universes without knowing where they come from. Did that happen to Lewis Carroll? Or did it happen the other way and we imagined Wonderland into being? But things have changed there, the Rabbit said. Wonderland/Underland, what's it like now?

Suddenly there was light below and Alice dropped into a pile of moss and dead leaves. For a moment she lay still, looking around while she recovered her breath.

She was in a dry, earthy hollow, the mouth of which was framed by tree roots. Above her everything faded into impenetrable darkness. There was no sign of the White Rabbit. She stood up, brushed herself off and re-buttoned her shirt. Then, cautiously, she stepped outside.

A huge oak tree towered above, the largest she had ever seen. It was set in a woodland of equal grandeur. Not Shifley's straggling collection with their peeling bark and stained leaves. These were far greener and thicker, rising from a verdant carpet of moss and grass, dotted with colourful splashes of improbably perfect flowers.

Alice took a few steps along a path that led away from the base of the great oak. The air was warm, the sky was bright. Bees buzzed, butterflies flitted. There was no sound of traffic or waft of car exhaust and not a single crumpled beer can or empty crisp packet in sight. It was almost too good to be true.

She stamped hard on the ground, sending a jolt up through her ankle. She ran over to a tree and slapped its trunk until her hand stung. It was all, overwhelmingly, real. She looked back at the hollow under the tree, wondering if she should try to get back the way she came. Could she climb up inside the trunk to the portal or whatever it was? Did she need the Rabbit's watch to open it?

Alice took a deep breath. She would not chicken out now. This was the start of an adventure and she would see it through. Boldly, she walked on along the path.

After a few minutes the wood opened out. In the clearing was a two storey red brick house with tall windows, heavy eaves and steep roofs, supporting several ornate chimney stacks. Surrounding the house was a rambling garden dotted with trees and bordered by low hedges. Under one of the trees was a long table covered with a white cloth and laid with plates of sandwiches and cakes, cups and napkins and a very large teapot. Three familiar figures were seated at the table.

The realisation of who they were made Alice catch her breath, then she shrugged and smiled to herself. Who else should she expect to meet here?

'Hello,' she called out as she walked up to the garden gate.

'A visitor!' the Hatter said. 'Come in, come in and take a seat!'

It was a more civil reception than she remembered the fictional Alice getting. She went into the garden and sat down at the table opposite her hosts.

The Dormouse, the size of a pudgy child, was slumped over the table asleep as expected. After her encounter with the Rabbit, its appearance did not seem so odd.

The Hatter was not as grotesque as she remembered from the Tenniel illustrations. His nose and eyes were a bit prominent, but otherwise he was not bad looking, she supposed. The hat would have looked better at Ascot, but the cut of the coat was back in fashion again. She was not sure while he was sitting down, but she got the impression he was quite tall. The March Hare seemed only a little bigger than the White Rabbit. He was wearing a brightly coloured Hawaiian shirt and, like the Rabbit, had hands rather than paws.

Having invited her to join them, the Hatter now appeared to ignore her, as did the Hare. Watching them drink, Alice suddenly realised how thirsty she felt.

'Excuse me, but could I have a cup of tea, please?' she asked, after a minute.

'I only invited you to sit down,' the Hatter said. 'I didn't ask you to drink as well.'

'Well, can I have some tea anyway?'

'And a cake as well, I suppose,' the Hatter said.

'Yes, please.' She looked at the pile of cakes hungrily.

The Hatter shook his head. 'Quite out of the question, I'm afraid.'

'Far too much trouble,' the Hare agreed.

'Much trouble,' the Dormouse added sleepily.

'How can it be too much trouble?' Alice asked.

'Our food is too adventurous for visitors, you see,' the Hatter said.

'Too uninhibited,' the Hare added. 'It may lead to consequences.'

' 'sequences . . .' muttered the Dormouse.

Alice was beginning to get annoyed. 'Look, the Rabbit said I could come here. He tested my –' She hesitated. Did they have any idea what the Rabbit had made her do? '– suitability,' she finished lamely.

'Oh yes, come by all means,' the Hatter agreed. 'Come here, come there. But consumption is quite another thing.'

'A whole new ball game,' said the Hare.

'You mean I can't have anything to eat or drink here?' Alice asked.

'There are plenty of nuts, berries and mushrooms in the woods,' the Hare said. 'They probably won't do you too much harm.'

Alice had no idea what wild food was safe to eat back home, let alone in Underland.

'Of course, the rules allow you to sign a declaration,' said the Hatter.

'A what?' Alice exclaimed.

'A declaration saying you won't blame us if you don't like the consequences. An odd rule, perhaps, but it avoids litigation. We have our own peculiar ways in Underland.'

'So I heard,' Alice said. 'What if I don't sign?'

'Then you get hungry, or you return the way you came,' the Hatter said with a shrug. 'It's up to you.'

Alice sighed. It seemed crazy to have to sign a piece of paper before she could eat, but then what else should she expect here? 'Where can I get one of these declarations?' she asked.

'There's probably one in the house,' said the Hatter. He prodded the Dormouse awake. 'Mouse! Find a declaration for our guest.'

Muttering darkly, the Dormouse slouched into the house and returned a minute later with a scroll of paper tied with a red ribbon and an old-fashioned quill pen and inkpot. The Hatter untied the scroll and handed it to Alice.

The document was decorated with flourishes and curlicues. Under the heading: OFFICIAL UNDERLAND VISITOR'S DECLARATION it read:

> I herewith agree, that it was all down to me, and not the fault of he, she or them. Whatever may come, even a pain in my tum, I won't point and say they're to blame. Should things get worse, I'll not moan or curse, but stay silent and take what follows. Be it good or bad, I promise not to be sad, because I was already told: The rule is the rule, even if it seems cruel, and it must be obeyed to the letter. It's the Underland way, so I'll never say, it's not what I was expecting. If I don't like what I find, I won't think it a grind, knowing full well such could happen.

There was more of the same making the same point. The type got steadily smaller as it went down the scroll, which was a good two metres long, until it became almost microscopic. At the very bottom was a space for her signature.

Alice blinked at the ridiculous document. All that so she could have tea and cakes! Still it was funny in its way. And it was true, back home, that people were suing for compensation all the time. Somehow the idea must have spread here. Anyway, she was willing to take her chances. She could always refuse anything she did not like.

Carefully she signed her name. The Hatter and Hare beamed in satisfaction.

'A wise decision, if I may say so,' the Hatter said. 'It's best to get these legal details out of the way. Now we can enjoy ourselves, knowing exactly where we stand. Do help yourself to tea and cakes.'

The tea tasted fine. Alice was about to bite into a cake when she hesitated, recalling her namesake's experience with Wonderland confectionery.

'This won't make me change size, will it?' she asked, trying to make it sound like a joke.

Her hosts smiled.

'A different recipe altogether,' the Hatter assured her with a chuckle. 'I can promise you will be exactly the same size after eating these cakes. Apart from a few calories, of course.'

Alice nibbled cautiously at the cake, which turned out to be pleasantly gingery. She finished it and took another.

She sat back, feeling content, and looked around. For the first time she noticed that though the sky was bright, glowing with a warm pearly radiance, there was no sign of any actual sun. Where was the light coming from?

As she was puzzling over this, the Hatter said: 'Forgive my manners, we haven't been properly introduced. I am Busby Topper, and this is my associate, Lepus Capensis. May one enquire your name?'

'Alice Brown,' Alice said, in between bites of cake.

'*Alice*,' Topper said. 'Now that is a name that will take you far down here.'

By now feeling warm and very relaxed, Alice unbuttoned the top of her shirt.

'Do make yourself comfortable,' Topper suggested. 'If you wish to give your breasts an airing, we shall not mind in the least.'

How considerate, Alice thought. She unbuttoned her shirt all the way, letting her breasts spring loose.

'What pretty mammaries you have,' Lepus complimented her.

'Thank you,' Alice said, feeling flattered. Idly she toyed with her nipples with one hand while eating cake with the other.

Topper and Lepus applauded this feat of dexterity. 'More, more!' they said.

Alice stood up and unhooked her skirt, slipped it off and waved it over her head.

Her audience cheered.

Everything suddenly made sense to Alice. Here she could be totally free and do anything she wanted. Her panties followed her skirt and she began tugging off her shoes. In seconds she was completely naked, the air fresh on her body.

She ran and skipped and jumped around the garden, her breasts bouncing prettily. The grass was soft under her feet. She turned a cartwheel, flashing her private parts for all to see, which was both hilariously funny and hugely exciting. A warm tingle was growing in her loins and spreading through her body, reminding her of the unfulfilled arousal the Rabbit's examination had kindled within her.

Then Topper and Lepus were either side of her, holding her arms. Topper was very tall and his hands were very strong. Alice squirmed and giggled happily in their grasp.

'I think she's ready,' Topper said.

'Hot and ready,' Lepus agreed.

'Ready for what?' Alice asked dreamily.

'We'll show you,' said Topper.

They guided her round the house and through a small side gate. The back garden was enclosed by a tall fence pierced halfway round by a second double gateway.

Through her blissful haze Alice saw shedlike buildings lined up against the fence that looked a little like oversized rabbit hutches. How odd, she thought. Surely all the animals here lived in houses. Other unidentifiable constructions of wheels and posts and frames were scattered about the lawn. In the middle of these were two tall wooden posts, joined at the top by a crossbeam. Several ringbolts had been fixed to the posts, from which hung ropes and pulley blocks.

'Oh, what's that?' Alice asked, as they led her towards it.

'A device we like to try on all our special visitors,' Topper said. 'We're going to show you how it works.'

Docilely, Alice let them stand her between the upright posts and watched with detached fascination as they buckled broad leather cuffs about her wrists.

'What are these for?' she wondered.

'To hold you steady while we imprint you,' Topper explained.

'Oh, I've never been imprinted before,' Alice said. 'Is it fun?'

'Once imprinted, never forgotten,' Lepus promised.

They hauled on the ropes. Pulleys rattled, dragging Alice's arms upwards and outwards until she was standing on tiptoe. Her pectorals stood out tautly, lifting her breasts high and proud. A second set of cuffs, fastened to ropes running to the bases of the posts, were buckled round her ankles. Topper and Lepus drew on these ropes, lifting Alice's feet off the ground and spreading her legs wide until she hung like a starfish in the air.

Alice shivered in her bonds, luxuriating in the novel tension they imparted in her muscles. It was exciting to be so stretched, displayed, and open. She felt important, the centre of attention. Topper and Lepus began to examine her, and she squirmed delightedly at their touch.

'Firm and fresh,' Topper declared, feeling the weight of her breasts, then squeezing and rolling them to test their resilience. He pinched and stretched the nipples and let them snap back, causing Alice to gasp and giggle. He slid stiff fingers past the gaping lips of Alice's lovemouth and into the wet tunnel of her vagina, bringing forth a new groan of pleasure. 'She's no virgin, but she is tight, hot and juicy,' he reported.

Lepus had been examining Alice's bottom, prying apart her buttocks to reveal the secret orifice between them. He tickled the pucker of her anus, then forced an inquisitive finger into the passage beyond, making Alice give a big 'Oh!' of surprise.

'Deep-cleft and tight here as well,' he observed.

'It's always the rear with you,' said Topper.

'An entrance more suited to my size,' Lepus admitted. 'And she does have a fine posterior, though it could be improved with the addition of a tail.'

The White Rabbit appeared through the side gate and came up to them. Alice favoured him with a slightly unfocused smile.

'Look at me, I'm tied up and sexy!' she laughed.

He glanced over her bound and naked body, then turned to the others. 'Did she give you any trouble?'

'None at all.' Topper said. 'This one's a splendid specimen. Well done, Ory.'

The Rabbit shook his head glumly. 'I'm just a common procurer.'

'Not at all,' Topper insisted. 'You have a talent for sniffing out suitable girls. And the ruder you are and the more you try to dissuade them, the more they want to come here. We couldn't run the business without you.'

'Don't worry,' Lepus added, taking an oil can from its hook on one of the posts and sliding the spout into Alice's bottom hole, 'you'll get your turn with this one once we've broken her in.'

Topper rubbed Alice's cleft again and smelt the exudation glistening on his fingers. 'She's roused sufficiently,' he declared. 'We can begin.'

While Lepus brought over a wooden box step and positioned it behind Alice, Topper unhooked a bamboo cane from the post and swished it experimentally through the air. Alice watched with wide eyes.

'Oh, have I been a naughty girl?' she simpered.

Topper smiled coolly. 'It doesn't matter whether you've been good or bad anymore, Alice. I'm going to cane your pretty titties and soft stomach and pouting cunny just for the fun of it, and also to begin your education in Underland ways. And while I'm doing so, my friend is going to sodomise you . . .'

Lepus had climbed on the box, bringing his groin to the level of her bottom, and clasped her hips. Now he spread his feet and braced himself against her taut body. From under his gaudy shirt a slender, glistening bright red pizzle extended stiffly from its furry sheath. A drop of lubrication sparkled on its tip. He rubbed his member up against the pale moons of her buttocks and then into the cleft between them, questing for the oiled mouth of her anus.

Alice was frowning and shaking her head, as though trying to make sense of what was happening.

21

She tugged at her bonds, squirming in the air. 'Will I like this?' she asked uncertainly.

'You'll learn to,' Topper assured her. 'Rabbit has a nose for your sort.'

Lepus's penis forced open the tight pucker of her arsehole and slid inside, violating her most private recess.

Even as Alice gasped at the shock of the intrusion, the bamboo cut across the undersides of her prominent breasts with a thwack. The heavy globes lifted under the shivering impact, then dropped back with a tremulous bounce.

Alice shrieked with the pain of the stinging blow, then choked as Lepus thrust deeper into her rear passage. The bamboo swished across her stomach, crossing the smooth well of her navel. Gasping, Alice jerked backwards by reflex only to impale herself onto the rampant pizzle. The third blow of the bamboo was lighter, but its target was the most sensitive part of her body, swinging upwards between her widestretched thighs and onto the fleshy pouch with its deep cleft furrow, bestowing a stinging kiss on her pubic lips. Alice yelped and squirmed and twisted in her bonds, but there was no escape and her wriggling hips only served to encourage Lepus, who increased the speed of his thrusts, his hips jerking faster, reaming out Alice's rectum.

Alice threw back her head and sobbed helplessly, unable to escape the rod of flesh pistoning in and out of her backside or the searing cuts across her front, which were etching a latticework of blushing red lines into her pale skin. She was a pretty piece of flesh strung out for the amusement of her captors.

So why was a new knot of arousal tying itself in her loins? Why was her tortured cunt dripping her juices onto the grass and her clit so hard it seemed like it would burst?

Somehow her suffering was turning into something she had never experienced before. The pain was terrible and wonderful. She was being buggered, which was disgusting and horribly exciting. She had never felt so aware of her body or intensely alive in her whole life. It was raw stimulation of all her senses.

Lepus grunted and his hot sperm blossomed deep inside Alice in fitful spurts. Topper ceased his caning to allow Alice to savour the release of every drop.

After a minute Lepus withdrew his pizzle from her rear. Oil and semen trickled out of Alice's bottom hole and began to run down the insides of her thighs.

Alice groaned in frustration. She felt deliciously soiled, but she had not reached her own release. Through her tears she looked imploringly at Topper. 'Please . . .?' she whimpered.

He smiled, dropped the cane and unbuttoned his flies. A huge erect penis sprang free of the constraining fabric, the foreskin half rolled back to expose the glistening purple plum at its head.

Topper stepped up to Alice face to face. She read masterful humour in his strange features, and knew he would do exactly what he wanted with her, which at that moment seemed entirely proper. The tip of his erection pressed against her lower stomach. He was so tall he had no need of a box to stand on to reach her like Lepus. His big hands grasped her hips. He dipped slightly, his cockhead sliding down her furrow, then thrust upwards.

Alice shrieked as he penetrated her, the shaft of his penis forcing its way up her hot, slick-walled passage, stretching her wide as it went. Rabbit's umbrella had not prepared her for anything so large. Then she was filled and could take no more. She was impaled on Topper; mounted on him, fluttering like a butterfly on a pin.

Topper looked into her eyes, grasping her hair in both hands so that he saw every shade of expression as it crossed her face. Behind her Lepus picked up the bamboo and swung it hard across her soft round bottom.

Topper watched Alice's eyes bulge and her mouth gape at the fresh assault. Her buttocks clenched and her inner muscles contracted spasmodically about him as she jerked forwards. Lepus swung again, drawing a new scarlet stripe across the pale resilient flesh and making it shiver.

Alice gasped at the terrible perfection of it. She was being caned onto Topper's cock, a living sheath for his manhood, a helpless receptacle for his desire. She cried out in wretched delight as she sucked on him with her lovemouth, pulling on her arms to rub against him, flattening her breasts against his chest, working herself up and down that massive member filling her insides.

She saw Topper grit his teeth in primal delight even as she felt the thick rod twitch and pulse within her. He jerked his hips, thrusting upwards even harder until Alice thought she would be split in two. Then he ejaculated, pumping his seed into her in thick, triumphant spurts.

As her passage flooded with his come and dripped to the ground, the knot in Alice's belly finally snapped.

Hot raw release burned through her like exploding fireworks and a bursting dam of pleasure. She shrieked with the force of it. For a timeless instant nothing else mattered in the world. Then, exhausted, she sagged limply in her bonds and sank into warm darkness.

TWO

Alice gradually returned to awareness.

She was lying on her side. The skin of her breasts, stomach, bottom and genitals seemed to burn gently, tingling in waves, while her passages, front and rear, felt hot, slick and swollen. Her shoulders and back ached and bands around her wrists and ankles were sore. In all, she had never before been more conscious of so many parts of her body at the same time.

There was something around her neck. She reached up and her fingers touched a collar. It seemed to be made of leather with a solid clasp at the front from which hung a large metal ring. As she moved her arms she felt the weight of leather bracelets on her wrists which also jingled with rings. She shifted her legs and saw that the same ornaments enclosed her ankles. Odd, she thought in vague puzzlement. She had never worn anything like them before.

Memory slowly returned. The tea party, her striptease, the posts, the caning, sex with Topper and Lepus. She groaned and sighed dreamily. It had been incredible . . . hadn't it?

She shook her head, trying to clear her mind. What had she been thinking? She had been drugged, tied up, raped and beaten! Now she was collared like an animal.

25

Filled with sudden loathing she tore at the collar, but it remained fast. The bracelets on her wrists were cuffs and equally secure. She sat up with a jerk and almost hit her head on some sort of low ceiling. For the first time she took in her surroundings.

She was in a boxlike enclosure just long enough for her to stretch out flat and only a little higher than her head while sitting. The floor was covered in straw and was, like the roof, made of wooden boards. There was a sort of low shelf along one end of the room, but otherwise it was completely bare. All four walls were formed of narrow metal bars set together. Through the bars she could see Topper and Lepus's back garden, with the empty whipping frame silently mocking her.

She was in one of the 'hutches' set along the garden fence.

Alice scrabbled over to the bars and tugged at them without effect. There was a small barred door set into the front of the hutch and she shook it frantically. It rattled but remained secure. She pressed her face to the bars, eyes swivelling desperately from side to side as she tried to see somebody who might be sympathetic to her plight.

'Help!' she called out. 'I'm locked up! Please, let me out!'

'Nobody's going to let you out,' said a voice from somewhere close by. 'But you'll get used to it.'

Alice looked round in surprise, then shuffled to the end of her cage.

Sitting in the hutch beside hers, little more than an arm's reach away, Alice made out the figure of a slim, dark-haired girl. She was also naked, collared and cuffed.

'Who . . . who are you?' Alice asked.

The girl smiled. 'I'm Valerie. What's your name?'

'Alice.' For a moment she felt so faint with relief at

finding a friendly face that she was speechless. It took an effort to ask, 'How did you get here?'

'The same way you did, I guess,' Valerie said with a shrug. 'I followed Oryctolagus cuniculus – the White Rabbit. He's a busy bunny.'

'But why have they locked us up?' Alice asked, clenching the bars of her cage.

Valerie gave a dry chuckle. 'Can't you guess after what they did to you? There's a lot more of the same to come. They use us for sex and work and any kind of fun they want.'

Alice shuddered. 'Who's "they"? Topper and the Lepus?'

'Not just them. Have you read the book all this comes from? Bet you did with your name. Well, most of the people and animals from the book are here for real, only here the animals are the people. Here, we're the real animals. They even have a special name for us: "girlings".'

'There are more like us?'

'Hundreds, from what I hear. Maybe thousands. They don't all come this way, but Topper and Lepus handle a lot of the market.'

'The market?'

'Their business is catching and breaking-in new girls, then selling them on. They also do obedience training classes for girlings, like you can send dogs to. That's what this place is for. They'll break you and train you, then sell you at auction.'

Alice had been listening to Valerie's matter-of-fact explanation with growing horror. Now she buried her face in her hands, shaking her head. 'It's not true! It's a nightmare. I must be dreaming!'

'It's OK,' Valerie said sympathetically. 'I know it's hard to believe at first. I had trouble too. But like I said, you'll get used to it.'

'No way can I ever get used to this!' Alice sobbed, banging on the bars.

'You will because it's right for you,' Valerie said simply. 'They're very careful who they choose.'

'What . . . what do you mean?'

Valerie sighed. 'Look, I guess you weren't happy with your life. Feeling restless, things not right at home, that sort of thing?'

'Maybe,' Alice admitted grudgingly.

'You felt you didn't quite fit in. A little shy, a bit bossed around at times. You wanted to get away, do something wild, but you couldn't quite get up the nerve to do it?'

It was such an uncannily accurate description of her feelings that Alice couldn't deny it. 'Yes.'

'And you like sex.'

Alice managed a weak smile. 'Yes, I do.'

'And then, just by chance, hah!, you met the Rabbit. He needs a bit of persuading but eventually agrees to bring you here if you pass his test, 'cos Underland's no place for children, right?'

'That's . . . about it.'

'So he got you to strip off and touched you up and you loved it!'

'It was so . . . humiliating!' Alice protested.

'But be honest, you still loved it. I did,' Valerie admitted unselfconsciously. 'Anyway, you get here and walk right into the Mad Tea Party. In ten minutes you're dancing about starkers –'

'They drugged me! The cakes –'

'That was just to loosen your mind and stop you putting up a struggle. You knew what was happening all the time. It didn't change your response deep down. Being tied up and caned and screwed front and rear was the biggest turn-on you ever had. I saw it all. You came so big you passed out. They even had time

28

to collar and cuff you before they put you in there. Face it: this is the place for you.'

Alice shook her head. 'It can't be true! I hate what they did to me. I hate being locked up like this!'

'That's just habit talking,' Valerie assured her. 'It's how you were brought up to think. How could any decent girl admit she gets a serious kick out of bondage and kinky sex? But it's in your genes somewhere, and Ory can sniff that sort of thing out. Trust me. I've talked to other girls and it's always the same way. It starts bad, but it's going to be the best thing that's ever happened to you.'

'No!' Alice shouted. 'It's not true. I . . . won't let them do this to me. I'll get away . . . somehow.'

Unexpectedly, Valerie nodded and smiled. 'Of course you'll fight it. You can get high on all that fear and shame and resentment, because you know you're going to be broken in the end. Then you can enjoy surrendering even more. Then the guilt cuts in and you start working yourself up for the next time. You'll see.'

Before Alice could reply, the door of the house opened, and Topper and Lepus emerged.

'Just let it happen,' Valerie whispered quickly. 'Enjoy yourself!' Then she crouched on her bed of straw in a subservient posture: head down and bottom up.

The odd pair walked right up to Alice's hutch and peered in at her. Alice shrank away, covering her breasts and pubes with her hands in a sudden rush of embarrassment. She saw that Topper was now hatless and in shirtsleeves. Like Lepus, he now wore a broad leather belt, from which hung keys, a riding crop and a length of chain.

'So you're awake at last,' Topper said. 'Time to begin your training.'

Alice mustered as much defiance as she could manage. 'You can't keep me here like this. It isn't right. Give me back my clothes and let me go right now!'

Topper laughed and Lepus exclaimed in mock dismay, 'Let a fine girling like yourself go? Now why in Underland should we do that? Besides, we have the law on our side, girl. You agreed to be our slave.'

'What?' Alice said. 'That's not true. And anything I did while I was drugged doesn't count.'

'Oh, this was before you touched one of our uninhibited cakes,' said Topper. 'You signed the declaration of your own free will, did you not?'

A horrible suspicion began to creep, over Alice. 'B . . . but that was just so I could eat and drink . . .'

She realised that Topper was carrying the scroll she had signed, rolled through so that it showed a section near the bottom. He held it up against the bars so she could see and pointed.

'You should always read the small print,' he said with a broad grin.

Alice could just make out the tiny lines of type:

. . . diverse potions I herewith allow, for any purpose and by anyhow, may upon my person be administered. When placed under sexual duress, by every orifice which I possess, I may freely and often be entered. Neither will I mind, a beating on my behind, even if it afterward turns rosy. By chain, rope or strap I'll happily be bound, also gagged to ensure no sound, of protest ever escapes me. Make me a slave, strictly teach me to behave, all this I willingly submit to . . .

'All perfectly legal in Underland law,' Lepus assured her smugly.

30

As Alice gazed at the words in disbelief, a shiver passed though her, accompanied by a perverse tingle of anticipation in her loins. She'd signed herself into slavery. They could do anything they liked with her . . .

Lepus slid a long board out from its resting place under the raised floor of her hutch. Clear of its runners, the board folded down to make a ramp, crossed by thin slats for grip. Producing a key, Topper unlocked the hutch door.

'Out,' he commanded.

'Please . . . my clothes,' Alice begged feebly.

'Girlings don't wear clothes in Underland,' Topper said bluntly. 'Nor do they speak out of turn. Now move!'

Trembling with shame, Alice obeyed.

She found that she could just pass through the small door on her hands and knees. As her head emerged, Lepus caught her collar ring and snapped the end of a chain leash onto it. Like a dog she was made to shuffle down the ramp, her hanging breasts bobbing and swaying, and then onto the grass. She felt so naked and exposed in this humiliating posture, acutely aware that anybody could look at her bared breasts and rolling buttocks, and all that was displayed between them.

'Remain on your hands and knees,' Topper told her. 'This is your first lesson. You're just a girling now, and that's where you belong. Everybody looks down on you and you look up at them, if they permit it. Understand?'

Alice didn't answer quickly enough. Topper unhooked his riding crop and slashed it across the convenient target of her out-thrust bottom, adding a fresh stripe of scarlet to the pink flush it still bore. Alice yelped and said shrilly: 'Yes – I understand!'

'Master', Topper corrected her. 'I am your master, Lepus is your master.'

'Yes, Master. Sorry, Master,' Alice whimpered.

'Kiss our feet and address us properly, so you will remember,' Topper commanded.

Miserably, Alice obeyed, kissing the shiny toes of Topper's boots and the tops of Lepus's furry hind-paws. Each time she choked out, 'Master . . .'

'Now stay,' commanded Topper, and Alice sank her head to the grass.

The two began discussing her training programme over her head as though she was invisible, or rather, that her opinion was of no importance. That was the truth, really. An image of how she must look to them came to her: pale, naked, leashed, on all fours, just like an animal. That was what they would make her – a girl-animal. Was there no end to her degradation?

As if in answer, Lepus idly began to rub the tip of his crop up and down the cleft of her pubic pouch, where it pouted from between her thighs. Alice whimpered, then groaned in disbelief as she felt the warm wet flush seep between her nether lips, called forth by the rasping of the knotted leather. Her nipples, which moments before had been shrivelled and cold, pulsed with renewed life. How could she be aroused by this? But she was. She could not help herself.

'A chain and ring to keep her down to begin with?' Lepus was saying. 'Stimulate her cunny at the same time?'

'A capital idea,' Topper agreed.

Lepus looked down at Alice and laughed.

Alice was pushing her bottom back and forth in tiny jerks to increase the friction of the crop between her labia. When she realised they had seen her, she froze again. But it was too late.

'It seems she has acquired a taste for the leather already,' Topper said.

Lepus lifted his crop and sniffed its tip, darkened with Alice's juices. 'We've got a hot one here and no mistake. She's going to bring a good price on the block.'

'Then let us get started,' said Topper.

They led Alice, shuffling along on hands and knees, over to what she had taken to be a garden table, set at one end of the line of hutches. Closer to she saw that it was a workbench of heavy, grey-weathered timber, with several hooks, rings and dangling chains bolted to its sides and top.

Heart pounding, she was made to climb up onto the bench and lie on her back. With practised efficiency, her masters stretched her out, dragging her hands together over her head and securing her cuffs with snap links, then spreading her legs wide and fastening them in the same way. They pulled a chain tight across her belly and hooked it into place. They bent her knees and turned her legs outwards, forcing them almost flat against the bench top, then drew chains across the insides of her thighs to hold them in place. Alice shivered at the cold bite of the metal links as they cut into her soft flesh and whimpered as the big tendons of her groin were stretched to their limits.

In seconds it was done and she lay in enforced immobility, the natural resistance of her straining body held in check by the unyielding bonds, its posture now shaped by forces beyond her control. The hills of her breasts, capped by the hard pink cones of her nipples, quivered like jellies. The swell of her stomach was deeply incised by the chain cutting through it. Her pale mound of Venus, exposed as it never had been before, rose over the diverging slopes of her wide-parted thighs and was crowned by its own wispy soft pubic thatch. The soft-lipped bowed cleft that cut through the mount gaped pinkly, exposing its intimate glistening ribs and furrows.

As Alice trembled in her shackles, a drop of exudation trickled from the lowest reach of her slit and ran over the narrow bridge which separated that orifice from its close neighbour. Alice's anus had been opened by the stretching of her thighs and now gaped like a tiny mouth caught in an 'O' of surprise. Into this the trickle of fluid ran. Topper observed the display with interest.

'She's certainly lubricating well, indeed, she oils her own rear passage,' he said. 'I think she can take all the stimulation we can give her. Let's put a nipple bar on her as well.'

From what was evidently a storage shed, Lepus brought out what looked like a large tin of paint, together with several smaller items and laid them on the bench. Wide-eyed and fearful, Alice tried to twist her head round to see what they were. She felt as though she were on an operating table, about to have some unknown procedure performed on her. The sensation was different from when she had been strung up on the frame. Now her mind was absolutely clear, she knew with stark certainty that she had never been so nakedly open or helpless before. Every nerve in her body seemed to be tingling and she was overwhelmed by a dreadful fascination about what was to come. What would she have to endure? It was all so horribly . . . exciting?

Topper picked up a short slim metal bar with a large ring set in the middle and small, toothed spring clamps at each end. He bent over Alice's taut body, clasped and squeezed a breast so that its engorged nipple stood up high, and slipped a clamp over it. Alice gasped as the metal teeth bit into her flesh but she did not protest, knowing that it would serve no purpose. When both clamps were in place, their teeth not quite breaking the skin, Topper pulled on the bar now linking her breasts. Her nipples stretched, tugging her breasts out into fat cones. Alice stifled a whimper of pain. Topper let the bar snap back, leaving her nipples pulsing hotly within their new restraints.

The weight of the bar rested on the plump cushions of her breasts, pinching them together to form a cleavage even as she lay flat on her back. What would the boys back home think to see those 'tits', 'melons' and 'bra busters' they had so admired bared and bound, their nipples clamped and standing rigidly to attention? She gulped as the image sent a renewed thrill of perverse excitement coursing through her.

While Topper had been attending to her breasts, Lepus had climbed onto the bench between her widespread legs. He was holding a black rubber dildo with a ring set in its base. With his small dextrous hands, he pried the soft lips of Alice's nether mouth open wide to fully expose her vaginal tunnel, and slid the head of the dildo up her. When it was lodged in place, he began twisting the ring in the dildo base which was swivel mounted. Alice gave a shudder as she felt the head of the device swell within her. A screw mechanism inside the dildo was forcing the soft rubber outwards as it drew in its tip. Alice groaned. She was being stretched wider than she ever had before! What was worse, as the dildo contracted, it pulled the base and twirling ring deeper inside her. Lepus stopped and gave an experimental tug, but the dildo held fast, jammed in place between the ribs of her passage.

Meanwhile, Topper had opened the tin of paint and dipped a brush into it. Moving to the head of the table he said, 'Hold your hands out, fingers together.'

Alice obeyed, and he proceeded to paint her hands all over up to her wrists with some viscous black, glistening fluid. Whatever it was seemed to dry in seconds to form a thick, rubbery coating. Alice tried to pull her fingers apart but they were held fast, as though rubber gloves had melted onto her hands. Topper then briskly applied more of the solution to her knees, shins and over her toes. Alice realised it was intended to protect her skin while she was on all fours. But how long would that be for?

They freed Alice's legs and arms, only to clip them together using short metal rods with ring holes cast in their middles and snap-link ends. A length of chain was run from her wrist links to her collar, and a second from wrists to the ring of her nipple bar. They drew her legs up and clipped a longer chain onto the rod between her ankles, then ran it up her body, passing it through the ring now deeply embedded in her vagina, up to her breasts and through the bar ring that hung between her nipples, then clipped it to her collar.

Releasing the rest of her bonds, Topper lifted Alice off the bench with a casual display of strength and dropped her onto her hands and knees on the grass. It was now impossible for her to stand or even straighten her legs. The long chain running from ankles to collar was not long enough. She could lie curled up on her side or stay on all fours, but that was all.

'Move!' Topper commanded, flicking his crop across her buttocks.

As she was driven across the grass Alice discovered the new degrees of torment and stimulation her chains induced. She could only move her arms and legs a short way and her motion was awkward and uneven. Every shuffling 'step' seemed to jerk the chains fastened to her nipple bar or pull the links running through her cleft. Now she understood the reason for her peculiar and intimate attachments. The torment of her most sensitive parts every time she moved would serve as a constant reminder of the completeness of her bondage.

They stopped her by the side fence in front of a pile of roughly trimmed sticks, of the size that might make firewood kindling.

'You are to move these over there,' Topper told her, pointing to the opposite fence where a small lean-to shingled roof protected a stack of logs.

It was a menial task presumably designed to teach her basic obedience, but Alice could not see how she could accomplish it. She could not carry the sticks with her fingers encased in their rubber coating, nor scoop them up in her arms, restricted as they were.

Then she understood.

She was being taught what it meant to be a girling, to be reduced to the status of an animal. She would not be expected to use her hands. How appropriately degrading.

'Yes, Master,' she said simply.

Steeling herself, she crouched down and carefully picked up a stick in her teeth. Now she noticed all the sticks had tooth marks about their middles. How many other girls had been put through this same challenge before her? She lifted her head to see Topper and Lepus exchange nods of satisfaction, then turn away to attend to some other task. They did not warn her of the penalties for slacking. There was no need.

Alice started off, weaving her way between the strange devices set out on the lawn. She reached the far fence and carefully dropped the stick beside the logs, then turned back for another. At the best speed she could manage, she estimated the round trip would take her at least a minute. From the size of the pile, she reckoned the job might take a couple of hours.

And they would be long hours!

Every movement made her more acutely conscious of her tormenting bonds. The clamps of the bar hanging from her nipples pinched and stung as her heavy breasts swung like udders beneath her, and if she shuffled her hands too far forwards, the chain from her wrists to the bar gave them an extra painful tug. Meanwhile, the long chain from her collar to her ankles worked back and forth through her vaginal ring and the channel of her cleft, the links rubbing and teasing her already swollen clitoris. She was aware of its every movement, and shamefully conscious that the links were already glistening with her lubrication. How bad, or how good, would it get?

She reached the pile of sticks and picked up another in her teeth. As she turned about she managed to yank her nipples painfully. Her reflex flinch jerked the chain hard though her cleft, causing her to shudder in guilty delight. This was going to be torture!

Desperately she tried to take her mind off the clash of pain and pleasure within her. Without slowing her steady pace, she watched Topper and Lepus as they moved about the garden. They were opening up more of the hutches and releasing their human captives. Soon six girls, including Valerie, were kneeling on the grass. All were young, attractive, naked, collared and cuffed as she was.

After a few minutes' discussion, Lepus escorted two of the girls into the house, driving them on with flicks of his crop. They scampered in front of him on their hands and toes, holding their prettily rounded bottoms up for his delectation. Meanwhile Topper began placing the remaining girls on various pieces of apparatus about the garden.

Two girls, both brunettes of similar height and build, had their wrists clipped together into the small of their backs. From the storage shed, Topper brought out leather bridles, fashioned for human use and complete with bits and blinkers, which he fastened over their heads. He then positioned the girls on either side of a thick wooden post which had long hinged arms extending at various heights from it. A chain from their collar rings ran to the post itself, preventing them from moving more than a few steps away from it. Topper extended and positioned two more arms in front of each girl, one before their breasts, the other behind their bottoms. On the end of each arm was a vertical board which bristled with dozens of sharp nails that had been hammered through so that their tips projected clear. There was only a hand's breadth between them and the soft flesh of the tethered girls.

Topper touched some control on the post and it started to rotate. There were two muffled squeals of pain as the rear nail boards swung into the girls' buttocks. Each started quickly forwards, lifting their knees high with each step in the manner of trained show horses. But they dared not get too far ahead of the rear pad or else their bouncing breasts would be impaled on the board before them. They had to maintain an exactly even pace in time with the rotation of both the pole and each other.

Alice's stomach knotted at the sight of them. An image came into her mind of the two girls in the future – harnessed like ponies to some sort of cart, each trotting along in perfect step. They were being turned into docile, submissive slaves. Was that her destiny? What would it feel like to live only to serve, to suffer pain or pleasure at somebody else's whim?

Anger briefly flared within her as she realised how foolish she had been. She should have got away when she had the chance, but instead she had signed that declaration thinking it was a joke! She had taken what Topper and Lepus said at face value because they were being so obstructive. They had virtually told her what the cakes would do. The Rabbit had used the same method. She would have become suspicious if he suggested she visit Underland, but instead he had been rude and difficult, making her even more determined. They had let her play right into their hands. Perhaps she deserved what happened to her now. No! She was not a slave, not like the other girls. Somehow she would escape.

As she shuffled back and forth she watched Topper take a redhead with very pale skin to a solitary post, which had a long rounded peg of wood jutting up at an angle from one of a row of holes in its side. He pulled the girl's arms over her head, wrist cuffs together, and hooked them to a ring bolted high up the post. She stood on tiptoe facing the post with the peg digging awkwardly into her stomach until Topper's large hand clasped the cleft of her buttocks, his fingers sinking into her groin, and heaved her up and forwards. She whimpered as the peg found its destined hole and slid up her vagina. Then she was hanging against the post, squirming her hips about the shaft that impaled her. Topper pulled her legs wide apart so her feet left the ground and clipped her ankle cuffs to rings set in a horizontal beam bolted to the base of the post.

Now the girl was suspended just from her wrists and the peg on which she was skewered, her body forming a shapely inverted 'Y'. Topper patted the clear soft roundness of her bottom, then stepped back and briskly administered half a dozen lashes with his crop, the sharp cracks ringing about the garden. Each brought a yelp of pain from his victim, followed immediately by a moan of pleasure as her buttocks contracted and she jerked herself against the post, driving the peg even deeper. One by one, the fresh red stripes glowed starkly into being on the pale flesh. Alice watched each one applied with helpless fascination, even though she knew next time it might be her mounted so cruelly.

When he was done, Topper patted the girl again and spoke a few words in her ear: 'When I come back, I want to see that peg soaked in your juices, understood?'

'Yes, Master.'

She was left to hang trembling against the post and experience whatever joy or despair her helpless posture allowed. Alice shuddered as she tore her eyes away, recalling her own response while she had been filled with Topper's cock and Lepus had wielded the bamboo cane on her backside. (Was that only an hour ago?) Even under the influence of the uninhibited cakes, how could she have pleaded for it? Was the red-haired girl going to be transported to the same heights of shame and delight? And why was her own lovemouth pulsing hotly?

Now there was only Valerie left to be placed. As Topper led her past, Alice saw her new friend properly for the first time.

Valerie had a beautiful slender figure with nice legs and a neat pink bottom. She carried small, perfectly rounded breasts capped with little brown pointed nipples high on her chest. Her pubic delta was as dark as the page-boy bob of hair on her head. Her face was oval and nose slightly snubbed. Deep-set dark eyes looked out over pale cheeks with quiet intensity. She bore an expression of serene resignation, as though to say: Yes, I know I shall suffer, but this is how it is supposed to be.

Topper secured Valerie by her wrists and ankles between two posts a little taller than she was, spreading her arms and legs but leaving some slack in the upper set of chains. The tops of the posts were linked by a horizontal metal rod with a knurled wheel set in its centre. The ends of the rod engaged with vertical pulley wheels set in the top of each post. Hanging from these by thin cords on the outside of the posts were cylindrical weights, which fitted like pistons in the tops of two tall upright, thick glass tubes. Currently the cords passed over the pulleys and hung limply on the inside of the posts. On their ends were spring clips similar to the ones clamped around Alice's nipples. Topper gathered up these clips and fastened them to Valerie's small hard teats, so that the cords formed slack curves.

Beside the posts, on a heavy piece of board, stood a waist height vertical brass tube formed out of two telescoping sections, capped with an open rubber nozzle ring. Rubber hoses snaked from the base of the tube to the bottoms of the glass cylinders.

Topper positioned this odd device between Valerie's spread legs so that the tube top nuzzled at her bottom cleft. He then pressed the top section of the tube down as though against the resistance of an internal spring, positioned it carefully, then let it rise again. Valerie's eyes widened and she gave a little gasp as he slid the tube nozzle past the mouth of her anus and up into her rectum. When it was deeply embedded in her bowels, Topper stepped back with a satisfied nod and turned the wheel on the linking rod.

This must have released a friction brake on the cords, for the weights immediately began to sink down into the cylinders with a hiss of escaping air. As they did so the slack was taken up from the cords fastened to Valerie's nipple clamps. Alice stifled a gasp of sympathy. The bar clamped to her own nipples was uncomfortable enough, but if the weights descended all the way to the bottom of the cylinders, Valerie's breasts would be stretched upwards and outwards to an agonising degree.

But Valerie was already bending her knees and squatting down firmly on the shaft lodged within her. There was a flatulent escape of air, but Alice saw the weights slow the speed of their descent. Valerie straightened, accompanied by a sucking sound, then pushed down again. The weights stopped falling and began to rise slightly.

The brass tube was an air pump linked to the glass pistons. As long as Valerie could force enough air into the cylinders she could prevent the weights falling and so pulling on her nipples. But it was obviously hard work driving down the pump head so intimately lodged in her bottom hole. The effort showed in her face, together with transient gasps and blinks in time with the almost comic sounds it made. Valerie's own anus formed the closure of the pump head, and Alice saw her buttocks clench and stretched muscle ring squeeze tight about the tube top in an effort to keep the seal complete. But it still slipped slightly in and out of her as she moved, losing a little compression each time. Air leaked both ways past this living valve to further torment Valerie's efforts, blowing and sucking at her bowels, which must have been a disturbing if not painful sensation.

Yet she pumped away, triumphantly lifting the weights back up to the top of the cylinders. For a few seconds she was able to rest, hanging limply from her wrist chains and even flashing Alice a smile of satisfaction.

Alice was so hypnotised by the sight that she forgot where she was. The crack of Topper's crop across her bottom reminded her.

'Sorry, Master!' she yelped, cowering down on the grass.

'Hmm. Perhaps you need some additional motivation,' he mused. 'Do you think what's being done to these girlings is cruel? Speak the truth!'

'Y . . . yes, Master.'

'Very well. When you have finished your task, their lessons shall end also. Do you understand?'

Alice gulped. 'Yes, Master.'

'Go, then!'

Back and forth across the garden Alice went as fast as she could move. Her shoulders, back, hips and thighs began to ache, then throb, then fill with hot needles. The taste of wood filled her mouth and the muscles of her jaw began to tighten. In the warm air she felt the sweat gathering between her shoulder blades and trickling down her spine. Her fringe was plastered over her forehead and she blinked and shook sweat from her eyes. Some found its way between her bottom cheeks to sting her anus and chain-sore cunt lips.

Sweat was lathering the other girlings as well. She could smell it and the musky aroma of their helpless arousal every time she passed close by their straining bodies. It glistened on the two brunettes as they continued their high-stepping circles, mingling with the bloody pinpricks on the breasts and buttocks. It shone off the pale, red-striped bottom of the red-haired girl as she hung from her straining arms and grinding hips, masturbating herself on the peg that transfixed her. Rivulets ran between Valerie's small, proud breasts and bejewelled her dark pubic bush and pink vaginal lips beneath, which gaped every time Valerie squatted down on the pump shaft, now oiled with her secretions.

Alice's eyes kept coming back to Valerie: her pretty face creased with effort, her teeth gritted, yet not looking at all resentful of the ordeal she was enduring. How could she accept such treatment?

Alice shuffled on, her body now screaming for relief, but knowing none would come until she was done. She ran her tongue over salty lips and longed for a drink. She marvelled that while her mouth was dry, she could produce so much lubrication from her swollen, pulsing, chain-cleft vagina, which teased her with its readiness. Was sex more important than comfort for her?

Gradually, numbed by pain and repetition and confused by her induced desire, her mind wandered. She had to accept that she was humiliated yet aroused by her situation. Perhaps, if she simply ignored the shame and did what she had been told, it would go easier for her? Maybe she could make a sort of bargain with herself. All other responsibilities had been stripped from her along with her pride, leaving only obedience. Do not make a fuss. Enjoy it. That was what Valerie had said.

Finally, Alice found herself staring at the place where the pile of sticks had been. It was empty. She looked around but could see no more. Oh, she thought muzzily, I've finished. Then she collapsed onto her side into semi-consciousness.

Alice was roused an unknown time later by the Dormouse standing over her and splashing water over her face. She looked round the garden and sighed with relief when she saw that the posts and frames were no longer occupied.

'Drink this, girling!' he commanded, thrusting a tin mug of water at her.

She took the mug clumsily between her rubber-sheathed hands and drank it down. Only then did she realise somebody had taken the dildo, long chain, nipple bar, wrist and ankle rods off her. She could stretch and straighten her legs! She squirmed ecstatically on her back, groaning as she worked the cramps from her knotted muscles. But despite the pain, Alice felt an unexpected glow of satisfaction at having accomplished her task without faltering. Perhaps she had more determination within her than she thought.

The Dormouse was looking down at her with considerable interest, his whiskers twitching. It seemed unlikely that a creature with the basic facial anatomy of a rodent could leer, but he managed it. He took the empty mug from her hands and then with unexpected agility, sat himself astride her, his fat furry body coming down heavily on her chest. Alice gasped, half winded, raising her arms to push him off. Then, biting her lip, she let them drop placidly to her sides again.

'That's right, girling,' the Dormouse said with a toothy grin, 'you remember your place.' He squeezed his legs together, bunching up her breasts so he could admire her cleavage. 'Great tits. I could really have fun with them.' He rocked back and forth and Alice saw a bright red pizzle tip protruding from between his furry thighs. 'Maybe later . . .'

He scrambled quickly off her chest, then turned and kicked her in the side. 'Move, Melon Tits!' he said impatiently.

On her hands and knees, still aching all over, Alice was herded across the grass. She saw a regimented row of female buttocks facing her, striped and glowing from the crop, with their dark quim mouths peeping from between their thighs. All six of the other girls were kneeling on their hands and knees before a low wheeled frame supporting some sort of deep metal tray. The Dormouse prodded her towards a space at the end of the row where a short length of chain dangled from the side of the frame. He pulled her head down and clipped this chain to her collar ring. Alice found her head now hung over a bare metal trough. She twisted round to look down the line of girls and found Valerie was secured beside her.

'Are you all right?' Alice asked anxiously. 'That pump-thing didn't hurt you too much?'

Valerie smiled. 'My arse and nips are a bit sore, but that's nothing new round here. It was more like an exercise to keep my hole stretched but tight.'

Alice looked at her in amazement. 'How can you talk about it like that? It was so cruel!'

'Like I said, you get used to it.'

'You mean, you really enjoyed it?'

'It was a turn-on,' Valerie admitted. 'You won't believe how juicy you can get having a rod up your rear. The only trouble with being chained is that you can't finish yourself off. But then, they like to keep us a bit frustrated. Makes us livelier when we get a proper screwing. But what about you? Trying to impress the masters? Nobody's ever shifted the sticks as fast as that before.'

Alice suddenly felt embarrassed and a little foolish. 'Well, Topper said he'd let you all down as soon as I'd finished. And I thought you looked so uncomfortable . . .' She trailed off.

Valerie looked surprised, then smiled warmly at Alice. 'That was really nice of you. I'll tell the others. But actually we don't want saving from anything. We don't expect things to be easy. We've got used to it that way. You'll learn too.'

Alice shook her head. 'Not me. I'm going to get out of here . . . somehow.'

Valerie grinned. 'We all said that at first.'

Alice took a deep breath. 'Wait and see.' She looked about her as well as she could. 'What's going to happen now?'

'We're going to be fed, of course. You didn't think they'd let us sit at a table? We're animals, remember? Pigs at a trough. Except don't insult pigs round here, because one day you might find one giving you a good porking!'

There was laughter from the other girls along the line. Alice found herself joining in rather light-headedly.

The Dormouse came out of the house carrying a large steaming pot, which he tipped out into the trough under their noses. It was a sort of thick vegetable stew. It smelled surprisingly good, reminding Alice how hungry she was. But while Valerie and the other girls dipped their heads and began to wolf down their portions, she held back. To eat like this seemed too degrading.

Valerie turned a cheerful, gravy-smeared face towards her. 'Don't worry about getting messy. Eat up. Look, I'll lick you clean afterwards if you do the same for me, OK?'

Hesitantly, Alice dipped her head and, as neatly as she could, picked up a piece of potato between her teeth and swallowed it down. Yes, it did taste good.

As they were eating, the Dormouse brought out what looked like a metal watering can with a funnel attached to the spout and carried it behind them.

'Our chance to pee neatly,' Valerie told Alice between mouthfuls. 'Make yourself go if you can, otherwise you could wet yourself in the middle of some lesson and the masters might get annoyed.'

Relieving themselves while eating, Alice thought. That was what animals did. But then, that was the probably the idea. She had an image of what they must look like from behind: a row of bare bottoms and pouty little cunt mouths with golden fountains spurting obediently from them in turn. When she felt the rim of the funnel cup her mound, Alice screwed up her eyes and tried not to think of anything as she let her bladder go loose. Another little milestone on the road of humiliation.

They had to lick the trough clean before the Dormouse would tip out the pudding: apple and custard. It was even messier to eat than the stew but by then Alice no longer cared. It was while they were finishing this that a bell sounded from outside the double gates at the bottom of the garden.

The visitor was a squirrel. He wore a bowler hat, dark jacket and bow tie, and was leading a naked girl on a leash. The girl had dark hair tied back in a ponytail, heavy breasts and a chubby bottom. Topper and Lepus both came out to converse with the squirrel. The girl was pinched, prodded and generally examined. Finally an agreement was reached. The squirrel raised his hat and departed, leaving his girling slave, now looking distinctly unhappy, in the care of the professional trainers.

Topper considered her thoughtfully for a moment, then glanced over at Alice and the others, still chained to their feeding trough. 'Bring them over so they can watch. It will be a useful lesson.'

While Topper and Lepus brought out new items from the storage shed, the Dormouse released the girls, slipping a single long chain through their collar rings as he did so. He led them over on their hands and knees, the chain pulling their collars close together and forcing them to scramble along after him in a jostle of naked flesh. He clipped the end of the chain to a ring on the side of the bench so they could watch every detail of the plump new girling's treatment.

A large barrel, some lengths of hose and other items were being prepared. First they fitted the girl with an odd sort of rubber face mask, trailing buckles and straps. It had an angled section of metal tube protruding from the front, so that one end stood upright while the other was forced into the girl's mouth. The mask also had an integral nose clip, a little like a diver's mask, which Topper ensured was pinched about her nostrils. Once in place, the mask was firmly buckled about her head, leaving her wide and uncertain eyes staring out past the erect tube.

Topper bent the grotesquely masked girl forwards over the bench while Lepus picked up a length of thick hose with a screw thread about its tip. Prying apart the girl's fleshy bottom cheeks, he screwed the end into her anus, to the accompaniment of several muffled squeaks and squeals. When it was firmly in place the hose hung from her rear like a tail.

She was turned round and bent backwards over the bench. Parting her legs and spreading the thick outer labia of her golden-crowned pubes, Lepus positioned a length of thinner hose ending in a small ovoid metal funnel, so that it cupped the folds of her inner lips. Spring clips fixed to the sides of the funnel pinched her peachy flesh tightly, holding the device in place.

Awkwardly trailing her new attachments, the girl was made to climb, with evident reluctance, into the upright barrel. Reaching inside, Lepus fed the ends of the two hoses out through bung-holes set low down in the side of the barrel. Topper produced its lid, which had two notches on opposite sides of the rim. Holding her hands before her, the girl's wrists were put into the notches and secured with straps extending from blocks set on the inside of the lid. Holding the barrel lid over her head like a fantastically broad-brimmed hat, Topper guided the girl's mask tube through a bung-hole.

With some prodding she was made to kneel down in the barrel. They had a last glimpse of her anxious eyes, then the lid closed over her. Lepus snapped spring clips across the rim and the girl was sealed inside with only her hands and the trembling spout of her mask tube projecting through the lid. Topper produced an ordinary conical funnel which he slotted into the mask tube. Taking out a small screw-topped can, he poured a measure of some oily substance into the funnel.

The girl's hands clenched and there came a muffled bubbling sound from inside the barrel. Unpleasant as it was she had no choice but to drink the oil down to keep her breathing tube clear.

Topper turned stern eyes towards the huddle of girls, who had been watching the procedure with rapt attention.

'This girling has been secretly eating more than her ration,' he explained. 'Now she's grown too plump for her owner's liking he's asked us to reduce her. After flushing out she'll stay in the barrel on bread and water until she learns to be grateful for what she's given. Unless you want the same treatment, you'll show proper gratitude at all times, do you understand?'

He was answered by a sincere chorus of: 'Yes, Master!'

While he was speaking, the Dormouse had placed a couple of small buckets under the ends of the hoses where they projected through the sides of the barrel. As they watched the barrel began shaking and they could hear muffled moans from within. The girl's hands began clenching and unclenching desperately.

51

The groans rose to a forlorn shriek, then subsided into choking sobs. A stream of urine ran out of the smaller tube into the bucket, while brown sludge plopped heavily out of the larger tube.

Alice felt Valerie tremble by her side. 'All the time she's in there she won't even be able to touch herself,' she whispered huskily.

Alice sensed they all shared that sentiment and she shuddered in sympathy for the plight of the girl imprisoned in the barrel, being purged through the tubes so intimately secured to her body. Yet beneath the fear was an insidious curiosity about what she felt having her labia clamped and a hose screwed into her anus, and wondering how well they might cope in her place with the dreadful need that would inevitably grow with the passing hours.

For the first time Alice smelt the helpless excitement of slave girls identifying with the degradation of their own kind; the uncontrollable scent exuding from the exposed lovemouths of the warm female bodies beside her. Then she realised, to her shame, that she herself was contributing that most intimate perfume.

But the lesson had been well given.

Alice silently vowed she was going to be a perfectly obedient slave. She would submit to anything rather than that sort of isolation. Then, at the first opportunity, somehow she would escape.

Three

The squirrel's girling was taken out of her barrel after a second purging and two days living on a mush of bread and water poured down her breathing tube. She looked thoroughly miserable and completely cowed by her treatment. After the hoses had been removed and life had returned to her stiff limbs, she was put in a treadmill to work off the excess fat she had accumulated.

Naturally the treadmill was no simple exercise machine. It resembled a giant version of a wheel one might find in a hamster cage. The girl was put inside with her arms pulled behind her and the axle of the wheel passing between the small of her back and her crooked elbows. Her lower arms were then drawn forward and a chain passing across her stomach between her wrist cuffs held her in place.

An ingenious device ensured the girl maintained a steady pace. A zigzag frame of wooden battens, looking rather like the letter 'Z', was mounted on the axle between the girl's elbows. The 'Z' frame pivoted about the joint between the upright and lower horizontal arm so it was free to rotate. The upper horizontal passed over the girl's head and from its end hung a pair of heavy spiked balls, dangling just in front of and below her out-thrust breasts. The lower horizontal arm had a broad rubber paddle on its end, which brushed against the slats lining the inside of the wheel. Hanging over this arm was an iron weight that could be slid forwards or backwards as desired.

Once the girl was set running, the rubber paddle was lifted by friction against the wheel slats, so rocking the frame forward and moving the spiked balls away from her. But if the counterweight was moved back along the arm away from the axle, the friction of the paddle was unable to support it and the frame tipped backwards, bringing the spiked balls up and back towards the girl's breasts. She had to run harder to turn the wheel faster to increase the paddle friction and so restore balance. The rapid slap of the paddle against the wheel slats became a rasping burr that filled the garden.

Topper and Lepus showed the arrangement to the girl's owner and told him she would be suitably slimmed-down in about ten days. Between her own training sessions Alice looked at the unfortunate girl: her pounding legs sent shivers through her sweat-streaked chubby buttocks, and she wondered if anybody would ever employ such drastic measures to reduce weight back in her world. A few people might be just desperate enough to try it, she decided.

Not one to let spare energy go to waste, Topper connected one end of the treadmill's axle through chain gears to crankwheels supported on an iron frame. The wheels drove two piston rods on each side of the main shaft and angled downwards at about thirty degrees. On the ends of the rods were ribbed rubber phalluses. Dawn and Linsey, the two brunettes Alice had seen being trained to run in step on her first day in Underland, were brought out and placed kneeling on the ground on either side of the crank frame, their bottom clefts in line with the phalluses. Their faces were pressed into the grass and their wrists were pulled under their bodies where, together with their ankles, they were clipped to a single spreader bar. The piston rods were screwed out until the heads of both phalluses had penetrated the girls' tight anus rings.

The gears were engaged and the phalluses began to pump, first one side and then the other. Groans rose from the girls as they were alternately buggered by the relentless mechanical sodomiser.

Alice was chained to the crank frame with her wrists clipped behind her and an oil can in her mouth, with orders to keep the phalluses well lubricated. Every few minutes she bent forwards and carefully dripped some oil onto the steadily oscillating ribbed shafts and watched as they forced their way deep into the girls' rectums and then withdrew, making little sucking sounds on the way.

Since Alice had spent much of that morning hanging on the impaling frame being urged to pleasure herself by Topper's crop across her bottom, this made a pleasant change. It was a simple task she could perform without risk of punishment, giving her time to think, to plan a possible escape. What she did not expect was how distracting the regular motion of the crank could be.

Gradually she became hypnotised by the sight of the girls' muscle rings expanding and contracting about the ribbing of the phallus shafts and the expressions passing across their faces as they rested their cheeks on the grass: a frown of discomfort as they were stretched open, a grunt as the phallus reached maximum penetration, then a strange almost wistful look as it was withdrawn.

Of course Alice knew it was an outrageous indignity to impose on anybody, but by the logic of

Underland it was perfectly reasonable. A girling had to learn to accept the repeated use of any orifice and, if Lepus was any example, the local animals preferred using girls' rears, so they had to be well exercised.

A dew was forming on the lips of Dawn and Linsey's flushed and pouting vaginas that was not entirely due to excess lubricating oil. Alice could smell female excitement and arousal and realised with a shiver that she was in the same state. After her morning on the impaler she thought she would have been incapable of responding to any sexual stimulus, but apparently this was not so. She was getting a perverse thrill from watching the two girls suffer, if suffering it was, and she now found herself wishing she could ease her own tension. Had she no pride left, she wondered? On the other hand, after so many enforced orgasms, why not for once take a little pleasure when she wanted? It would make no difference to Dawn and Linsey's treatment one way or the other. But with her hands cuffed behind her back it was impossible even to touch herself.

She was groaning with frustration until her eyes fastened onto the large rounded hexagonal nut securing the protruding end of the crankshaft to its socket in the supporting frame. It was turning smoothly against its washer. Dare she do it? She looked about the garden, but there was no sign of any of their masters. If she stood on tiptoe . . .

Carefully she eased herself forwards against the end of the frame until the nut nuzzled into her cleft. Its blunt angles churned and rippled her labia as it spread the fleshy lips, still tender from her earlier exertions, aside. Dawn and Linsey were both looking up at her with knowing grins. Emboldened she pushed harder against the nut so that it ground into her swollen clitoris. Yes, that was heavenly! Just a minute of this and –

Crack!

A riding crop burned across her bottom.

An unseen hand took her by the hair and jerked her away from the sodomiser frame so that she was sent sprawling, landing heavily and dropping the oil can. A large furry foot pressed down on her head, holding her face to the ground.

'Taking a little unauthorised pleasure I see,' said Lepus. 'Does the sight of buggery excite you that much, girl?'

'Yes, Master. Sorry, Master,' Alice whimpered, unable to deny the simple truth.

'Well never let it be said we do not reward our girls' enthusiasm . . .'

Ten minutes later Alice was secured in Dawn's place, gasping and sighing as a phallus reamed out her rear passage. She could not complain since this was one punishment she really had brought upon herself. Perhaps it was what she wanted, or at least was being conditioned to need. Was that a frightening thought? Whatever the reason, she came twice before she was released.

Though her treatment at the hands of Topper and Lepus was strict, at least they never inflicted cruelty for its own sake, Alice conceded. The Dormouse, however, was undeniably a mean and spiteful character, resentful that he was only a cook and general assistant and not a full partner in the business. Whenever he had the opportunity he delighted in taking out his frustrations on the girls. Though he was not allowed full use of them, he found other ways to satisfy himself.

The next afternoon was warm and still. Some of the girls were in their hutches, resting aching limbs and well-used passages while the others were fastened to various pieces of training equipment, undergoing their assigned exercises. Topper and Lepus were out on business and the garden was quiet, apart from the occasional jingle of chains and moan from a girl surrendering herself to another orgasm.

Alice was curled up on the soft straw in her hutch, nursing her sore vagina and tender buttocks. She was feeling completely drained. That morning the shaft running off the treadwheel had been fitted with a pair of geared counter-rotating disks set in tandem. Each disk was tipped with splayed rubber prongs and was set close enough to the other for them to intermesh. She had been made to stand between the two disks so that their prongs pressed into her groin and buttock cleft, and then her feet had been chained wide to the ground. When the disks were engaged with the drive shaft they began to turn upwards into her body, and she had been unable to resist the little rubber fingers as they relentlessly brushed and teased her orifices.

From her hutch she could see Valerie mounted on the machine just as she had been earlier, except that Valerie was obviously not fighting the pleasure it gave her. Alice wondered once again at Valerie's cheerful acceptance of her status as a sexual slave, even as she worried about her own increasingly rapid response to sexual stimulation. Even without the assistance of uninhibited cakes, she was climaxing more often and more intensely than she could have imagined possible. Was that the result of her training, being in Underland, or simply her natural capacity for pleasure coming to the fore?

The Dormouse banged on the bars of her cage, jerking her out of her reverie. He had a small wheelbarrow outside loaded with tools and a bundle of straw.

'Got to clean your hutch out, Melon Tits,' he said gruffly. He walked round and peered into her toilet pot, which hung under the hole cut in one end of the low board shelf which ran along one end of the hutch. The pot could be removed from outside through a small port let into the bars that was far too small for a girl to get through. On the other end of the shelf rested a folded blanket, a washing bowl, a pitcher of water, tin mug, soap, flannel, small towel, toothbrush, toothpaste, comb and toilet roll, which at that moment represented the sum total of Alice's possessions.

'You want to use this again before I empty it?' the Dormouse continued.

Alice didn't particularly, but already knew better than to displease the Mouse. She sat herself over the hole in the board, well aware that her bottom and pubic lips pouted below her before his eyes looking in from outside. Of course he enjoyed her discomfort and watching the water hiss from her. When she was done she wiped herself off, dropped the paper into the pot and made to get off.

'Stay put,' he commanded. Put your hands through the bars. Might as well keep you there while I clean up.'

Biting her lip, Alice squeezed her hands back behind her through the bars and felt him clip her cuffs together. Of course he could have tidied her hutch this morning while it was empty, but this way he got to exercise some personal control over her.

She waited while he took away the pot and cleaned it out. Before he put it back in place he reached in through the slot in the bars and pinched the soft swell of her vagina. Half expecting it she stifled a yelp.

'Nice plump puss, Melon Tits,' he observed. 'I bet a lot of people are going to enjoy themselves in there.'

His fingers toyed with the round pucker of her bottom hole, one slipping past the ring of muscle as it suddenly relaxed. Alice gasped, surprised how easily she had let him in. A new reflex she had learnt. The sodomiser had done its work well. 'And in there, too,' he continued. 'Really nice and tight and hot, that feels. A dormouse could have a lot of fun up there. One day, girl, one day . . .'

He let the sentence trail off ominously, withdrew his finger and replaced the pot. He pulled the ramp out from under the hutch, unlocked the door and ducked through. He was small enough to stand upright inside. With a rake and broom he cleared out the old straw, then brought in a bundle of fresh straw which he scattered around. When he had finished he brushed off his whiskers and turned to look at Alice, who was still fastened in place squatting on the toilet hole.

Her knees were pressed together and she was bowed forward as far as her wrist cuffs would allow to avoid catching his eye. However, this caused her breasts to hang full and free from her body. At the sight the Dormouse's eyes glittered. He stepped up to her, caught her by the hair and pulled her head up so that she had to look at him.

'All done, Melon Tits. Aren't you going to thank me for giving you all this nice clean straw?'

'Thank you, Master,' Alice mumbled.

'You can do better than that, Melon Tits.'

'Thank you for giving me all this nice new straw, Master,' she said loudly.

'That's better, Melon Tits. You don't mind me calling you "Melon Tits" do you?'

Alice bit her lip. 'No, Master.'

'Because you have got big ones, haven't you?'

'Yes, Master.'

He dropped her head and reached down with his small hands. Clasping her breasts he squeezed and kneaded them together as though working dough, forcing her to rest with her face pressed to his furry fat belly.

'Lovely big tits,' he said dreamily.

She felt something warm and wet pressing against her cleavage, then sliding into the valley of flesh. At the same time the Dormouse began to jerk rapidly against her. The little beast was tit-fucking her! But there was nothing she could do but let it happen. She was a girling. It was her purpose to be used. What else did she expect?

Hot sperm spurted out from between her breasts and splashed down her stomach, a few drops falling on her pubic bush. With a satisfied grunt, the Dormouse let her go and stepped back, his bright red pizzle still dripping. After admiring the glistening trail he had made down her front he stepped forward again.

He was going to make her lick him clean! she thought in sudden horror.

But instead he took hold of her hair and bent her forward, using it to wipe off his member. Then he gathered up his tools, climbed outside, locked the door and moved on to the next hutch. He left her there, cuffed and soiled, for an hour – only freeing her shortly before Topper and Lepus returned.

The sign read:

TOPPER AND LEPUS
Girling Brokers
All Breeds Handled
Training & Obedience
Lessons
(Ring for Service)

It hung from a tall gibbet-like post set beside the double gates at the front of the house, past which meandered the lane which led to the village of Margrave. The sign was suspended by means of thick ropes running through pulley blocks and then down to a windlass bolted to the base of the post, allowing the sign to be raised and lowered as required. Access was necessary because the sign was double-sided, with the individual letters cut out and mounted on thin horizontal metal rods. These two panels formed the opposing sides of a narrow box frame, one face of which was hinged so it could open like a door, allowing just enough room between them to sandwich a girling. One was put in the sign first thing in the morning and hung there to lunchtime, when she would be taken down and replaced with another who stayed there until the fall of the twilight that passed for night in Underland. All through the daylight hours, therefore, the sign held imprisoned within it a living example of Topper and Lepus' trade.

This morning it was Alice's turn.

As the sky brightened she had been taken from her hutch, fed and watered, a special ball-gag had been strapped into her mouth, and then she had been led outside the gates. The empty sign had been lowered to the ground and opened up. She had lain down inside it spreadeagled, and her wrist and ankle cuffs had been clipped to the inside corners of the frame. Two angled brackets extended down from the top of the frame with just enough room for her head to rest between them. Screw clamps passing through these brackets were tightened against her temples, ensuring she kept her head facing forward and her chin up while she was on display.

The front panel of the sign was closed and locked shut, pressing her tightly into what was effectively a narrow cage. This caused her pale, crop-striped buttocks to moon from between the third and fourth rows of letters on the reverse of the sign, while her heavy breasts squeezed out between the bars supporting the second and third rows of letters on the front. Even with these constraints, being in the sign would have been preferable to many of the indignities and subtle tortures being inflicted on her sisters on the other side of the gates, were it not for a few small but significant details.

The ball-gag filling her mouth was made of metal mesh in two screw-together halves. Inside it was a piece of uninhibited cake mixture, which slowly dissolved against Alice's tongue and trickled down her throat. The dose was much less than she had taken on the day of the tea party, but it was enough to make her feel warm and tingly inside and increase her awareness of every part of her body.

Then there was a slot in the base of the sign frame between her spread legs through which ran the rod on which the bell hung. The ring at the top of the rod hung from a hook mounted on the end of a thick plug, incised with a deep screw thread, which was literally screwed into the tight pucker of Alice's anus. When hoisted aloft the whole weight of the rod and solid brass bell hung from her rear passage. An additional torment was provided by a short arm extended forwards from the top of the rod between her legs and curved up to the exposed lips of her vagina. Once the sign was vertical, the bell hung free, swinging in the wind or with slight movements of her own body as she tried to ease her posture. This caused the bristling, rubber-pronged ball mounted on the end of the arm to part the soft folds of flesh and tease her clitoris unmercifully.

Alice tried to remain still, but it only took a few jerks of her hips to set the sign swaying. Then the momentum of the bell and the influence of the cake seemed to take over and she had to respond to it: working the prongs up and down her dripping cleft deeper and harder, unable to resist masturbating herself even though she hung in full view of anybody who might come along the lane.

If a caller rang the bell while she was building to a climax, the vigorous motion of the swinging bell combined with the movement of the anal screw inside her, would be enough to bring her off, and the visitor would be ushered through the gates to the accompaniment of her desperate gag-muffled groans and gasps. After each climax, while she sagged limp and blushing in her bonds, she marvelled at the way her pride and inhibitions were being stripped from her. What better advertisement could there be for Topper and Lepus's skill and ingenuity at breaking in girlings?

In between these helpless – if pleasurable – diversions her thoughts wandered. Being in the sign was still a good place to think.

She worried about her parents and how they would be concerned about her. Were the police looking for her now? She had been gone a week. Or was it more? She was not sure how long days in Underland lasted, and her watch had been taken away along with her clothes.

But it was hard to focus on her old life when Underland seemed so much more real and intense. Even something as normally mundane as the traffic passing by was fascinating to watch.

Much of it was of the local animals going about their business as people might walk along any country lane. They were at the same time bizarre yet familiar, as many of them awakened memories of the illustrations from the Alice books. She still could not work out which had come first – the actual place or the story, inspired or shaped by some subtle inter-dimensional influence. And how had Wonderland mutated into Underland? Was it natural evolution or a response to a more cynical world? Whatever the truth, there they were before her: some wearing slightly dated waistcoats and hats, others carrying walking sticks; a lizard, a dodo, a squirrel, a mouse, an owl and more.

Most of them, whatever their original form, were much the same height, standing no taller than her shoulder. Like the Hare and White Rabbit they had slightly humanised upper bodies, together with ordinary, if rather small, hands. And though many were dressed in coats, none wore anything below the waist. Of course as they were decently covered by fur and feathers and since it never seemed to get cold in Underland, it hardly mattered. But was it significant, somehow?

Then two things struck her at the same time.

Firstly, so far she had only seen one of each breed of animal. Secondly, they had all been male. Thinking back, she could not recall any female animals in the Alice books, at least none playing significant parts. And if those stories shaped life here, did that mean there were no female animals at all? But then how did they reproduce? There was no hint of sex in the original books, but that was not surprising considering they were written in the shadow of Victorian morality. Of course, that had provided a front for a good deal of hypocrisy where sex was concerned, and the local animals certainly enjoyed sex for pleasure as she knew only too well. But then what might be called the laws of nature were different here. Perhaps Underland simply continued timelessly as it was. Without mates of their own species the animals turned to girlings for both pleasure and service. Yes, there was a certain echo of true Victorian values in the idea of young women being used for sex and heavy labour. Or quite literally in Underland as beasts of burden, Alice thought, as she watched an old-fashioned four-wheeled farm cart loaded with potatoes go past.

Its driver was a hamster, wearing a flat cap and loose waistcoat. He sat on a small seat at the front of the cart, occasionally flicking the reins across the hindquarters of the two naked dark-haired girls who were hauling it along. They were bent over on either side of the cart's single shaft and yoked to it with a double set of padded hoops, which served the same function as horse collars and held them with their bottoms slightly higher than their shoulders, so they moved along with their knees bent but not touching the ground. One of the hoops went round their necks, the other about their waists just above their hips, presumably so they could apply all their strength to drawing the cart. Their heads were encased by the straps of a bridle, supporting blinkers and cheek rings which held bits between their teeth. Thick coats of the same sort of black rubbery material Alice wore encased their hands, shins and feet, protecting them from the ground and perhaps giving them extra traction. As they moved, their sturdy, sweat-sheened thighs and buttocks swelled with effort and spittle ran from the corners of their bit-stretched mouths, yet they continued on along the lane in a purposeful, determined manner, like docile working animals contented with their lot.

The cart reinforced this strange inversion of the normal order of things. It was built to suit its driver and so was only two thirds or half the size a similar vehicle would have been in the 'real' world. It made the women seem bigger in proportion, almost like (Alice could not escape the analogy) dray horses. Like horses they were larger than their master, who walked upright while they went on all fours. He was decently covered by cloth and fur, while they were naked. He could talk, while their mouths were stopped with bits. He could employ the full mobility of his hands, while theirs had been reduced to things hardly more dextrous than hooves or paws. Girlings really were the animals here and the animals people.

Not long after the cart passed, Alice heard a discordant clonking of bells coming down the lane. A ferret carrying a long stick was driving half a dozen girlings along before him. The noise came from what looked like old-fashioned cow bells hanging from their collars. Chains running from their ankle cuffs passed through a large anal ring, ensuring they shuffled along on their hands and knees, having to pull one leg forward to give enough slack to extend the other. As they got closer she saw they all had very large but perfectly shaped breasts capped by proportionately prominent nipples. Glossy and taut as though full of milk, their mammaries swayed pendulously beneath them as they moved.

No, surely not! Alice thought. But there was a horribly seductive logic to it. She had seen girlings used as horses, so was it surprising these should serve the function of cattle? Were they being taken to a new pasture or to a milking parlour? Yet for all the indignity she imagined them suffering, their faces showed the same look of placid acceptance she had already seen on her fellow slaves. They passed her with hardly a glance, contained in a tight group by taps from their drover's stick.

A spasm of panic ran through Alice as she watched them go, making her tug at her bonds. They would

67

not turn her into a milk-cow! But her struggles only set the bell-rod swaying and the teasing rubber prongs resumed their insidious work. As she surrendered to its pleasures she knew the truth was she no longer had any control over her fate. She might yet end up in a herd of girling cattle.

Was 'herd' the right name for such a grouping, she wondered as her mind spun and hips jerked. What was the correct collective noun for enslaved girlings? A string, perhaps, or a squeeze? Maybe a truss, a bind, a gaggle or a giggle, a covey, a cunny . . . a come? A come of girlings? That said it all, she thought wildly as she came to herself. Was she going mad or was it all a dream?

When she was taken down at lunchtime, the Dormouse gave her a few quick flicks with his cane to encourage her to move her stiff limbs and crawl back through the gates. The stinging pain brought Alice back to her senses. She really was in Underland, where every day was a mad dream.

Four

If the devices in the garden compound served to
break the girls into a life of slavery with mechanistic
relentlessness, subtler lessons were taught inside the
house. One day Alice was taken to Topper's bedroom
to learn the art of individual and personal submission
on a one-to-one basis.

For the most part his room fitted the Victorian
period. It was high-ceilinged, lined with flock wallpaper, and thick curtains framed the window; there
were gas lamps set on curving brackets; an open
fireplace with a chunky brass fender topped by a
mantelshelf crowded with ornaments; glass-fronted
paintings hung from a picture rail; side tables, a
bookcase and armchairs were of dark polished wood,
while the bed-frame was of heavy tubular brasswork;
chains coiled round the bed railing and a selection of
canes and crops hanging from a row of hooks on the
wall were the only obviously atypical items.

A second glance, however, revealed several anach-
ronistic additions. The spines of some of the books on
the shelves clearly belonged to modern paperbacks, a
couple of audio cassettes lay amongst the clutter on
the mantelpiece and one of the framed pictures on the
wall showed the latest English test cricket team. Alice
assumed Topper must have picked them up during

trips to her world, since it was hard to imagine the Rabbit or Hare walking into a shop and buying them.

Alice knelt in the middle of a thick tufted rug. She was sitting back on her heels with her hands clasped behind her neck and knees widespread in accordance with the dictates of correct slave posture, which stated that it was both thoughtless and offensive for a girling to adopt any posture that would hide her private parts, particularly when she was alone with her master. Clad in slippers and a long silk dressing gown patterned with an oriental design, Topper paced round her while he lectured.

'Forget any of your modern, Overland notions of rights and propriety,' he told her. 'You signed those away when you put your name to the visitor's declaration. Now you are just another girling, and a girling's first and only purpose is to serve her master in whatever manner he desires. Do you understand?'

'Yes, Master,' Alice replied meekly.

'And your master is represented by the cock, be it a man's or animal's. Think of it as an icon worthy of reverence, to whose needs you must at all times be ready to submit. Any orifice may serve as its sheath, whatever passing discomfort it may cause you. Accept that simple fact and your time as a girling may not be unpleasant.' He smiled. 'Indeed, if you surrender yourself totally to its service, you may find unexpected contentment. '

With a dry mouth, knowing what was to come, Alice responded dutifully: 'Yes, Master.'

'Then show me how you would demonstrate proper respect to your master.'

He dropped his robe to the floor. Underneath he was naked. Alice looked at him in awe. He did not have pumped-up muscles like a bodybuilder, he was simply made on a larger and far more impressive scale than any man she had ever seen before. And nestling heavy and potent in a thick mat of hair covering his lower belly was his manhood itself.

Alice gulped. Even flaccid it was an impressive sight. Had she really taken that inside her? And in proportion below it hung testicles she could swear were the size of tennis balls.

But even as she felt herself helplessly, slavishly, responding to the sight, part of her held back. Since her initiation – her 'imprinting' as they had called it – she had only been penetrated or stimulated by mechanical means. Now she was going to have a live cock inside her once again. I can't fight the inevitable, so I might as well get it over with, she told herself. After what she had endured in recent days this was almost normal. Had that been the point of her training? To break down her resistance and heighten her sexual response so she would readily accept 'normal' sex. How long would it be before she no longer had the will to try to escape, until it was easier to accept her situation and become just like her fellow trainees, or those girling cows on the lane? Of course they had seemed curiously content. I must play along, biding my time until the right opportunity comes up, she countered desperately. But was not that kind of rationalisation the first step on the path to total submission?

Alice abandoned this tangle of confusing thoughts, took a deep breath and let herself go. She might as well co-operate with the inevitable without assuming the extra burden of guilt or shame. Her doubts melted away as she let the reflexes her body had so recently learnt take over. She looked uncritically at the massive genitalia displayed before her and realised Topper was right. In a crude way a cock was an icon, better yet a totem, worthy of reverence, even adoration. And she knew instinctively what its worship required.

She shuffled forwards, rising on her knees to reach, and carefully bestowed a kiss on each lobe of his ball sack. His musky, exciting male scent filled her nostrils. She pressed her face into the thick coils of his pubic hair and began to lick the base of his penis. Immediately it began to stiffen and rise. She had never seen such a thing happen up close. The great column of pulsing flesh flopped across her face as it uncoiled like a snake. Its single eye momentarily transfixed her before lifting towards the ceiling into proud erectness. God, it was a monster! She could not have encircled it with the fingers of one hand. And the harder she worked the larger it got and the more she would be stretched when, inevitably, it would be thrust inside her. She was engineering her own forthcoming discomfort. How perverse! But she was at the mercy of her instincts now, kissing and licking her way up the shaft of flesh, feeling the hardness beneath its silky smooth skin. Blood pulsed under her tongue as it did into her own nipples, turning them into tingling cones. Her stomach was knotting in anticipation and warm slickness filled her vulva. The massive member lifted a little higher and the foreskin began to roll back from the purple plum at its crown. She had to rise from her knees to get her mouth to the top and take it inside, stretching her jaws wide to do so. She would choke if he wanted oral sex, and anal would split her in two!

Suddenly Topper grasped Alice by the hair and hauled her upright so he could look into her flushed face and slightly unfocused eyes. He must have been satisfied with what he saw, because he said, 'You have an artful tongue, girling, and have roused me well. But what of yourself?'

He cupped his hand over her hot breast and squeezed, testing her own arousal. Only a finger spread as large as his could have held so much of her full tits in one go. She was like a toy in his arms. His hand slid down across her stomach through her pubic bush into the wetness of her cleft and two large strong fingers slipped up inside her passage, stretching her open and making her gasp.

'Yes, you are full ready. What a lusty creature you are, to be sure. How fortunate Ory found you. Fancy all that passion being wasted in your world. Now, will you serve me as a girling should?'

'Yes . . . Master,' she choked.

'You can plead more prettily than that.'

'Have me, Master! Screw me, put it up my cunt, please!'

She was too far gone to care that she had been made to beg to be used. All that mattered was consummation and relief from the terrible need that was filling her to bursting.

Still holding her by the hair, he dragged her across to the bed and threw her onto the sheets. Heart pounding, she rolled onto her back and parted her legs wide, opening her engorged pussy lips and offering herself to him like a slut in heat.

'Do you expect to couple like a free woman?' he asked.

Alice reached up and grasped the rails of the bedhead.

'Chain me, Master,' she pleaded.

He snapped the waiting chains to her wrist cuffs and drew them tight, then did the same for her ankles. In a few seconds she was spreadeagled – perhaps the most submissive and vulnerable posture a woman could be put into. Topper loomed over her, his cock standing up like a flagpole. Automatically

73

she lifted her hips in mute appeal, showing him in the most basic way that she had a hole that needed filling. He climbed onto the bed between her legs, the springs creaking beneath his bulk, the heat and power of his body overwhelming her senses. His elbows came down on either side of her head and she found herself staring up at the hair of his chest. He was too big for them to couple face to face, or perhaps she was so very small. Just a toy, really. A mere girling. The head of his cock was probing her cleft, pushing aside her sex lips as it found the entrance to her passage. He was bearing down, flattening her breasts, then she squealed as he drove up inside her, on and on. The length of him! Would it never stop? It would come out through her navel! But somehow she contained him, making herself a sheath for his manhood. Then the thrusts began, jerking her against her chains and making the heavy bed creak and rattle. She cried out in pain and delight, telling him he was going to burst her open and that he must not stop, but her words were muffled as she was crushed beneath his weight and skewered on his cock. Then he was emptying himself into her, the sperm squirting out in the tightness between his flesh and hers, and she was spasming and shrieking incoherently as the universe exploded within her.

For some minutes afterwards Topper lay unmoving on top of her and she had no choice but to bear his weight. But then why should she expect any consideration for her comfort, she thought dizzily, as rational thought only slowly returned. She was only a girling. This was the place for her: chained to a bed under her satisfied master. Then she whimpered. She must fight such thoughts. But she knew now what it was like to be a completely dominated and subservient slave, and

74

how total surrender to another's will felt. A new level of sexual experience and pleasure had been revealed that she found impossible to resist. Perhaps she was a natural sex slave. Valerie said the White Rabbit chose his subjects carefully. No, she told herself. She might lose control in the excitement of an orgasm, but the rest of the time she still yearned for freedom. But could that state of joyous surrender expand to fill the space in between, so that she lived perpetually in the afterglow of the last high and in anticipation of the next?

Her personal tuition continued the next day in Lepus's bedroom. The furnishings were similar to Topper's, except that the bed was a wooden four-poster and set lower to the ground to accommodate its owner's smaller stature. The anachronisms were also more obvious: several garish printed T-shirts hung carelessly on an open rail; a portable CD player sat on a shelf; and posters rather than framed paintings hung on the walls, including one of the latest girl band and a female tennis player rubbing her bare bottom.

Another difference was that Alice was not alone with her teacher.

Valerie knelt beside her, hands cuffed behind her back as Alice's were, their collars linked by short double chains. Valerie had flashed her a bright smile as they had been led in and whispered: 'Don't worry, this won't hurt. Everything'll be fine.' Now she was listening to Lepus's lecture with studious attention. Alice kept giving Valerie's intent and pretty face sidelong glances, wondering how she could be so fascinated by Lepus explaining how best to please any animals they might find themselves serving. Would she end up taking her own training so completely?

'You will find,' Lepus was saying, 'that animal masters will tend to use more restraints on you than humans. There are various reasons for this. Firstly, you are larger creatures than we are and might inflict injury by reflex response to, say, some punishment you were undergoing. Of course, a properly trained girling will rarely turn on her masters, but there's no reason to take chances when an additional chain or strap renders her incapable of any significant physical resistance. Bind her tight and she'll serve you right, as we say in Underland.

'Secondly, even a docile and tractable girling needs to be constantly reminded of her place. It helps to keep her mind on her duty, and saves her from making careless mistakes which will only bring her a beating anyway.

'Lastly, it is simply a pleasure for us to have absolute domination over such pretty creatures as yourselves, and chains and ropes and suchlike are the outward symbols of such mastery. This is especially satisfying since you are of the same species as the gentry.' He wagged a finger significantly. 'Ah, yes, the gentry. I'll tell you more about them another time. For the moment it is enough that you realise you may encounter some resentment because of your closeness to them, and perhaps some harsher treatment than you deserve. There is nothing you can do to prevent it, of course, and the only way of limiting such treatment is by total obedience and submission. Show you accept the rightful mastery of animals, and it may go easier on you.

'Another fact you must appreciate is that we animals enjoy seeing girlings coupling with each other. Knowing you are normally shy about such things, and especially performing them in public, only adds to the pleasure. Also, two girlings rutting vigorously can generate fragrant scents and secretions that your poor noses cannot fully savour.

'Remember, however, that although a show of embarrassment or distress when you are commanded to perform together will generally add spice to the act, you must in truth have no inhibitions between yourselves whatsoever. As you will learn, there is no part of you that cannot be kissed, nor any orifice beyond probing. Any sexual position or combination between two or more girlings that you are called upon to adopt you will do so. You are creatures beyond the bounds of shame or humiliation. Your only purpose is to give pleasure and service.'

Alice swallowed hard, glancing sidelong at Valerie as she guessed what was coming. The other girl appeared unconcerned gazing seriously up at Lepus while slowly nodding her head.

He picked up a plate from a side table. 'First, a little something to ease your way.' On it were two cupcakes, looking very similar to the 'uninhibited' cakes Alice had already sampled. Lepus saw her expression and smiled. 'No, a slightly different recipe, girl. Now open wide.'

He crammed the cake into her mouth, forcing her to chew and swallow it down. Alice tasted orange mixed with the warm ginger base. Valerie accepted her cake more delicately and without apparent hesitation.

Lepus separated their chains, reversed their collars and ran each length about their wrist cuffs before clipping the end back on their collar rings, thereby pulling their wrists high up their backs and leaving a short length rather like a handle that he could use to control them. He then turned the girls to face each other so their spread knees were nearly touching.

Alice gazed anxiously at Valerie, who smiled back and mouthed, 'Don't worry.'

At least it would be with Valerie, Alice thought, in an attempt to steady herself. She had been so kind to her from the first, and she was very pretty. What would it be like to make love to her as though they were lesbians? She had joked about such things in the past with her friends. Now it was going to happen.

Alice licked her lips, suddenly feeling flushed and light-headed, a warmth flowing through her. Valerie was gazing at her seemingly all eyes. Pretty brown eyes. Now she was smiling at her – a wide happy smile. Lovely lips. Soft and moist, she imagined. So very kissable. She shook her head. It was the cakes making her feel this way, of course, but knowing made no difference. The image of Valerie was filling her mind the longer she stared at her. So delectably slim, such pretty little breasts ... tits. So neat, so different from her own monsters. Hard brown nipples standing up, pointing at her. She realised her own nipples were in the same state of arousal.

'Do you want her?' Lepus asked.

'Oh, yes please, Master,' she said huskily. Whether it was artificially induced or not, there was no doubt in her mind that she was ready to make love to Valerie. Her pussy lips were dripping wet and pulsing and need was knotting her stomach. It was similar to the feeling aroused in her by Topper, yet also subtly different. This was not submission to another but a mutual sharing of joyful pleasure. How strange she had ever had any doubt. Thank goodness her inhibitions had been stripped away from her.

'Do you want her?' Lepus was asking Valerie.

Valerie smiled. 'I do, Master, very much.'

She and Valerie were each almost unconsciously bending towards each other, tongues flicking over their lips. But Lepus held them back by their chains, making them whimper in frustration.

'Simmer a moment longer, little dumplings,' he told them.

They tugged and whined and pleaded with him piteously. Once again they were being made to beg for their release. They were girlings in heat and would take their pleasure only at their master's choosing.

Suddenly he let them go with an encouraging slap on their bottoms. They lunged at each other, covering each other's faces with passionate kisses. Unable to use their hands to exchange caresses, they had only the friction between their bodies and their busy lips to express their desire. Alice was overwhelmed by the taste and scent of Valerie, the litheness of her slender body pressed to her own, the play of soft/hard muscles and the promise within her. They rolled over on the mat, desperately trying to interlock their legs to rub their groins harder together.

Lepus looked down at them with satisfaction, and said:

'Nipples pressed to nipples and mingle your bushes.
Fannies hard a'wiggling; you grind and she pushes.'

With prods and tugs on their chains he arranged them to his liking.

'Now you turn about and her sweet lovemouth find.
That smile perpendicular's what I have in mind.'

Alice lay on her back with Valerie reversed on top of her, so that they were each licking the soft lips pouting from between the other's thighs. It was Alice's first taste of another girl's most intimate

79

succulence. Valerie reminded her of honey and wild woods. She gasped as Valerie buried her face in her engorged and slobbering cleft.

'Plumb her depths and tongue her, far as you can go,
Tickle, lick and cunny her, make her juices flow.'

Lepus pulled back Valerie's head so he could dip his fingers into Alice's golden cleft and sample her excited outpourings. He sniffed and nodded approvingly, wiping his hand clean on Valerie's hair. Pulling off his shirt he went round to the other end of the beast with two backs that writhed and moaned so ecstatically on his carpet. From under his furry belly his pizzle was rising.

He lifted Valerie's pale tight bottom, exposing Alice's flushed and glistening face below it, and thrust an exploratory hand into Valerie's dark-haired delta. The sticky exudate he recovered was also to his liking. After inhaling it deeply he pushed his hand into Alice's hungry mouth and she licked it eagerly from his fingers.

Lepus parted Valerie's legs a little wider and squatted down with his feet on either side of Alice's head. He clasped Valerie's jiggling buttocks and pried them apart, opening the way to the tightly crinkled hole concealed between them.

'Open that secret way to me, my pretty girling bum,
Parted shall your anus be, and riddled your rectum!'

Alice, her head enclosed between the soft flesh of Valerie's thighs and the Hare's furry belly, saw his slender red glistening pizzle almost touch her nose as it probed her lover's anus. Of course, she thought dizzily, they were not going to be allowed to have each other to themselves. They were here to be used.

Valerie gave a little gasp as the hard rod of flesh slid inside her, then resumed her tonguing of Alice's cunny. Lepus began to pump in and out of her. His dark, thinly furred testicles, held tight between his legs, brushed across Alice's forehead. Overwhelmed by the scent of lust around her, both human and animal, Alice tilted her head back and licked the rapidly jerking balls.

'That's a good girling!' he cried.

She lapped at the grinding genitalia before her face, shamelessly licking round her lover's stretched anus and the slender pizzle that penetrated it. Thus locked together, the two girls and their animal master rode to a triumphant climax.

Alice was still enveloped in the afterglow of her coupling with Valerie as they were led out of the house. Shuffling along the hall on hands and knees, brushing against each other with shy smiles and giggles, they passed the door of a small box room which was slightly ajar.

'We like to think of this as our trophy room,' Lepus said with a chuckle, pushing the door open so they could see clearly.

The walls were filled with pigeon-hole shelving. Each niche contained a bundle of clothes, sometimes with shoes, tied up with string from which hung a brown parcel label with a girl's name on it.

'Never let it be said we are careless with your property,' Lepus continued. 'We are interested in your bodies not your clothes. They remain here if required, though few girls have ever asked for them to be returned.'

Her past life had been reduced to one small bundle of clothes, Alice thought. Was it as insignificant as that?

The garden table was set for a feast far grander than the tea party Alice had first sat down to. The girlings had been scurrying to and fro for an hour, under Topper's strict guidance, to lay gleaming cutlery, fold napkins, polish glasses and decanters, and arrange place settings.

'Anybody who purchases a girling from us knows she has been trained to serve her master in every situation, private or public,' he told them proudly.

'Under the sheets or by the table,
She is always bright and able.'

As an assortment of invited village animals arrived they were bowed in through the garden gate by two girls chained to the posts in kneeling postures. As each animal entered, the girls touched their heads to the ground and said, 'This humble slave welcomes you, Master.'

Alice's task was to take a tray of drinks round to the guests before they sat down to their meal. Since her hands were cuffed behind her back, however, she could not hold the tray in the normal fashion. A scalloped cutout in the tray pressed against her chest hard under her breasts so they rested upon it, held in place by straps running over them from the sides of the tray and causing them to swell like fleshy balloons. Two small crocodile clips rising from the base of the tray held her nipples stretched into sharp points. The outer edge of the tray was supported by two chains that ran up to the ends of a short wooden rod she held clenched between her teeth. It would be acutely painful if she let the rod go and the tray tipped over while fastened only to her breasts and nipples, to say nothing of the punishment she would receive for such carelessness.

She had to go down on one knee before each guest, keeping her back straight and the tray level, and mutely offer a drink. Sometimes the guest would also examine and prod her, tweaking a taut nipple and pinching a rounded buttock. She could only endure the handling with tears pricking the back of her eyes, knowing that she, like the rest of the girls, was being displayed before potential buyers.

None of the guests were humans, Alice realised. She had heard from the other slaves that Topper was something of an oddity in Underland, preferring the company of animals to his own kind. Humans formed the ruling class here as they did in the original story where they were mostly portrayed as titled, ruled by a King and Queen. It was rumoured amongst the slaves that Topper also had a title, which he had renounced long ago. Topper's behaviour was tolerated because he provided many of the girlings the gentry also took as slaves. Girlings were considered by both animals and humans to be inferiors. It was probably the most they had in common.

The Rabbit, looking slightly dishevelled and already smelling of drink, was one of the last to arrive. He had called at the house a few times during her training and, Alice noticed, he seemed increasingly morose. Apparently he had not been able to find any suitable new girls since he had lured her to Underland. She recalled how he had said he disliked being a 'common procurer', and supposed that was bad enough without losing the talent for it as well.

As the guests took their places at the table, Alice hurried back to the house. She passed Valerie and another girl coming in the other direction. Valerie, now a beautiful beast of burden, was on her hands and knees with a large tray strapped to her back holding covered bowls and platters. She flashed Alice a bright, gag-stretched smile which made Alice's tummy flutter, and then continued on.

The Dormouse was in the kitchen supervising the despatch of the dishes. Alice waited patiently while he sent off the next laden girl and he turned his small black eyes impatiently to her.

'What is it, Melon Tits?' he snapped.

Alice wiggled her tray mutely.

'Oh yes, the red wine. I suppose I have to do everything in here while those two stuff themselves. Hold still, girl!'

She had been offering fruit juice and white wine from her tray, but red wine was to be served with the meal and the guests' glasses were to be kept topped up. The Dormouse unstrapped her tray and replaced it with a wine bottle in a sling dangling from her neck ring so that it hung in her cleavage. A loop strap squeezed her breasts around the bottle, warming it with her soft flesh.

The Dormouse pinched her nipples and slapped her on the rear, sending her back out into the garden to where the animals dined and the girlings served beneath the shade of the oak tree. Here she took up position to one side of the table and watched the diners. As soon as a glass was drained she hurried forward and asked, 'More wine, Master?'

A curving spout capping the bottle allowed her to pour it out neatly, though it had taken hours of practice with plain water to master the art without using her hands. Inevitably, bending low over the table invited curious hands to caress her buttocks and tickle the soft cleft of her vulva as it pouted from between her thighs. She twitched and gritted her teeth at these minor indignities, but continued pouring the wine smoothly.

She felt a frisson of triumph when, by the end of the meal, she had not spilt a single drop.

The guests had departed and the table was cleared. The girls knelt loose-chained in a row on the grass before Topper and Lepus. They felt nervous and excited at having been on show before so many locals and relief the ordeal was over. All that remained was their masters' verdict.

'That was well done,' Topper said.

The girls sighed and exchanged relieved grins. Even Alice felt elated and strangely proud.

'You moved most prettily as girlings should,' Lepus added. 'You deserve a reward.'

The Dormouse brought out a punchbowl and set it on the grass before them. The remaining wine was poured in, together with some slices of fruit, and drinking straws were arranged about the edges.

'Enjoy yourselves,' Topper commanded.

A little while later, Alice lay amongst the sprawled string of girlings with her head resting on Valerie's soft stomach. She was feeling warmed by praise and wine and the sweetly-scented body under her. As she looked about at the dreamy tranquility of the timeless Underland afternoon she thought, a little muzzily, that it wasn't all bad being a slave.

Gradually she became aware of Topper and Lepus standing a little way off, looking at her.

'We might sell them as a contrasting pair,' Topper said.

'They coupled well and lustily,' Lepus agreed.

They meant her and Valerie, Alice realised. They might be paired as slaves, as lovers?

Alice twisted her head round to see that Valerie had also overheard their masters' words and was grinning at her happily.

'Would you like that?' she said. 'We could have such fun serving together.'

As Alice stared into her eyes, she began to believe it might even be possible.

Their training as a pair began that very night when they were put in the same hutch.

Alice had wondered if their intense lovemaking under Lepus's guidance had been purely the result of the uninhibited cakes they had eaten. That first night as they huddled under the blankets, giggling and kissing and exploring each other's bodies, convinced her otherwise.

She had to accept that she enjoyed having sex with a girl, at least with Valerie, as much as she ever had with a boy. Yet she did not start thinking of herself a lesbian. This was just another facet of the amalgam of emotions and physical interactions encompassed by the deceptively simple word 'sex', which, as she was discovering every day, was actually far more complex than she had imagined.

In the real world her relationship with Valerie would have been, at least to begin with, largely clandestine and developing only gradually; strained by guilt and anxiety over what families and friends would think if they ever found out. Here they were being groomed as a girling pair without any inhibitions where sex was concerned. What they did together voluntarily in the non-privacy of their hutch, or under orders in the training yard or bedrooms of the house, was not only tolerated but encouraged. In a strange way they had more freedom than they would have had back in the real world. But the speed with which friendship had developed into something deeper was disconcerting. Alice didn't know if she truly loved Valerie, with all that entailed, but whatever it was they shared was intense and exciting and its passion drove almost all other thoughts from her mind.

They did make an interesting pair physically, Alice conceded. Though Valerie was more slender and had such distinctly smaller breasts, they were the same height and their hair was of similar length and cut, emphasising the contrast between black and blonde. Their training was now designed to made them work and respond in similar emotional harmony.

Their collars were often linked by a short chain, and they were either secured to the same piece of equipment, or else on two apparatuses placed close together so they could be swapped about while watching each other's pleasure and suffering. The bond between them was both tested and strengthened by a new rule their masters imposed, namely that any fault one of them made earned a punishment for both. This led on more than one occasion to tearful apologies and forgiveness afterwards. The intended consequence was of course that they became even more attentive and obedient than before, increasing their potential value when the day came to sell them.

It was one night in their hutch, as they lay folded in each other's arms, that Valerie talked about what would happen when their training ended.

'I wonder how long it will be before we find our perfect master,' she mused aloud. 'I suppose it's too much to hope for that he'll be the first one who buys us.'

'What's a perfect master?' Alice asked.

Valerie grinned. 'Exactly the right one for you, obviously. He might be an animal, but I think mine would be a man. He must be kind but strict as well. Somebody you can give yourself to completely and suffer anything for to show how much you loved him.'

A lump came to Alice's throat. 'I thought you . . . loved me.'

'Of course I do, silly!' Valerie exclaimed, kissing and hugging her more tightly. 'You're special and I'll always love you and I want us to be together for ever. But loving a perfect master isn't the same thing. And that's what every slave really wants.'

It was then that Alice realised the difference between them. Though loving her, Valerie had surrendered herself to slavery, while she, on the other hand, wanted to be with Valerie and free. How could they both have what they wanted?

Five

One morning a few days later, Alice and Valerie were toiling round the perimeter of the garden under the weight of a wooden double yoke locked about their necks. They were dripping with sweat and their backs and legs ached under the load, but they were keeping their spirits up by exchanging smiles, jokes and comforting words. There was a special pleasure, Alice had discovered, in sharing a burden, quite literally, with the one you cared for.

Then the White Rabbit hurried in through the side gate, looking even more flustered and dishevelled than usual. He raced over to Topper and Lepus and immediately launched into some urgent exposition. One phrase floated over to Alice and Valerie as they plodded along: '. . . the Duchess is coming . . .'

'Does he mean the Duchess from the story?' Alice panted.

'I suppose so,' Valerie said, licking her dry lips. 'I've heard the others mention her. Topper doesn't like her but he has to be polite . . . Shhh!'

They dropped their heads deferentially as Topper, Lepus and Rabbit came towards them. All three were in the middle of an acrimonious debate.

'She'll do what she did before,' Lepus was saying angrily. 'Look over the stock and buy any she fancies cheap before we send them to auction and the Queen's agents see them. Mean with her money like all the gentry.'

'We can't stop her coming, but perhaps we can keep the best of girls out of sight,' Topped suggested.

'We can hardly pretend we've got none in stock,' Lepus pointed out. 'She knows how many we usually have in training.'

'And she could be here within the hour!' the Rabbit interjected, consulting his watch. 'Whatever we do it must be soon.'

Topper glowered, his gaze fixing on Alice and Valerie. 'Halt,' he commanded, and they gratefully obeyed, sinking down onto their knees. 'At least we should keep one of the pairs out of sight, and I think these two are more valuable than Dawn and Linsey. We must save them from being split up.'

'Agreed,' said Lepus. 'But where do we put them? What if she goes snooping about the house or grounds? You know how nosy she can be.'

'Then let us hide them in the woods,' said the Rabbit impatiently:

'In some secret hollow where none will follow,
Trussed and bound so they can utter no sound.'

'We can't risk that,' Lepus said. 'They'd need to be watched all the time, and we don't know how long the Duchess will stay.'

'What about the village?' Topper suggested. 'They can mix with other girls there.'

'Housing such a distinctive pair in the village might attract attention,' Lepus pointed out. 'There are some there who court the Duchess's favour and know her tastes, who might tell.'

'Then we'll split them up. At a distance Valerie

might be mistaken for Vulgaris's girl after slimming down. Who's to know we aren't returning her to him? I'm sure he won't mind having the use of Valerie for a few hours.'

'Let it be days rather than hours,' pleaded Rabbit. 'The Duchess might be suspicious, ready to pounce on any she thought had deceived her.'

'A couple of days, then,' Lepus allowed. 'And where do we lodge Alice?'

'Ory can take her,' Topper said.

Rabbit looked alarmed. 'But she's not fully trained yet.'

'Nonsense,' said Topper. 'She's well broken in and won't give you any trouble. Take extra restraints and secure her so that she can't move if it makes you feel safer. Just keep her out of sight. You can do that, can't you?'

'But if the Duchess should find out I was hiding a choice girling from her . . .' Rabbit whimpered.

'We'll give you a bill of sale for her dated a week ago,' Lepus snapped in exasperation. 'If you are challenged you can show her that. No blame will come to you.'

'Can I treat her as my own?' Rabbit asked hesitantly, eyeing Alice up and down.

'Naturally. You were due the use of her soon anyway. Really! You'd think we were asking you to mind a snapping Nile crocodile instead of an obliging young girling. Do as you like as long as you keep her hidden until the Duchess is gone.'

The Rabbit mopped his brow with his handkerchief and appeared to gather his resolve. 'All right, I'll do it.'

'Good. Then let us make haste.'

Alice and Valerie were freed from their yoke and hurried across to the equipment shed. Lepus looked thoughtfully at Valerie. 'I'll put a muzzle and blinkers on her,' he said. 'It'll make her less easy to identify.'

'Good idea,' said Topper.

The muzzles were small baskets of thick wire mesh shaped like face masks and held in place with straps running from chin to crown and around the back of the head. Leather flaps extended forwards on either side of the eyes, limiting the field of view. Alice watched as it was slipped over Valerie's head and buckled tight, making her look even more like a beautiful captive animal.

Lepus clipped a lead to Valerie's collar. 'Right, I'm away. I'll go across the fields.'

'Be quick,' said Topper.

Valerie gave Alice a quick smile over her muzzle before the lead jerked her head round. Alice had a last view of her as she trotted after Lepus through the garden gate, then she was gone. A sudden sense of emptiness came over her. They had been so intimate recently that it would feel very strange not to have her at her side even for a couple of days.

Topper was frowning at Rabbit.

'Are you fit to lead her?' he asked. 'No, you can hardly stand straight. It's the drink again, isn't it? You must pull yourself together, Ory! I'll get out the hobby horse and you can ride her back.'

The device he brought out of the shed did have a resemblance to the old children's toy. A small seat with a basket on the back was supported by bicycle-sized spoked wheels on each side. A wooden shaft extended from under the middle of the seat and curved upwards to a little over head height. On the top was a hollow horse head of painted wood that hinged backwards. Broad buckled leather straps hung from the front of the shaft. Set before the driver's seat a tiller-like steering rod ran through a sliding pivot mount set in the shaft and was capped by an upward-curving hook and set of spring clamps.

Alice was backed against the shaft, straddling the end of the tiller bar, and her hands were cuffed around it behind her back. Neck and waist straps were buckled tight, holding her firmly upright with her head up, the curve of the shaft fitting the curve of her spine. Topper slid the end of the tiller rod back and up until the rubber ball that capped the tip of the hook was lodged in her vaginal tunnel. He then fastened the crescent-shaped clamps set on either side of the hook to her inner labia, making Alice gasp as the sprung jaws took a firm hold of her soft, tender flesh. The handle of the tiller no longer hung loose but quivered in response to the trembling of the living socket into which it was embedded.

The head mask of the hobby horse came down over Alice's head, forcing the rubber bit bar that ran across its hollow interior into her mouth. She found herself peering out through the eyeholes of the mask and wondering how strange she must look: a girl's body topped by a horse's head.

Rabbit climbed into the driver's seat but she felt no extra pressure on the main shaft because he was sitting right over the wheels which bore his weight. As long as the ground is level and not too rough, I should be able to pull this thing along quite easily, she thought.

Then Rabbit took hold of the tiller and gave it an experimental turn. Alice yelped and bit down on the rubber bar separating her jaws. It was as though he had reached into her sex pouch, taken a good hold, and twisted. The tiller gave him extra leverage to stretch her tender flesh any way he wished. She stood very still, knowing he had absolute control over her.

Topper came out of the shed with a clinking bundle which he dropped into the basket of the hobby horse.

'There are the extra restraints for her. Now be off home. I've got to get the place ready for the Duchess. I'll call round when it's safe to bring her back.' He turned away, calling out, 'Mouse – where are you? Get to the kitchen. We've got an important visitor coming.'

Alice heard no more because the Rabbit pushed the tiller, and her inner labia felt like they were being yanked out of her cleft. She started forwards, drawing the hobby horse after her. The Rabbit twisted the tiller round, stretching her to the right and she turned to follow. They passed through the side gate and crossed the back garden at a steady trot, through the garden gate and out into the woods. Turning left, they struck a well worn path that wound away between the trees. With more pressure on the tiller Alice broke into a jog, setting her breasts bouncing and the hobby horse rattling merrily along behind her.

Of course she could not run away from the clamps and hook, but when she was going at a satisfactory speed the Rabbit eased off the pressure and the stretching of her labia became tolerable. It was an instinctive, direct and intimate way to control a girl, and made her very attentive to the slightest movement of the tiller. The trick, Alice quickly decided, was not to think for herself but just go where her cunt was taken.

Even so, it felt good to get out of the garden and really stretch her legs. There was a curious sense of freedom in running naked, though nobody could physically have been less free than she was at that moment. She felt the air blowing through her clamped vagina and realised how wet she was and how stiff her nipples were. Even though the tiller attachment was painful, she could not deny it was also perversely exciting.

94

They bowled along the pathway. Thicker woods lay on one side and small fields on the other, with the roofs of houses showing through occasional gaps in the trees. In one of the fields, bounded by low stone walls, half a dozen heavy-breasted girlings were on their hands and knees placidly feeding on some lush grass the same way cows did. A few of them looked up with mild interest as they passed. Alice did not feel quite the shock she had the first time she had seen them in the lane. They looked so content in their field it was hard not to think it was perfectly natural. Well she supposed it was in this topsy-turvy land.

The path curved round to an open gate set in a hedge bordering a lane. On the other side were fenced or walled gardens fronting very low houses, some with thatched roofs. They seemed ridiculously small until Alice realised they were built to suit the proportions of animals. Rabbit pulled on the tiller, causing the hook lodged inside her to dig into her passage. Alice came quickly to a halt, standing very still except for the heaving of her chest and the saliva from around her bit dripping out the open bottom of her horse mask onto the upper slopes of her breasts. Rabbit peered anxiously up and down the lane, but there was nobody in sight. He turned Alice into the lane and then almost immediately sharply right through the open driveway gate of a brick house with leaded windows, that stood a little taller than the rest. A brass plate on the gatepost read: O. CUNICULUS, ESQ.

There was probably no logical reason why animals went by their Latin names in Underland, it was just so. *Cuniculus* was punningly appropriate, considering the Rabbit's job.

He drove her round the house and into the small walled rear garden, with its unkempt lawn and weed-choked flower beds, and pulled her up by the back door. Through her mask she saw a little lean-to brick and glass structure built against the wall that seemed oddly familiar. Alice shivered as she recognised it as an old-fashioned cucumber frame – a detail straight out of the original book. The plants inside were withered, she noticed.

Rabbit had climbed out of his seat and was looking at her uncertainly. In his hands was the bundle of restraints Topper had given him. With a nervous glance round he pushed back the head of the hobby horse, lifting the bit from her mouth as he did so.

'Now, we must get you inside, girl, quick as we can,' he said in a quavering voice. 'The neighbours mustn't see you, oh dear me no!' He tried to sound masterful: 'You'd better not give me any trouble or it'll be the worse for you, understood?'

Alice, who had no intention of causing trouble while she was so intimately fastened to the hobby horse, said: 'Yes, Master. I'll be good, I promise.'

She wondered how he could be so different now from the cunning creature who had so cleverly manipulated her with his words when they first met, so that she had humiliated herself before him, then followed him to Underland. Of course, any animal might be wary of a girl a head and shoulders taller and twice his weight, but surely not one as experienced with handling slaves as the Rabbit. His self-confidence must be close to rock bottom. It was almost sad to see.

His disorganised state of mind was further demonstrated by the quantity of restraints he piled upon her, despite the delay this entailed in getting her out of sight. By the time the tiller clamps were released, causing her to whimper as the blood returned to her pinched pubic lips, she was on her hands and knees with a short chain hobbling her wrists and a bar linking her ankles, and chains running both between them and her collar. The bar spreading her ankles was long, forcing her to splay her thighs and making it impossible even to shuffle forwards at any great speed. In addition, the Rabbit had fastened a discipline leash to her. Instead of clipping directly to her collar ring, the leash chain was fed through it, branching into two short lengths, each attached to a flexible metal disk with a star-shaped hole punched out of its centre. These disks went over her nipples, the Rabbit pulling her hard nubs of flesh through the holes with his small quick fingers.

Alice felt the springy metal tines pressing into the sides of her nipples and stifled a groan of discomfort. He gave an experimental tug and Alice gasped aloud. The tines were angled upwards to form shallow cones, so that they would dig in even deeper if any attempt was made to pull them off. They could only be removed by being carefully flexed apart – impossible for her to do while her fingers were confined within their rubber sheaths. Under tension the tines would not loose their grip even if her nipples softened. Not that there seemed much chance of that as the disks' constant pricking kept her nipples disturbingly stimulated, pulsing hotly within their new restraints.

The Rabbit locked a small padlock on the chain below the collar ring, so that it could not slide through even if the disks were pulled off her nipples. Alice realised that the greater the length of chain between the lock bar and disks, the less painful the leash would be, since before her nipples were stretched too far, the padlock would reach the collar ring and transfer the force to that. To her dismay the Rabbit had placed the padlock only just above the point at which the chain branched.

Finally satisfied that she was suitably restrained, he gave the leash a tug, which had the effect of dragging her nipples upwards and together, yanking her breasts with them.

'I'm coming, Master!' Alice yelped.

In an awkward shuffle she followed after him, her chains jingling, as he led her through the back door and into the kitchen. After an anxious glance outside, Rabbit closed the door behind them and then sank gratefully into a chair. Alice squatted on all fours beside him and looked around her.

The kitchen was furnished with heavy wooden cupboards, a large black-leaded open range, a plain square table with a check cloth on which rested an oil lamp, and a rectangular china sink fed by a single tap. The fittings were animal size and height, but the ceiling was tall, presumably to accommodate human visitors. There were more indications of neglect in the room. The bare floorboards were dusty, dirty crockery almost filled the sink, half a loaf of bread and a hunk of cheese lay uncovered on the table beside a cluster of wine bottles, only one of which held any wine, and a single unwashed glass.

With an unsteady hand the Rabbit filled the glass with wine, gulped down half of it, and then sat back with evident relief. The sight reminded Alice of how dry she was after her run and the session carrying the yoke. She asked cautiously, 'May I have a drink please, Master?'

He blinked at her. 'What? Oh, yes. Must keep you fed and watered.'

After some rummaging he drew out a cream and brown china bowl from the cupboard under the sink, ran some water into it and then placed it on the floor by the kitchen table. The bowl was inscribed: GIRL-ING.

Alice had to spread her knees wide and hunch forwards, bending from the hips over her pinioned hands with her nipples brushing the floorboards, so that she could get her mouth to the bowl. The posture reminded her of a family dog lapping up water from its bowl by the kitchen table. She knew girlings were used here for pleasure and as working animals, but she had not until now thought about them being pets. But why not? Would she be taught tricks? Fetch the stick, girl! Roll over and play dead! Beg . . .

Well, for the next couple of days at least she was Rabbit's pet, and she would have to accept what came. She glanced up at him as he sat moodily toying with his wine glass and wondered what he would expect of her. Suppose his depression got worse and he began mistreating her? She shivered. He could make her life hell – Topper and Lepus would never know. Then she saw it the other way round. For the first time since she had been enslaved she was in an ordinary house with a single overseer, and one not currently at his most keen-witted. Could this be her chance to escape?

Alice buried her face in her bowl, sucking and lapping intently lest her expression betray her thoughts. She would have to choose the means and the moment carefully. If her attempt failed she would probably be secured so tightly she would never have a second chance, to say nothing of the severe punishment she would undoubtedly receive.

For a moment, fear of that hypothetical retribution caused her to hesitate. How much easier not to take the risk – to be a meek, obedient girling. In a few days she would be reunited with Valerie. If they were sold to a reasonable master they could be happy serving together. Perhaps the pleasure would make the rest tolerable. It had been pretty fantastic at times. Alice screwed up her eyes. No! Sex was not everything and she would not be its slave. Somehow she would get away from the Rabbit and hide in the woods around the village. From there she could find out where the Squirrel lived and try to rescue Valerie. Then they could be together and free.

Holding on to that sense of resolve, Alice considered her next move. There was no chance of escape, secured as she was, and the Rabbit was unlikely to remove her restraints in his present state of mind. Therefore she must boost his confidence while making herself seem more helpless than she was. She must appear to be a willing slave, completely broken in and eager to be of service.

A strange thrill coursed through her. For the first time since she arrived in Underland she would, coldly and calculatingly and without any external stimulation, act the part of a true submissive. She would do whatever was necessary to convince the Rabbit she was genuine. Fortunately she had no shame or inhibitions left after what she had already been put through. In a way that was her strength: a willingness to sacrifice her pride, to accept any humiliation while using the allure of her body to achieve her goal. And she had two days at the most to do it.

Alice lifted her head from her bowl, licked her lips, shuffled round to face the Rabbit and asked in her meekest little-girl voice: 'Would you like me to clean up in here, Master?'

'What, cleaning?' he replied vaguely. 'No, Mary-Ann is my domestic.' He looked round in puzzlement. 'Where is the girl? Mary-Ann, Mary-Ann . . .?' Then he clasped a small hand to his brow, frowning. 'No, I sold her a month ago . . . oh, dear . . .'

'I'd be so pleased to do it, Master,' Alice continued with deferential persistence. 'I can wash the dishes and clean the floor, or dust. Whatever you wish.' She smiled brightly. 'I'm here to serve.'

He looked at her doubtfully. 'I've got to keep you safe and secure. Mustn't let the Duchess know you're here.'

'Of course not, Master. She sounds a terrible woman. I wouldn't like to belong to her. But that needn't stop you getting your house cleaned. Make use of me while I'm here. I could use a broom or a dustpan and brush if you don't have a vacuum.'

The Rabbit looked about him. 'I suppose it could do with a spring clean. There are implements in the cupboard, I think . . .'

As he rummaged in a tall cupboard Alice felt a thrill of hope. She could not clean properly chained as she was and with her hands sheathed. He would have to remove some of her bonds.

He turned back to her with a dustpan and brush and her heart sank again. Their handles had leather loops fitted, obviously to allow a sheathed girling hand to hold them. Patience, she told herself. The Rabbit did at least lengthen the chain between her wrist cuffs, but the chain linking her collar to the ankle-spreader remained, so she could not straighten up.

With the Rabbit holding her leash she set to work, making a show of doing a thorough job, grateful for the rubber sheathing on her knees. As she swept methodically round the room she purposely kept her bottom towards him, presenting the split peach of her mount of Venus, her pale buttocks and, when she bent a little lower, the crinkle-edged pit in the cleft between them. She had seen enough of the other girls similarly displayed to know how arousing such exposure could be. The Rabbit had to think of her as an obedient sex object, not a threat. She must make herself as open and vulnerable to him as possible. And if he wanted to she was ready to give him the best anal sex ever.

Her resolve induced a sudden helpless fit of giggles which she had to struggle to subdue. Whoever would have believed she could have thought of such a thing just a few weeks ago. Yet it was the simple truth. Her anus had been well exercised by Lepus, the sodomiser and other devices, and she had no doubts about her ability. After all, it was what she had been trained for.

To her surprise, Alice found she was getting excited at the thought of sex, becoming aware of a growing warmth and slickness in her vagina. If the local animals were as sensitive about such things as Lepus had said, the Rabbit could already smell her arousal. If so, she hoped the scent would please him. It would make it easier when the time came.

She finished the kitchen and, with Rabbit's approval, continued on into the hall, sweeping round the dark-stained boards either side of the strip of carpet. The sitting room held two large overstuffed chairs, several small side tables and an upright piano. The ashes of an old fire lay in the iron grate. All the surfaces were covered with china, and metal ornaments and heavy oil paintings hung on the wall. A couple were simple landscapes but the last showed a sporting event: animals by the side of a track were cheering and waving as girlings harnessed to small pony traps raced past.

By the time Alice had swept out all the ground floor rooms of the house her back and thighs were aching, but she hid her discomfort. In the kitchen once more, she bent down low before the Rabbit, trying to appear as small as possible.

'Is it to your satisfaction now, Master?' she asked humbly.

Another glass of wine and the sight of her hard at work had eased his fears. In a distinctly mellower mood he nodded with approval. 'Yes, it's much better. You're really quite an industrious little girling when you get started.'

'Thank you, Master,' Alice said. 'I'm just sorry I can't do the washing, but I couldn't hold anything properly.' She lifted her sheathed hands by way of explanation.

'That can't be helped,' he said amiably.

'Of course,' Alice added with calculated lightness, 'if I could kneel straight and my hands were free, I could see to all those dirty cups and dishes. You wouldn't need to let me off my leash, of course, Master, and I wouldn't do anything you didn't want me to with that clipped to me. It's so firmly fastened. See how hard it's keeping my nipples?' She pushed her hands up under her breasts, lifting the heavy globes as though offering them for his approval.

The Rabbit goggled at them for a moment, then reached out and stroked and fondled their full curves.

Alice gasped and moaned softly, fluttering her eyes as though in ecstasy. 'Oh, that feels nice, Master. Please don't stop, Master . . .' She surrendered to his touch, recalling the perverse pleasure she had felt the first time he had handled her. At this moment she must play the part of a willing pet wholeheartedly. Her nipples pulsed and burned inside their constraining collars.

'Such a nicely developed girl,' the Rabbit said wistfully, giving her a pinch and tweak. 'You responded to my probing, I recall:

' "Pretty titties with nipple'd prows,
Swelling out of schoolgirl blouse.
Two plump pillows for my bed,
On which to rest a weary head." '

103

'If you wish, Master,' Alice said huskily, 'I'd be honoured to please you.'

'But not until you've put this place in order, girling. Work before pleasure. If you're so anxious to please, let me see you clean those dishes. And mind you don't break anything!'

He used a bottle of solvent to remove the rubber sheaths from her hands. It turned the material into a soft jelly which simply slid off. Alice flexed her fingers gratefully. The sheaths had been removed every couple of days during training, but only while she was in her hutch. The next morning a fresh coating had been applied. This time she hoped it was gone for good.

The kitchen sink and wooden draining board was low enough so she could work at it while kneeling. The Rabbit moved her long chain round so that it ran from the back of her collar to the middle of her ankle-spreader bar, meaning she still could not stand upright. Her wrists also remained chained, if loosely, allowing her just enough freedom to manipulate the crockery and old-fashioned dishmop. The Rabbit had the key to those chains in his pocket. She would either have to remove it stealthily or else overpower him and take it by force. But she dare not attempt that while still hobbled, because he could easily evade her if her first attempt failed and then lock her in while he got help. Of course, even if she could get out of the chains, her collar and cuffs would still remain and their keys were back at Topper's house. Well, that was another problem. First she must escape from the Rabbit's clutches.

He sat by the kitchen table watching her work. Every so often he would tug gently on her leash, which now ran over her shoulder, lifting and stretching her tender nipples. It was a reminder that he controlled her, an encouragement to keep working, an amusing minor torment and a means of keeping her aroused.

The last surprised Alice, but it was true. Was she learning to find pleasure in such painful stimulation or had she simply immersed herself in the role of a willing slave? The latter of course. And excitement at the thought of escape. It must be empowering. It was as though a sexual potential was growing within her, setting her whole body tingling and making her vagina feel hot and swollen. She was ready for anything.

At last the sink was empty and a gleaming stack of plates, dishes and cups rested on the drainer. Alice shuffled herself round to face the Rabbit, her legs splayed by the spreader bar and her hands, wrinkled by soap and washing water, resting demurely on her thighs, and asked, 'What do you wish me to do next, Master?'

He beamed at her, merry with restored confidence and half a bottle of wine, looking her up and down with the interest of a connoisseur.

'Clasp your hands behind your neck,' he commanded.

Alice obeyed. The change in posture thrust out her breasts, the chains linking her confined nipples dangling in her cleavage. Alice sat back on her heels a little further, boldly displaying herself. She was ready. The sooner he had her the better. It would be another step in winning his confidence.

He got up and walked round behind her. There was a click as he locked the middle of her wrist chain to her collar ring, securing her hands behind her neck. He stroked her hair, then ran his hands down the curve of her back and gave her bottom a pinch. Alice trembled, breathing rapidly. He continued round until he stood between her splayed legs, toying with her breasts, tweaking her imprisoned nipples and watching the little grimaces of pain contort her features.

'As I recall, I left you in a state of unrequited need at the end of our first meeting,' he said reminiscently.

'That's right, Master,' Alice gasped.

'You'd become quite attached to the handle of my umbrella when I was using it to give you a riddling, and didn't want me to stop.'

'Yes, Master.'

'Quite the shameless little slut, weren't you?'

'I was, Master.'

'And now you're a wanton girling eager to please.'

'Yes, Master.'

He went over to the sink, took an old-fashioned fly swatter off its hook by the kitchen window, and swished it experimentally through the air, causing Alice to gulp. 'I want to hear you beg to finish what I started,' he said.

'I do, Master. Please will you – aww!'

Swish, smack! The metal mesh blade of the fly swatter whipped across the side of her left breast, leaving a burning grid on her skin.

'Beg with more feeling, girl,' he advised her, raising his arm again to deliver a backhand blow. 'Tell me what you want me to do to you.'

'Please fuck me, Master! I – ahh!'

This time it was her right breast.

'Such fine, plump targets they make,' the Rabbit observed. 'I want to hear you grovel!'

'Have me up my bottom, Master – ouch! Bum-fuck me, please! I'm hot and tight – aww! A dirty, slutty girling – uhh! Make me come – eek!'

Stinging blows set her breasts shivering and put a rosy blush on her pale flesh, punctuating the words

106

that tumbled from her lips without any artifice. Calculated readiness had now become an agony of need denied. At this moment, kneeling in chains, naked and helpless, receiving his chastisement, Alice knew she was the Rabbit's absolute slave and he was her master. Even if she escaped from him that very day, nothing would change the truth of that.

She made no attempt to turn away from the stinging swatter but held herself stiffly erect. Was this just self-restraint because she still had to allay his suspicions, or was it because she knew the Rabbit had every right to punish her? Punishment made a girling more receptive and ready to please. But she did not want to be a girling . . . did she? She thought of the expression on Valerie's face the first time she had seen her mounted on the anal pump. That look of calm resignation and acceptance of her suffering was necessary to who, and what, she was. Was this who she was?

With pain and pleasure mingling in her body and confusion filling her mind, she realised the swatting had stopped, leaving her breasts burning and vagina hollow and aching. The Rabbit was standing before her with a glistening red pizzle rising stiffly from between his legs.

He stroked his erection proudly. 'It's been a while since a girling's excited me as much as you,' he told her. 'Now I'm going to make up for lost time . . .'

Unsnapping the long chain from her collar he then removed her ankle bar. Wrapping her leash round his fist, he dragged her to her feet, holding her head low so that she had to walk doubled over, hands still chained to her neck.

Up the narrow stairs they went, Alice stumbling on the short, shallow steps. At the top was a landing with an animal-height ceiling. Ducking through a doorway she found herself in a bedroom equally low-ceilinged and lit by a small window, but which was dominated by a brass-framed human-sized double bed. Its presence puzzled her for a moment until she realised from the sight of chains dangling from the corners of the frame that it was intended to accommodate a girling.

'Get on,' the Rabbit commanded. She obeyed, kneeling at the foot of the bed.

He pulled the old-fashioned long bolster cushion from under the pillows, laid it across the bed and then pushed her forwards over it. The bolster lifted her bottom up while her face was pressed into lavender scented sheets. He pulled her ankles wide and chained them to the foot of the bed, opening the divide of her buttocks. He stripped off his clothes, picked up a can of girling oil which had been gathering dust on the windowsill, and climbed onto the bed behind her.

For a moment he squatted between her legs, savouring the view of her exposed backside: the smooth firm roundness of her pale bottom cheeks, the ripe pouch of cleft flesh beneath them and crinkled eye of her anus. He thrust his fingers between her engorged lips and withdrew them glistening with her scented juices, which he sniffed with delight and then wiped across her haunches.

Alice gasped, despair and frustration making her breathing ragged. 'Put it up me, please, Master . . .!' she begged. She was quivering and lewdly pushing out her bottom towards him, lost in the thrall of her carnal need.

He fed the spout of the oil can into her rear passage and pumped in the lubricant, watching the ring of muscle twitch in response. Removing the spout, he positioned his own erect member before the now prepared orifice and forced its tip inside. The pliant anus gave before his thrust and he slid deep into the hot elastic tightness of her rectum.

Alice groaned and bucked. 'Thank you!' she whimpered.

The Rabbit drove into her faster and faster, his furred haunches banging against her inner thighs. Alice felt his slender hardness rapidly pumping in and out – a living thing deep inside her body violating her most secret places. She was being used in the crudest way by an animal for its pleasure and it felt disgusting and wonderful. The dam of passion burst within her and she writhed and jerked and yelled in blissful release, even as spouts of hot animal sperm spurted into her bowels.

The Rabbit rested hunched over Alice's limp body, his pizzle still lodged inside her, caressed by her pulsing anus as his sperm bubbled out around it. As he felt her trembling with post-orgasmic aftershocks he thought what a delightfully lustful and passionate creature she was! All it had taken was the right handling. Perhaps he had not lost his old talent. After a few minutes he found himself stiffening once more. Taking a fresh grasp of her hips, he began to sodomise her again . . .

Outside the drawn curtains of Rabbit's cottage was the half-light of Underland night.

In the small upstairs bathroom Alice half knelt, half squatted over the low toilet bowl to relieve herself. The Rabbit stood over her, the end of her nipple leash held confidently in his hand.

With a groan Alice expelled her soil mingled with his sperm through her sore bottom hole. He had come inside her at least half a dozen times in the couple of hours he had kept her on the bed, and not once had he completely withdrawn from her. Finally he had allowed her a break when she pleaded that her bladder was about to burst under the agitation it had received.

He watched her eliminate with approval as an experienced handler of girlings might note they were performing their natural functions properly. When she was done he wiped her clean, applied some soothing cream to her anus, and then introduced the oil can once again to ready her for further use.

Alice felt the oil spout within her and knew what it presaged. The surprising thing was that she did not at that moment resent either it or the Rabbit. With her primal need satisfied she felt herself curiously detached and content – but that was a feeling she had to fight! She reminded herself she was meant to be planning her escape and must be alert, ready to take advantage of the slightest opportunity. Yet it was so hard to motivate herself. Was she frightened of the consequences of failing, or simply finding excuses not to act because she liked what was being done to her? Valerie had said such a thing would happen but she had not believed her. She was horribly confused.

Grinning, the Rabbit led her back to the bedroom.

Six

Alice was woken by the morning light shining in around the curtains.

She lay on the covers at the foot of the bed with her back to the bed-frame. Her wrists and ankles were locked together and they in turn were chained to the brasswork. It was how Rabbit had secured her after finally having his fill of her bottom in the early hours.

The Rabbit himself was sitting on the side of the bed, clutching his head and groaning. It seemed that the wine and his exertions of the previous night had finally caught up with him.

Alice thought it best to lie quiet as he dragged himself along to the bathroom and then, a little while later, descended the stairs. For half an hour she heard sounds from the kitchen which suggested a meal was being made in a haphazard fashion. Her stomach rumbled, reminding her that she had not eaten since breakfast yesterday. Would he remember to get her some food?

Eventually he came back upstairs, still undressed but looking a little stronger, and carrying a glass of wine. Presumably he was trying the old 'hair of the dog' cure, or whatever they called it here. He sat down on the bed and regarded Alice with bloodshot eyes.

Not wanting to talk out of turn but feeling she must maintain her submissive demeanour, she said meekly, 'I hope I was pleasing to you last night, Master.'

He glowered at her for a dangerous moment, then said, 'You were all right, girl.'

'I would never have believed you could do it so many times, Master.'

'Really?' he grumbled. 'But isn't that what my kind are proverbially good at?'

'Pardon, Master?'

'Rabbits, girl. Haven't you ever heard them say lovers were "at it like rabbits" in your world? Isn't that what you expected from me: a multiple coupling?'

She caught the whiff of self-pity in his words. His confidence had obviously bombed again. She said hastily, 'No, Master, of course not. I don't mean I didn't expect anything. I was sure you could do it . . . and you did. My bottom feels so well used, but in a nice way, of course.'

To her dismay this compliment only seemed to infuriate him further.

'Oh yes, I'm a maestro at bottoms. That's all humans think we're good for – girling bottoms. Arseholes for the animals and cunt holes for humans. Is that fair?'

Alice, desperately trying to strike a reasonable balance, said, 'Well, you're smaller, Master, so a bottom is a better fit. I don't mean you're too small. I'm sure you're just the right size for a . . .' She trailed off hopelessly.

'For a rabbit,' he sneered. 'A silly, nervous rabbit who's always running late. Good for nothing but sniffing out girlings for training. Then if he's lucky, getting the use of their rear ends for a few days before they're sold to the richer animals or the gentry to enjoy. All those lovely, succulent pussies I never knew!'

This mixture of maudlin pity and anger was beginning to frighten Alice. 'But you've got me now, Master,' she said, squirming about and trying to open her legs to him. 'Use my cunt. I'm really tight. I know you can enjoy me as well as any man.'

A new light had come into his eyes. He tossed back the rest of the wine and fixed her with a wild stare. 'Oh, I can and I will, girl. We can be as good as anybody!'

Rising unsteadily to his feet he made for a small bureau standing in the corner. He pulled down the front flap and rummaged inside. Alice heard something click and saw the Rabbit draw out a couple of small brown glass bottles and a medicine measure, which he put down on the bedside table. They were labelled very simply: 'BIG' and 'SMALL'. He looked down at Alice as though momentarily uncertain of his actions. Appearing to marshal his resolve, he pulled off the silver ring he wore on his left hand and laid it on the table, unstoppered the bottle marked 'BIG', poured out a small quantity of pink liquid into the measure and drank it down.

'Now I'll have you like a man,' he growled, his voice deepening as he loomed over her.

The breath caught in Alice's throat. The Rabbit was growing bigger before her eyes.

He swelled like an inflating balloon, keeping the same proportions as he expanded in every direction. His ears brushed the ceiling and bent over, then he had to duck his head and hunch his shoulders to avoid striking his head.

In seconds the impossible change was complete. No longer a figure of fun or pity, he now bulked almost as large as Topper and appeared far more menacing. He clenched what had become broad and powerful hands and from out of his great furry head dark bulging eyes glittered in manic triumph. As he stood over the bed and looked down at Alice's naked and chained form, his pizzle twitched with renewed potency, swelling into a carrot-like rod of pulsing red flesh.

Alice found her voice, which sounded like a squeak in comparison with his. 'Oh ... you're so big ... so magnificent, Master!'

She had not intended to voice such a compliment, but now she had it seemed the right thing to say. Letting instinct guide her tongue she continued brightly, 'This is going to be so special, Master. Do you want to take me from behind or have me on my back? I can be more open for you then. It's how a man would have me and you said that's what you wanted, Master.'

They were slavish, submissive words perhaps driven by fear, but they came with surprising ease. Why not? It was the natural thing for a girling to say before her master. Of course, she told herself, she had no choice anyway so it made sense to co-operate and keep him happy.

'I'll have you on your back, girl,' he rumbled.

He unchained her from the bed-frame, leaving her wrists cuffed together but freeing her ankles, then casually picked her up and threw her lengthwise on the bed. She shivered at this demonstration of strength. It was exciting to be handled like that. Almost eagerly she splayed her legs wide as he chained her ankles to the corners of the bed-frame. As he did so she became aware of the wetness at the top of her thighs and the tingle in her vulva. Despite the exertions of the previous night her body was readying itself for sex again.

Smiling, she put her cuffed hands above her head for the Rabbit to secure, but he ignored them. There was no possibility of her overpowering him now.

Impatiently he climbed onto the bed, making the frame creak. Alice gulped as she thought of his weight bearing down on her. His face was almost nose to nose with hers – an intimidating thing to see so close when grown to such proportions. She could smell the wine on his breath. He sank down, pressing her into the mattress with its furry bulk. His pizzle probed her wet slit and found her entrance. With a cackle of triumph he moved up into her. Alice gasped as he stretched her passage to its limits. He was almost as big as Topper.

He began pistoning in and out of her, almost driving the breath from her body. She had to grasp the bars of the bed-frame to brace herself, her knuckles turning white. He rested on his elbows so he could watch her face contort with each thrust, hearing her grunt and yelp and groan in testament to his absolute mastery of her, enjoying the sight and sound and feel of his human slave bucking under him.

Alice came with a shriek, even as she felt him discharge his sperm into her in fitful spurts. His furry body shuddered with each ejaculation, filling her already tightly plugged passage. Then with a final gasp of satisfaction he collapsed, his chest flattening her breasts so she had to turn her head to one side to breathe, his head resting on the pillows above her.

Slowly, what Alice hoped was common sense returned to her. The Rabbit was lying very still with his eyes closed. For a horrifying moment she thought he was dead, then she realised he was breathing, though his breaths were very shallow. A snore suddenly reverberated round the room. He was asleep! The

115

change of size on top of the drink must have knocked him out.

She tried to rationalise the apparently impossible thing she had just witnessed. It seemed beyond anything she had so far encountered in Underland. A distorted view of her own world she had come to terms with, but this seemed to break fundamental laws of nature.

A dose of 'magic potion', for want of a better description, couldn't add a hundred kilos to a body. Where did the extra mass come from, and how could a body rearrange itself to accommodate it so quickly? She recalled Simon Gately going on about an old black and white science fiction film that was one of his favourites, telling the story of a man who began shrinking down to the size of a mouse. He liked it artistically but not for its science. As he explained, it could not happen like that. Somehow removing selected atoms while keeping the same proportions would not work because a man reduced to the size of a mouse while still made of the same body cells would only have room for the brain power of a mouse. And even if you could change the size and mass of atoms in a body it could not absorb oxygen from normal air. Alice supposed growing in size raised the same objections. It was not possible.

Except she had seen it happen before her very eyes!

If she had not been weighed down by the Rabbit's all too real bulk she would have shrugged wryly. There was nothing for it but to accept that the laws of nature she was familiar with did not apply in Underland. Should she have been surprised? In the original Alice story the heroine changed size and shape several times under the influence of magic potions, cakes and mushrooms. And to think she had asked about just this sort of thing half jokingly at the tea party when she first arrived. Perhaps there were common things or processes in her world which would not work here. Maybe that struck a sort of balance.

Alice tried to shift herself into a better position while not disturbing the Rabbit, but apparently he was dead to the world. His pizzle had softened and retracted but his spent sperm continued to ooze out of her, making a wet patch on the sheets under her bottom and adding to her discomfort. She turned her thoughts to more practical matters. If only she could slide out from under him she could get the keys to her chains from his jacket which lay across the arm of a chair. But it was too far away.

Her wandering eyes passed over the bedside table, then swung back to the brown glass bottles labelled 'BIG' and 'SMALL' as a daring thought struck her. Cautiously she moved her arms, which had been folded over her head, towards the table, edging herself a little further out from under the Rabbit. Her cuffed wrists made it awkward but she could just reach the bottles. She hesitated. Would it work on her? There was only one way to find out.

Her hands closed around the 'BIG' bottle. If she grew larger than the Rabbit nobody could stop her.

She had actually pulled out the cork when she realised one unavoidable consequence. With a shudder she replaced it and put the bottle down. She had almost made a lethal mistake! The Rabbit had removed his ring before he took the potion. Unlike the storybook version it obviously did not affect inanimate objects. If she had grown bigger she would have strangled herself with her own collar!

Her hand moved to the other bottle. Presumably it was the counter-agent to the growth formula, but would it also reduce somebody down from their original size? If it did then she could shrink out of her collar and cuffs in one go, and there would be no need to sneak back to Topper's house for the keys. She tried to think the idea through, aware that the Rabbit might wake up at any time. The storybook Alice had got into all sorts of trouble getting stuck at the wrong size, and while that was not a sound guide to her current circumstances, it did remind her to stay in reach of the antidote.

She took a deep breath, popped the cork off the bottle and brought it to her lips, aware of the risks she was taking. She had no idea of the correct dosage, or if the result was in exact proportion to the amount drunk. She would need to be about half her size to slip out of her collar. Perhaps she should try the equivalent of a teaspoonful first.

Cautiously she took a small mouthful and swallowed it. It tasted slightly of peppermint. If the Rabbit's change was any guide it should take effect almost . . .

The bottle was growing and getting too heavy to hold and it slipped from her hand. The sheets were crawling under her as the walls of the room fell away. Her collar rose up in front of her even as it dug into the back of her neck and then flopped over her head. Pain stabbed at her chest as air rushed out of her lungs in a belch. Her ankle cuffs were dragging her downwards as they spread her legs even wider. She vanished under a mass of coarse fur. The cuffs slipped from her feet. Her stomach bloated and something viscous began squirting out of her vagina and down her legs. She shrieked in terror. She was being crushed, suffocated! The Rabbit's body was like the roof of a cave pressing down on her. There was just room between it and sheets like wrinkled canvas to squirm towards the light.

Sobbing and gasping, Alice pulled herself free and flopped down onto her back. Beside her the Rabbit lay like a beached whale, while his sperm oozed thickly out of her front passage by the handful and stickily lathered her legs. Her collar and one of her wrist cuffs, looking like something fabricated by heavy industry, lay against a boulder of a pillow.

She was now the size of a Barbie doll.

For several minutes Alice sat hugging her knees to her chest and trying not to give in to shock. Her eyes kept drifting to the seemingly monstrous form of the Rabbit. If he woke up now he could crush her with one hand.

Gradually she mastered her emotions. At least she seemed physically unharmed. Every part of her had reduced in the same proportion, so it might almost have been the rest of the world that had expanded about her. How it worked she had no idea, but she could still move, breathe and see perfectly well. And she was free of her collar and cuffs. Her gamble had paid off and she now must make the most of it.

Trying to get up, she found her thighs were gummed together by the Rabbit's sperm, which was forming a flaky crust as it dried. Gross! she thought, as she pried her skin apart. She scraped the slimy stuff from her legs and cleft in disgust and wiped it on the sheets. The sperm still inside her had retained its normal volume, so as her passage had shrunk, it had been forced out of her. It was an experience she would not forget in a hurry.

Walking over the yielding surface of the bed towards the side table, Alice encountered a new problem. There was a gap between the side of the bed and the table top, which was also higher than the bed. A small distance in reality, it now resembled a chasm, far too wide to step over, and with the floor an alarming distance below. Nevertheless she had to get to the 'BIG' bottle to regain her normal size and make good her escape.

There was no other way of bridging the gap so she decided she would have to jump. If she landed rolling, taking it on her shoulder, it should be all right.

Alice took a few steps back, measuring the distance with her eye, then sprinted forwards and leapt. But as she pushed off, her foot slipped as the edge of the mattress gave under it. Instead of clearing the edge of the table it caught her in the midriff. She hung on for a second scrabbling to get a grip on the polished wood, her feet kicking in empty air, then started to slip backwards. She twisted round to make a grab for the side of the bed and clutched the folds of the sheet. But the material slid through her fingers and she could only slow her descent. She reached the edge of the sheet, lost her grip, and, with a despairing shriek, dropped free.

She landed with a thump on the edge of the bedside rug, which fortunately cushioned her fall. Winded and trembling she looked up at the table top, which was now as relatively far above her as the roof of a house. Gingerly she got to her feet, rubbing her coccyx. She supposed she ought to be grateful not to have broken a leg or even her neck, but how was she going to reach the bottle of potion now? The table was supported by three splayed legs which merged into a single central column. Even if she could climb it, the table top overhung all round.

Alice walked around the base of the monstrous bed searching for a way back up to the top. But its shiny brass legs were too large and slippery to get a grip on, and looking round the bedroom she saw nothing she could move to make a step. It was ridiculous but it looked as though it would take a rope and grappling iron to get back onto the bed. It occurred to her that she might find rope – or at least string, which would serve her as well – in the kitchen. There might also be pins or nails there which she could use to make a hook.

She set off at a jog towards the bedroom door, which fortunately the Rabbit had left open, and passed through it onto the landing. At the head of the stairs she paused, looking down the daunting cavern of the stairway. The house had taken on the dimensions of a cathedral, and there were cracks between the floorboards on either side of the strip of carpet that she could have twisted an ankle in. But the stairs, being made for an animal's length of stride, proved relatively easy to negotiate. She vaulted down each in turn with the carpet softening her drop. Climbing back up would take longer, of course, but at least she was in good condition to make the ascent. Whatever else her girling training had done for her, it had kept her fit.

Reaching the hall, Alice made for the kitchen, trying to concentrate on finding what she needed instead of the surreal experience of scampering about naked through the vast house. It made her feel even more exposed, yet curiously liberated at the same time.

It was only when she reached the kitchen and looked about her that Alice realised her mistake. Cupboards and drawers were no longer the readily accessible repositories of handy domestic items she was familiar with, but vast constructions well out of her reach and ability to manipulate. The Rabbit's kitchen might be full of bits of string and bent pins that could be turned into grappling irons, but there was no way she could get to them.

Alice wandered aimlessly round in a circle trying to think. Where else would you find what she was after? A cupboard under the stairs? The same problem of access. A sewing box? Perhaps, but where would the Rabbit keep such a thing, assuming he even had one? The only other place she could think of was a tool shed, but how could she even get outside to search for one with the doors closed? Was there an open window she might risk jumping out of, and how would she get back in again if she did?

Just then she heard the tramp of footsteps and a shadow passed across the kitchen window. The knocker of the back door sounded thunderously and a booming voice called out: 'Rabbit, it's me. Can I come in?'

It was Topper.

For a moment she was gripped by despair. As soon as Topper found her discarded restraints and the reducing potion he would guess what had happened. No time for her to get back to normal. She had to escape as she was.

Topper knocked the door again. 'Rabbit, can you hear me?'

Alice darted across the floor to the angle between the wall recess and hinge side of the doorframe, where she flattened herself into the corner. The handle turned, the door swung open towards her, and Topper, looking like a veritable colossus, stepped inside.

'Don't say you're still abed, Rabbit,' he called, looking towards the door leading to the hall. 'The Duchess has gone and I think we've got away with it, so calm your worries . . .'

Even as he was speaking Alice rolled under the door which he still held open. She scrambled over the wooden sill, down the stone steps and dropped to the paved path. Leaping the cracks between the flag-stones she sprinted towards the back gate, which was set in a high brick wall. The door closed and Topper's voice disappeared into the house. She had a minute at most to get clear.

The back gate was of solid board, but there was room enough to squeeze under. On the other side a winding path fringed with docks and cow parsley meandered past back gardens. Beyond that rose the great green wall of the woods. She dashed across the path, waded through tufts of grass as tall as her waist, stalks scraping her bare thighs, and then into the concealing shadows under the trees. From behind her came a faint cry of dismay: 'Rabbit, what have you done!'

Alice did not stop running until the village was out of sight. Then she flopped down onto a bed of dry leaves in a hollow between the roots of a tree. Wiping the sweat from her brow she recovered her breath.

As she did so, a sense of deja vu came over her. Of course! The storybook Alice had escaped from the White Rabbit's house in the same shrunken state as she had, though her namesake had been lucky enough to retain her clothes.

Nevertheless it was a disconcertingly close parallel. Was she caught up in a re-run of the story? No, she decided. Specific events were not repeating them-selves, only similar situations created by related characters and places. In the story it had been size-changing cakes the Rabbit had in his house, while in her case it had been a liquid potion. Desperation had driven both she and her counterpart to take some. Though it had never really happened, since the other Alice was fictional. Or rather, she had been a real girl in a fictional story. Presumably . . .

Alice groaned, resting her head in her hands. She was no longer so certain of the boundary between fact and fiction. Which had come first: the story of Wonderland or the place she was now in which had apparently mutated from it? Maybe the same place could be fictional and real simultaneously, depending on your point of view. Was she herself just a character in another story? She shivered suddenly, though not from cold. This was not the time to try unravelling the interrelationships between parallel universes. Her first priority was to remain free. At least the woods provided plenty of cover.

Already greener and fresher than anything she had known before, they had been rendered even more magical by their relative change in scale. She was on the edge of a flowery glade ringed by a magnificent forest of giants, seeming vast and primeval, that spread their branches in an interlacing canopy of green against the bright sky, as high over her head as the tallest redwoods back in her world. But these were oaks and beeches and proportionately their girth was even greater, with their roots forming massive buttresses lifting the ground around them into small hills.

Entranced by the wonder of it, Alice left her hollow and walked down onto the floor of this magical glade. It almost made up for everything she had gone through. Nearby a clump of – to her – gigantic mushrooms stood like things out of fantasy. She half expected to see tiny windows and doors set in them. Of course in Underland that might not be so unlikely. In the clearing between the trees were starry wood anemones, primroses spreading their crinkled leaves the width of tables and clumps of bluebells standing taller than her head. She wandered between them, heady with their scent, their cool, lush, dew-fresh leaves brushing her naked body. In such surroundings her nudity almost seemed natural. Beads of dew the size of apples had gathered in the hollows of the leaves, reminding her how dry she was. Could she drink un-miniaturised water? Carefully she cupped one in her hands and brought it to her lips. The bubble of surface tension holding it together seemed to dissolve as she swallowed. It tasted fine and she drank several more until her thirst was slaked.

It took an effort to wrench her mind back to her own circumstances. There was no time for sightseeing. She was an escaped slave reduced to the size of a child's doll. What should she do next?

First: regain her normal size, which meant getting back inside the Rabbit's house and using the growth potion. That would be hard enough, but now Topper might be waiting for her. It depended whether, from the evidence, he believed she was still shrunken. If the Rabbit was not sure how much had been in the bottles to start with, Topper might conclude she had used the 'BIG' bottle to restore her size and left before he arrived. That meant she could wait for him to leave and then she would only have to get past Rabbit. But if Topper decided she was still reduced he might anticipate her return and lay a trap. Well, that was a risk she had to take. She had to get back to normal size as soon as possible.

Or did she?

Maybe there were advantages in remaining as she was for a little while longer. It might even help her sneak back into the Rabbit's house. Then, if she could get hold of enough of both sorts of potion, she could put it to further use. She could work her way around the village until she found Topper's house, wait until Valerie was returned and then free her. A dose of the shrinking potion and Valerie could simply walk out between the bars of her hutch!

Alice warmed to the ingenuity and daring of her plan. She imagined Valerie's surprise when she appeared like this, and then the two of them escaping together. Once they were free they could do, well, anything together.

Regretfully she came back to earth. First she must reconnoitre Rabbit's house and see what was going on there. After some thought, she found a patch of damp earth and smeared it all over her, adding streaks of crushed moss to complete her camouflage. Then she set off back the way she had come.

Alice was so excited with her plans and thoughts of the future that it was a good fifteen minutes before she began to wonder when she would strike the path skirting the back of the village. She stopped and looked about her. Nothing seemed familiar, but then she had been too concerned with escaping to note any significant landmarks.

Surely she was going in the right direction, though. She had left the flowery glade by the same route, so even if she veered a little off course she should strike her objective at some point. Or had she left the same way? She was unused to finding her way almost at ground level in dense woodland without a marked path, under a sunless sky that gave no sense of orientation.

Alice swore aloud, using words which would have shocked her parents. There was no point deceiving herself. She was lost.

Two hours later she was beginning to think the woods of Underland went on forever. They were certainly thicker than anything she had ever seen before, especially when viewed from her current eye level. She might have passed close to the village several times without knowing.

Just when annoyance was turning to worries about survival, a silky voice purred: 'My, my. What a thing to see a pretty girling in such reduced circumstances!'

Alice started and spun round, but there was no one in sight.

'Up here, girl,' the voice said.

She looked up. Draped over the branch of a tree above her was tabby cat wearing a supercilious grin on its crescent slash of a mouth. Alice's momentary surprise turned into a resigned shrug of her shoulders. She was bound to meet him sooner or later.

'Good morning,' she said, feeling she might as well be polite.

'Now that yet remains to be seen,' the Cheshire Cat replied. 'I wondered what you were when I came across your scent and followed you. And now I find a girling no more than a foot high. Where are you bound, girling?'

'My name's Alice,' said Alice. 'And I'm trying to get to the White Rabbit's house. I don't suppose you know the way?'

'As it happens I do,' the Cat said, smugly.

'And can you tell it to me, please?'

The Cat considered for a moment. 'Well if I were going there, I wouldn't start from here.'

'Very funny. Thanks for nothing.'

'As you will,' said the Cat. 'Do you have any other objectives?'

'I'd like to get back to my right size, but I don't suppose you can help with that either.'

'Ah, now I see your problem,' said the Cat. 'You have two goals, but you can't go two ways at once. Clearly a symptom of mental derangement, if not madness.'

'I'm not mad,' Alice said hotly, 'at least not yet.'

'Madness and sanity are merely what the majority defines them to be,' the Cat said. 'What you would call madness is quite common here. Weren't you warned before you came?'

'I suppose I was,' Alice admitted.

'And haven't you seen many examples of this madness since you've been here?'

'Er, yes.'

'Then why do you still respond with surprise when you encounter its manifestations?' The Cat shook his head sadly. 'Only a deranged person would do that, unless you are attempting to deny this reality. In either case you are mad.'

Alice pinched the bridge of her nose. The Cat was right. She was having a crazy conversation in a crazy place – circular, self justifying and therefore perfectly logical in Underland. What else did she expect?

'I'll just get on then, OK. Bye . . .'

'Wait, girling.'

' "Alice"!' said Alice angrily.

'As you wish: Wait, "Alice",' said the Cat. 'I may perhaps be able to assist you –'

He sprang down from the branch. Halfway to the ground he faded into thin air, leaving Alice gaping at nothing. Not even his grin remained. All right, she thought, keeping her nerve with an effort. So he can make himself invisible, or maybe teleport. I should not be surprised. Cats always seemed to be unnaturally stealthy.

'– if we can come to an agreement,' the Cat continued from right behind her.

'Shit! Don't do that!' Alice exclaimed with feeling as she spun about.

'Really, such language from one so young,' admonished the Cat. 'And you smelt such a nice, tender girl.'

He was sitting primly on the ground, looking much larger than he had appeared on the branch. Alice

128

became aware of the size of his teeth and the length of his claws. Apart from the slight anthropomorphism of his face he looked much more of a true animal than anything she had so far encountered, perhaps because he wore no clothes and went on all fours.

'What sort of agreement?' she asked cautiously.

'Why nothing but to join in a little game,' the Cat said.

He stood up and began to circle round her, sniffing and brushing close as he did so, daintily placing his paws with feline grace, his tail languidly flicking from side to side. Alice found having something the size of a furry carthorse wearing an insane grin while frotting her deeply disconcerting.

'The problem with Underland,' he continued, 'is the increasing difficulty for me to exercise my natural instincts.'

'Natural instincts?' Alice asked.

'By which I mean the thrill of the chase in pursuit of my prey, be it vole, bird, mouse or even rat. Such things as come naturally to me, you understand. The gentry do it all the time. They revel in a good hunt, so why should not I? But can you imagine, the local animals object to my exercising my natural desires. They claim kinship with the brainless creatures that haunt these woods, saying they are distant cousins and will not allow their blood to be shed. They argue that as they have overcome their instinctive tendencies, so I should also. But then most of them are herbivores, so what would one expect.'

'And where do I come in?' Alice wondered.

'Obviously, you are a mere girling, and one most fortuitously reduced to a convenient size. The animals would not care if I hunted you.'

'What!' Alice exclaimed in horror, shrinking away from him.

129

'Purely for sport, you understand,' the Cat said with a broader smile. 'I can imagine it now! The exciting pursuit, twisting and turning, the final spring, a little toying with my helpless prey, perhaps allowing a futile attempt to escape. The scent of warm flesh, the fluttering heartbeat under my paw. What joy, what bliss!'

'You must be mad,' Alice said, backing further away.

'Of course I am,' said the Cat in surprise. 'This is Underland, as I thought we had already established.'

'No way!' Alice shouted, and turned and ran.

'If not by agreement, then let it be by default,' the Cat called out. 'Tally ho!' and he bounded after her.

Alice sprinted through the wood, her thighs pumping, bottom flesh shivering and breasts bouncing. She was lathered in sweat and scratched about the legs from fallen branches and cuts from grass stems. Every few seconds she snatched a glance over her shoulder to see how close the Cat was. If only she could get ahead of him long enough to find a hiding place.

But he was bounding along in her tracks, grinning with delight. Gasping for breath, Alice ran on, thinking: This cannot be happening to me, it cannot be happening! But there was all too much of the hunting tiger in the Cat's pursuit to doubt his purpose. At least he was not using using his invisibility/teleportation trick to stalk her. Perhaps he wanted it to be a sporting hunt.

But as they darted between the trees, Alice realised he needed no supernatural assistance to catch her. Four legs versus two – it was no contest. The Cat closed the gap until he was springing along at her very heels. A paw, claws sheathed, hooked about her legs. Alice tumbled over, smashing into a clump of bluebells and adding their sticky pulp to the grime that already caked her. Before she could get to her feet the Cat pounced, one huge paw pressing down firmly on her chest as he crouched over her.

Winded, Alice struggled wildly, tearing at the paw that held her while looking up in sick horror at its great un-catlike grin exposing an abnormal number of white and very sharp teeth. Fear loosened her bladder and a shameful stream of pee coursed between her legs, even as a wretched feeble scream, sounding more like a squeak, burst from her lips.

'Please no! You can't! Don't kill me!'

The Cat's eyebrows rose as no normal cat's should. 'Kill you! What do you take me for? I would never kill a thinking being. I leave such things to the gentry. You should have let me finish explaining. Now be quiet, girl, or you will spoil the moment.'

His other paw batted her across the side of her head. Dazed and confused she lay limp except for the tremulous rise and fall of her chest.

The Cat appraised her with satisfaction. 'Ah, what a tasty morsel is this.' He sniffed her body, nuzzling into her crotch. 'A fine girling, so young and tender. She seems to have wet herself, poor thing. No matter. Now, how I shall feast off her . . .'

He prodded her arms and legs with its paw until she was spread wide, then crouched down over her, front paws resting across her arms. His huge pink tongue lapped out, up her belly and over her breasts which lifted under the insistent pressure. Still dazed, Alice shivered at the warm wet caress and the surprising roughness of his tongue. It was like a scouring flannel rasping across her skin. Not exactly unpleasant and infinitely better than being eaten.

She was not going to die, that was all that mattered!

Perhaps the thrill of that realisation explained why her nipples pricked up to receive a second lick.

'Ah, girling flesh,' the Cat purred, 'how succulent.'

The tongue worked down lower into Alice's crotch, suddenly rasping through her pubic hair, her labia parting under it, opening her to its caress, adding its own wetness to hers.

'The taste of excited girling,' the Cat said. 'Such sweet nectar.'

Alice stirred uneasily. What was he doing? She tried to rise but the Cat cuffed her back with a flick of its paw.

'It's no good struggling, girling, for I shall have my fill of you by hook or by crook.'

Alice squirmed but the Cat's weight was too great and she dared not risk annoying him. Heart pounding, she tried to relax. She had never imagined the chase would end in sex, but it seemed to be an obsession in Underland and . . . ohh . . . that did feel good. Weird but good. Hares, rabbits, now a cat. She was working her way through the menagerie.

'Warming up, are you, girling?' the Cat enquired lasciviously, licking his lips. 'I like to bring a smile to the face of my prey.'

Her arousal intensifying with every teasing tongue stroke, Alice's fears dissolved as she lost herself in bizarre delight. She had never felt anything like it before. Her cunt was sopping wet and her clitoris hard. It was probably a world record for oral sex. Her buttocks were clenching and hips lifting as she offered herself to the great rasping tongue that was working its way deeper and deeper inside her.

'Do you beg for release, girl?' the Cat asked.

'Oh . . . yes please, yes . . .!'

'Do you want it to be different to anything you have felt before?'

'Yes, yes! Bring me off, please!'

The Cat stopped licking and shifted his weight forward, its chest pressing her into the ground, flattening her hungry hips. No! She wanted to feel its tongue again – ahhh!

A pizzle that felt like a cucumber forced its way up inside her. She shrieked and flailed about, but she was spreadeagled and helpless under him. Nothing could stop the piston-like thrusts she thought would tear her apart even as his weight drove the breath from her body. He would split her, she could not take it! But she did take him, her sheath stretching wider than she had thought possible, the pressure frightening and exciting, her clitoris ground between the weight of his body and the hard plug of his pizzle. Then the cat came. It was like a hose filling her with hot cream and she thought she would burst under the pressure. But instead fireworks of sheer pleasure exploded in her belly and sizzled up into her brain, perversely made more intense by the pain. Sobbing in joy and confusion she blacked out.

Alice recovered her senses an unknown time later.

She lay sprawled on her back on the bare earth under a straggling holly bush that spread like a spiky green tent over her. She was utterly satiated. Little shivers of delight were still rippling through her as the Cat's ejaculate seeped out of her ravaged vagina and soaked into the soil. Had he damaged her? She must know. With a huge effort she tried to sit up, only to find she was paralysed! Her limbs were limp and useless. Even her vocal cords would not respond. Yet she could still feel, and realised a foolish rictus of a smile was frozen on her lips. What was wrong with her?

'It is a novel effect my seed has on girlings, and will wear off when it has drained from you,' the Cat said, looking up from licking his genitals and reading the dismay and confusion on her face. 'Meanwhile, you'll be safe enough here while you recover.'

Ignoring her indistinct grunts and twitches he completed his meticulous toilet, then lent over to look her in the eye. His grin was wider than ever.

'You are one of the most satisfying girlings I have ever had,' he told her sincerely. 'I could happily keep you in this state for a week and have you again at my leisure. But I have hunted well and taken my prize, and now I will leave you to your own devices. *Nulliforia transformassicus* is what you want, by the way. Small round orange and white spotted mushrooms. They're not common but a careful search will turn them up. Eat a piece and you'll return to normal size. You see, despite your doubts I have solved one of your problems.'

He turned as if to leave, then looked back at Alice still lying akimbo.

'It is a most curious thing, but nobody ever enquires why I smile so,' he confided. 'Perhaps now you can guess:

' "Why does the Cheshire Cat so widely grin?
Because he's supped the cream and the quim,
The pursuit of girlings is his lifelong joy,
Tricking and trapping 'em by ingenious ploy.
He licks and laps at their private parts,
Tups them right heartily and then departs.
Leaving smiles behind him almost as wide,
And fond memories of letting a cat inside!" '

And with that he sauntered away.

Alice lay there feeling filthy, helpless, used and yet still high on raw pleasure and perversely satisfied. What sort of a slut did that make her?

Was it simple delight at finding herself alive when she thought she was going to die? Did that compensate for being screwed by what was effectively a giant feline? After all, he had been very well spoken.

Hell, she couldn't think straight. Get a grip, Brown!

How could she accept the fact of it so easily? What did it tell her about Underland or herself?

The agreement she had signed, however unwittingly, the collar and chains and the orderly way she had been trained had given her treatment up to now a strange sense of legitimacy. But she had escaped from that and so declared herself free. Now she had been taken without her prior consent by what was certainly a sentient being. Was it rape? It did not feel like that. Was she a willing participant in a strange game – on some voyage of sexual discovery to test her own limits? She did not want to be a slave, but undeniably found erotic pleasure in being treated as one. Chained up, strapped down, front or rear, cock or rubber dildo, being caned, with or without uninhibited cakes, with man or animal she always came! And it was the most intense pleasure she could remember. Did that make her a nymphomaniac or a masochist?

Was it an impossible contradiction or simply what the Rabbit had sensed when he 'sniffed her out'?

Would accepting that she was special in some way help her survive in Underland? Perhaps. As an adult individual who had taken responsibility for her own life, the way she chose to respond to what happened here was up to her. Forget about rationality, fairness or conventional morals. Those abstractions did not apply in Underland, at least not in the way she had known them. It was a mad place, but if she learned to make the most of it, enjoying any pleasure it offered however bizarre without guilt, then that was her business alone.

Was that a good philosophy of life? Well, for now it was all she had.

An hour passed before the blissful paralysis faded and Alice was able to sit up unsteadily and examine herself. Her groin felt pummelled but there seemed to be no damage, only a curious hollowness inside her as her distended passage gradually contracted. The memory of that huge member would linger even longer than the Cheshire Cat's smile.

When she felt strong enough she crawled out from under the holly bush and set off through the woods once more. But now, thanks to the Cat, she was also looking for small round orange and white spotted mushrooms.

What she found was a bramble bush bearing blackcurrants the size of pumpkins, guarded by thorns the size of daggers. Alice had to twist like an eel between the stems to get to them, knocking the fruit down with sticks (twigs). Her hands and mouth were stained purple with their juice, but she thought she had never tasted anything so delicious.

The possibility that the berries might have something else in them besides vitamin C she considered briefly and then dismissed. She was too hungry to care. Now, sitting cross-legged in the shelter of the bush, enjoying her reward, she seemed to be suffering no strange effects. Whether she was getting any nutritional value out of the fruit in her shrunken state was uncertain, but at least they felt satisfying. It did not seem she was in immediate danger of starving or dying of thirst.

A few stones lay jumbled in the heart of the bush, and in a deep cleft between them she scraped out a simple shelter which she lined with dry moss and grass. As twilight fell across the wood she barricaded the mouth of her hideaway with a latticework of twigs and curled up inside to pass the night as best she could.

As she tossed and turned in her inadequate bed, missing Valerie's company dreadfully, she tried to plan for tomorrow.

Clearly there was no point in wandering about at random any further in the hope of finding either mushrooms, the village or Topper's house. She had to work to some methodical search pattern. Blazing a trail or in some way marking her path would stop her getting lost. There might even be a tree she could climb to help locate the village though, considering the giants around her, the prospect was daunting.

Eventually she fell into a restless half-sleep, jerked into anxious wakefulness every so often by nocturnal woodland noises, then dozing off again. In this curious state her mind wandered.

Could she weave a rope out of grass to help climb a tree? How stone age. Were her survival skills up to it? Images of the Rabbit's house came to her and she turned over ways of getting inside unnoticed. How would she get the bureau open to get at the potion bottles, assuming they hadn't been moved? It would need something like a crowbar. Why had he hidden it away so secretly anyway? Was he hiding it from his girling maids? She'd been a girling but now she was free. Free and lonely and a little frightened. Were there other things apart from freedom? Being a slave had its compensations – other people took responsibility for you – all you had to do was obey. How she missed having Valerie to curl up against. Their hutch seemed very homely right now. She finally found deeper sleep imagining Valerie's warm scented body in her arms.

* * *

137

Alice awoke with the dawn. She was stiff and cold and uneasy in her mind, but determined to see her plan through. She breakfasted on blackcurrants while wondering if she could find something else to vary her diet. Of course mushrooms were abundant in the woods but she dare not risk sampling them at random. What other berries were edible?

A scrape in the earth a little way from her shelter, served as a toilet. As she gingerly wiped herself clean she decided that natural moss had, once again, proved an inadequate substitute for the modern conveniences of life. The woods also seemed to be short on soap. She set off on her first excursion, thinking wistfully of extra smooth moisturised toilet paper and other essentials of feminine hygiene.

Determined not to get lost again, she used a stick to scrape arrows in the earth to mark her trail at regular intervals, or else bent over flower heads or tall stems of grass. She planned to travel for an hour, as far as she could judge, in a straight line. If she found nothing, she would retrace her steps, estimate a bearing forty-five degrees to one side of the first and repeat the process. By this method she should be able to find either the village, the lane or at least a well-used path.

But before she found any of those she came across a clump of half a dozen *Nulliforia transformassicus*, pushing out from under some dead leaves.

She examined them closely, assuring herself they were what she was after. Then she tore a hunk off one of the bulbous caps, that seemed to her like beach-balls, and brought it to her lips, only to hesitate. Should she keep the mushroom for later and make use of her current size as planned? If she regained her normal size she would have to build another camp for herself. But suppose she could not get into Rabbit's

138

house and obtain a supply of the regular potions. How long would the mushroom segment stay fresh and effective? Fungi were short-lived, and this clump might not be here very long.

No, she dare not risk losing the opportunity. As recent experience had taught her, she was the prey of everything larger than herself, and the next one might not be as reasonable as the Cheshire Cat. Besides, being normal size would help her find the village more easily. She would just have to think of another way to rescue Valerie.

Before she could argue with herself any further she bit into the hunk of mushroom and swallowed it down. The flesh was rubbery and almost tasteless. Would it work?

Nausea overcame her and she fell over. The ground seemed to be crawling inward under her. Her lungs felt crushed as she desperately gulped down air to fill their expanding volume.

In a few seconds it was over. She blinked up at trees that no longer seemed so impossibly tall. Beside her head was a tiny clump of orange and white mushrooms nestling between a few small leaves. Alice grinned foolishly and then laughed aloud as pent-up tension found release. She was her right size again! How she had regained her body mass, whether it had been with her all the time but in some way suspended round a dimensional corner, she had no idea.

But she was back to normal, and suddenly anything seemed possible once more.

Seven

It was on her second traverse through the woods that Alice came upon a small brook, trickling and burbling between the trees over a rocky bed. The water was so clear she did not hesitate to drink it. Then she splashed some over her face and squatted down and scooped handfuls up into her crotch to wash herself out. Greatly refreshed, she considered the stream thoughtfully.

It would serve as a better marker than any trail she could blaze, and might lead somewhere interesting. Certainly it would not hurt to follow it for a while. She set off along the side of the stream, enjoying its cheerful music. Five minutes later she came upon the signposts.

There was one on each bank, both bearing a white board facing away from each other. The sign nearest her read in bold black letters:

IMPORTANT! READ OTHER SIGN

What was so important, she wondered? She waded across the stream to the other bank. As she did so she saw there were a few words written in tiny letters on the back of the sign facing the water:

PRIVATE PROPERTY! NO TRESPASSING!

The front of the board read:

IMPORTANT! READ OTHER SIGN

Alice looked back the way she had come and saw there was also lettering on the back of the first sign. She recrossed the stream and read:

PRIVATE PROPERTY! NO TRESPASSING!

But which side of the stream was private? She gave an exasperated sigh. It was more twisted Underland logic. Well, there was nobody about to notice at the moment, so she might as well carry on.

More small rivulets joined the stream, swelling its volume. Shortly the woods opened up before her and she found herself by the banks of a small lake.

The water shimmered like green crystal under the bright sky, fringed by clumps of bullrushes and lazily drooping willow trees. Dragonflies darted to and fro on iridescent wings. The scene was so perfect that for a minute Alice just stood there drinking in the simple tranquility. You had to hand it to Underland, she conceded, the inhabitants might be strange but the scenery was perfect.

Suddenly she became conscious of how dirty she felt, even though the grime she had picked up over the last day had been thinned by her return to normal size. The lake seemed deserted, so why not have a swim?

The water was perfectly clear and just cool enough to be refreshing without being cold, she discovered as she waded in. The bottom sloped gently down without any long weeds. When she was waist deep she took the plunge and swam a few strokes. It was perfect. She ducked her head under again to soak her hair, and then worked it through with her fingers while she trod water. Some shampoo would be nice but this was better than nothing.

Lazily, she swam the length of the lake for the pleasure of moving her muscles in relaxing rhythm and the feel of the water flowing over her naked body. Then she lay on her back, just her face and nipples breaking the surface and floated. When she got back home, she would find somewhere she could swim nude. It would not be as perfect as this, of course. She must make sure she knew how to find the lake again. It might be a good place to hide.

Thoughts of her lover reminded her she still had to find the village. Regretfully she turned back to where the brook entered the lake when something on a nearer bank caught her eye. Mildly curious she swam a few strokes closer. Laid out neatly on the sloping grass were two sets of clothes with folded white towels beside them.

It took a moment for the implication to sink in, then she gave a start and twisted round with a splash, scanning the banks and clumps of rushes. Somebody had already been by the lake when she got here. But where were they now? Watching her from the shelter of the trees, perhaps?

Briskly, Alice swam on towards the spot she had entered the lake. She didn't want to risk any more encounters. Best that she leave quickly and quietly.

Something hard brushed her foot and she glimpsed a dark shadow skimming across the bottom. She twisted to one side and struck out in a different direction. What felt like a cold hand ran down her thigh. Fearfully she kicked out at the unseen thing and then made a desperate lunge for the nearest bank.

The water erupted in front of her and she shrieked and almost choked as a monstrous head bobbed up.

It was a great green frog, grinning broadly.

Alice splashed and kicked wildly, backing away from it.

There was a surge of motion behind her and the head of a brown frog broke the water.

'Not a mermaid, Temp,' the green frog said in a deep rasping voice, circling round Alice. 'But a pretty thing, nonetheless,

'No collar you notice, Esc, so she must be newly arrived,' the brown frog replied, circling in time with his friend. 'Otherwise she'd know this was private property.'

'But what of the signs?' the green frog wondered.

'Perhaps she can't read,' the brown frog suggested.

By this time Alice had managed to clear her throat. 'Who . . . who are you?' she spluttered.

'We are forgetting our manners, Temp,' the green frog said with a disconcerting grin. 'We must introduce ourselves. I am Rana esculenta.'

'And I am Rana temporania,' said the brown frog.

'I'm Alice Brown,' said Alice. 'And I'm sorry, I saw the signs but I didn't know what bank of the stream they meant was private property.'

'Why, both banks are private, girl,' said Esc. 'It's the stream that is not private property. If you'd stayed in the stream you wouldn't have trespassed. But now you have.'

'I didn't know this was your lake,' Alice said quickly. 'It looked so nice I couldn't resist a swim. I'll go right now.'

As she spoke she tried to edge between them and make for the bank, but with effortless kicks of their legs they slipped in front of her. There was no way she was going to outswim a pair of frogs.

'Please, I don't want any trouble, I just want to leave,' she said.

'This is no trouble,' said Esc, his great bulging eyes rolling as the corners of his huge mouth turned up.

'A long time since we had such a pretty thing like you to ourselves,' Temp explained, a pink tongue flicking out and running round his lips.

They were circling her more closely so that she could feel the touch of their bodies. Long-fingered webbed hands reached out and brushed her hair, her cheeks, her breasts. Underwater, curious fingers slipped between her thighs, tickling and probing. Alice gulped. No, not with frogs! she thought. But of course she knew only too well, even as she feebly tried to push them away, that she could if she had to. There was nothing she could not do if she let herself. It was her weakness and her strength.

'She's not used to Underland ways,' said Temp. 'Maybe I should teach her how a girling's expected to serve.'

'I saw her first,' Esc said quickly. 'I'll have her.'

'No, I saw her,' Temp retorted. 'She's mine.'

Esc gave a croaking laugh. 'Why are we arguing over a girling with two holes? We can both have her at once.'

Alice whimpered and shook her head, but it was far too late now. She was encircled within their double embrace. Esc's great frog face loomed before her, its protruding eyes at once grotesque and hypnotic. Large cold hands closed about her waist while others took hold of her wrists, supporting her even as they pulled the three of them together, sandwiching her between their smooth rubbery bodies. She was struggling from instinct even as she felt herself surrender to the inevitable. Valerie had said it was more exciting to resist. Was she right? Hard rods of flesh were nuzzling up into her groin and the cleft of her buttocks. What sort of sexual equipment did frogs have? Was it different in Underland?

They slid into her with surprising ease, their members slick and smooth. She gasped by reflex, but they were not much bigger than Lepus and her insides had been trained to accommodate far larger intruders in recent weeks.

The vigour of their thrusts increased and the curious suction of the water drawing on her bowels as they slid in and out added to the sensation. Alice began to relax, letting her body take over. It was not unpleasant. She could actually get off on this. Who would have thought –

Without warning, still locked together, the three of them plunged under the water. Rolling over and over they were propelled forward by the frogs' powerful legs, every kick driving them up into her in a remorseless rhythm. They broke the surface with Alice frantically gasping for breath.

'Not underwater . . .' she choked. But the pair were lost in a frenzy of coupling as was their nature. It was all she could do to gulp down more air before they ducked under again, sculling through the limpid green depths of the lake. Alice was soft and warm as they rolled over and over, the blood pounding in her ears as they had her again and again.

Alice lay sprawled on the bank where the frogs had dropped her, too dizzy and exhausted to move. Her lungs ached from holding her breath, her ears popped and sucked, sperm and water trickled out of her well-used passages onto the grass. Yet she also felt oddly proud. She had survived coupling with two frogs underwater! Surely the animals of Underland had no weirder way they could use her.

Meanwhile the frogs had wiped themselves off with their towels, strange as it was to see amphibious creatures taking such pains to get dry, and were now dressing. Whatever served them as penises seemed to have disappeared somewhere inside them. Vague recollections of reptile anatomy from school biology classes came back to her, along with the word 'cloaca'. Apparently like birds, frogs in Underland kept their genitalia concealed until needed.

Wearily watching them dress, Alice hoped they had finished with her. They knew she would not use their lake again. When she got her strength back she could get on with finding the village.

The last items the pair put on were old-fashioned curled and powdered white wigs, which complemented their frock coats trimmed with gold braid and knee britches. The whole ensemble seemed comic yet also strangely familiar.

They came over to her as she coughed and tried to sit up.

'What'll we do with her now?' Temp wondered.

'No, please, you've had your fun,' Alice protested.

Feebly she tried to crawl away but they caught her legs and dragged her back over the grass like a sack of potatoes. Esc took hold of her wet hair and turned her head from side to side so he could examine her face.

'We caught her trespassing on Her Ladyship's land, so she'll decide.' He gave a rasping chuckle. 'We'll do ourselves a bit of good bringing this one in. She likes them pretty.'

'Her Ladyship?' Alice gasped.

'The Duchess of Margravia, of course. All this belongs to her.'

Of course. The frogs were dressed as footmen.

She was not going to escape meeting the Duchess after all.

A curious sense of fatalism seemed to overcome Alice as the frog footmen led her through the woods. Her

146

brief spell of freedom was over, snuffing out her plans for rescuing Valerie and escaping from Underland. She was a helpless captive once again.

Yet she was bigger than the frogs and, though exhausted and light-headed from her recent exertions, she might have been able to break away from them. They were her betters in the water but surely she could outrun them on land. But somehow she could not muster the will to make the attempt. The most she could do was drag her feet and tug weakly at their restraining hands without effect. She was uncomfortably aware of her aching orifices and their sperm trickling down her thighs. They had caught and used her in the way a girling was supposed to be used. What else did she expect?

A mansion nestled in the woods, approached on one side by a gravel drive and enclosed on the other three by high garden walls. Temp and Esc, still gripping Alice firmly by the arms, led her through a gate in the wall and past manicured lawns, closely clipped hedges and regimented flower beds. The house was taller and grander than Topper's and loomed imposingly. An insidious suspicion was creeping over her that this was the sort of place where she belonged. No, she thought desperately, she had to fight it! Her only advantage was that the footmen had assumed she was newly arrived in Underland. She might be able to turn that to good use, though she had no idea at that moment exactly how. It depended on whether the Duchess's household was as mad as it had been portrayed in the story.

Steps by the side of the house led down to the sunken yard of a half-basement level onto which opened a row of windows misted over by steam. The frog footmen led Alice in through a door into a scullery containing several old-fashioned domestic items including a large sink, mangle, washboard and a wooden drying rack hanging from the ceiling. In strange contrast to these antiques, another wall held rows of hooks from which hung straps and chains and other items of restraint.

A red-haired girling was bent over a sink up to her elbows in steaming soapy washing. She was naked except for small white frilly maid's cap, a very deep black collar trimmed with lace, and a stiff black lace-trimmed corset running from the bottom of her ribs to the top of her hips, which was buckled tightly, pinching in her waist. Chains ran from rings at the back of her corset to wrist and ankle cuffs, apparently allowing her enough freedom to work but no more. As Alice was led past her she saw the girl's bare bottom was striped with a regular cross-hatching of narrow red weals. The girl flashed Alice a quick, curious glance over the broad strap-gag that closed her mouth and then bent over her work again. Alice wondered if the Duchess had obtained her cheaply from Topper and Lepus.

A second door led into the kitchen itself, the air misty with aromatic steam. It was fitted out in a similar period style to Topper's but was much larger. A vast woman in frilly white mobcap and floor-length aprons was standing over an iron stove, stirring bubbling pots. Two more girlings, harnessed like the one in the scullery, were at work washing and peeling vegetables and scrubbing the floor. The cook looked up from her work. A nose like a ski-ramp protruded from between her heavy jowls. She folded her brawny arms and sniffed in disapproval.

'Well, and what have you got here? Somebody lost a girling? I hopes she isn't stolen.'

'No, Mrs Braising,' Temp said quickly.

'We found her swimming in the lake,' continued

Esc. 'She doesn't belong to anybody. See, she's got no collar.'

Mrs Braising clumped over to stand in front of Alice. She was nearly as tall as Topper. Reaching out a big hand she caught hold of a fistful of Alice's hair, twisting and turning her head to examine her face. Her other hand slipped down to cup and squeeze Alice's breasts, her fingers digging into the heavy globes. Alice bit her lip but said nothing.

'A nice, full-breasted girling,' Mrs Braising said approvingly. 'Lean meat but well fleshed out where it matters.' Her eyes passed Alice's stomach and thighs. 'Firm belly and flanks . . .'

With irresistible force she jerked Alice out of the frogs' grasp and pushed her face down over the side of the big kitchen table amid the clutter of pots and sliced vegetables. The scarred boards, dusty with flour and smelling of onions, ground roughly under her skin. Mrs Braising's big hand slapped into Alice's bottom, making her pale cheeks jump and shiver.

'A fine bit of rump and chump here.'

She casually pulled Alice's legs apart as though she was handling a farm animal.

'Tight little parson's nose,' she observed, examining the fleshy split pouch between her thighs and then thrusting a long stiff forefinger up into depths of Alice's cleft while her thumb went up her rectum. She worked them in and out, exploring the elasticity of the fleshy passages and making Alice gasp. 'Juicy and tender and already well-oiled, it seems.' She withdrew her glistening fingers, sniffed them, then glanced accusingly at the frog footmen. 'Have you two been spawning with her?'

'Just a bit of fun, Mrs Braising,' they pleaded.

'Well, it looks like she can take a lot of stuffing.' She jerked Alice's head up so she could look her in the eye. 'What's your name, girl?'

'Alice . . . Alice Brown.'

Mrs Braising smiled knowingly. 'Oh, an Alice, are you? We always have particular fun with Alices. Do you belong to anybody?'

'No, I'm free,' Alice protested tremulously. 'Please let me go. I didn't mean to trespass. I wasn't doing any harm.'

'We'll let Her Ladyship be the judge of that, girl. Right, you two,' she said to the frogs, 'we can't show her upstairs in this state. Since you found her, you'd better clean her up.'

A few minutes later Alice was standing in a tin bath in the scullery with her arms outstretched and wrists tied to the overhead drying frame. One of the girlings brought out a large steaming kettle from the kitchen range and mixed it with a bucket of cold water, which was then poured over Alice with a jug. The footmen, who had taken off their jackets and rolled up their shirt sleeves, enthusiastically began sponging and soaping and scrubbing her down. The hard bristles scraped her skin. Their hands worked the soap into every fold and crevice, turning her into a slippery plaything. Yet she accepted it all passively. The soap and hot water felt good and the intimate handling brisk but not unkind. A few weeks ago she would have freaked out at something like this, but now she knew it was mild compared to what might be done with her.

After she was rinsed down she stepped out of the bath as it was dragged aside and stood placidly on a towel while they dried her off and combed her hair. The frogs were unexpectedly dexterous and now they had finished fiddling with her it was more like a careful grooming. She began to feel pampered. Surely any household that took this much care of a girling could not be too bad.

'Please, can you tell me what the Duchess is like?' she asked.

'Well, she's very particular about some things, girl,' said Temp.

'What sort of things?' Alice asked cautiously.

'Pigs, for instance,' said Esc.

'And pepper,' added Temp. 'Likes her dishes to be well seasoned, does Her Ladyship.'

'And she has very firm ideas about proper child-care.'

'And cabbages.'

'And Kings.'

'Not forgetting Queens, Esc.'

'Certainly not,' agreed Temp, then added bitterly, 'and keeping certain creatures under her thumb –'

'Enough of that, Esc,' Temp said sharply. 'Legs apart, girl . . .'

They lapsed into silence, concentrating on brushing and fluffing up Alice's pubic hair, which made her squirm and giggle. Was what they said true or simply more mad Underland talk? Though as she knew only too well, just because it sounded mad didn't mean it wasn't true in Underland.

'Anything else I should know about her?' she prompted.

'Everything in the house has to be kept spick and span,' agreed Esc.

'Oh yes, a regular tyrant about the dusting and polishing being done properly, is Her Ladyship,' Temp agreed.

'And order. Everything in its place and a place for everything. Got to be neat.'

Well, being houseproud was not a bad thing, Alice thought. She sounded a bit saner than the Duchess in the original story, though she was no longer sure how useful a guide that was. She remembered the Duchess

151

had been portrayed as being particularly ugly. Well if she was she would go out of her way not to notice and try to be as polite as possible. The underlying morality of Underland, though obviously pretty twisted, was essentially Victorian, when good manners counted. If she made the right impression maybe she could persuade the Duchess to let her go on her way. She might even persuade her to give her some clothes. Should she call her 'Your Ladyship' or 'Ma'am'? Despite her situation Alice stifled a giggle as the absurdity struck her. Did you curtsy to a Duchess even if you were stark naked?

At last the frogs stood back to inspect their work. Alice stood before them feeling unexpectedly refreshed. Her hair shone bright gold, the dirt had been scraped from under her nails and her skin glowed pink and clear. Despite being naked and outdoors for so long she seemed not to have tanned at all, which she supposed was because there was no proper sun in Underland.

'Now, nipples up, girling,' Temp said. 'Show you're excited to be here and pleased to see Her Ladyship . . .' He and Esc pinched and rolled her nipples until they swelled into plump, blood-red cones.

Untying Alice, they took her back into the kitchen for Mrs Braising's approval.

'She'll do,' the cook said, after looking Alice up and down. 'Her Ladyship'll be in the drawing room, I expect.' She flicked a finger sharply at Alice's nipples. 'Keep them up, girl, if you want to make a good impression.'

With one footman on each side holding her firmly by an arm, they led Alice upstairs.

Passing though a green-baize door they entered a grand hall, all dark shiny wood, panelled walls and plaster mouldings, with an imposing staircase running up to a big open landing. Everything was spotlessly clean and the smell of wood polish lingered in the air. The frogs led Alice across the hall to a large door with gilt handles and entered without knocking.

The room beyond was light and airy, with a high ceiling and large windows looking out across the gardens. Chairs and side tables were arranged in neat regular groups. Marble pillars flanked a big fireplace while four small semi-circular alcoves were let into the wall opposite. Two of the alcoves were currently occupied by naked girlings – harnessed, chained and strap-gagged and standing straight and as still as statues while staring rigidly ahead of them.

The Duchess herself was sitting in a chair reading. She was resting her feet on a living footstool. A naked girling was kneeling hunched over on the floor in front of the Duchess's chair with a cushion strapped to her back.

'Your pardon, Your Ladyship,' said Temp deferentially, 'but we came across this girling swimming in the lake. She has no collar and claims she is free. We think she may be newly arrived in Underland.'

The Duchess looked up with interest. 'Really. Bring her closer,' she commanded in a deep, hearty voice.

The footmen ushered Alice over to stand beside the Duchess's chair.

Though not as ugly as she had been portrayed in the original book illustrations, the Duchess was certainly not beautiful. Built on the same larger-than-life scale as the other humans Alice had so far encountered, she was also stocky, with huge bosoms rising under long trailing robes richly patterned in red and gold, which she wore wrapped about her toga fashion. These, together with a peculiar turban-like headdress, gave the impression that she was preparing for a fancy dress party as some old-fashioned oriental potentate. Perhaps they were her lounging robes. Alice vaguely recalled some wealthy Victorians had a thing about wearing oriental dress in private. Under the turban, the Duchess's heavy brows hooded deep sharp eyes, a large nose and a wide straight mouth set in a square no-nonsense jaw.

She had been inspecting Alice in turn, waving a hand to the footmen to turn her round so she could see her from all sides. Now she looked her in the face again and nodded in approval.

'Yes, a pretty little thing, and so well endowed with fine upstanding nipples. What is your name, girl?'

'Alice Brown, Your Ladyship,' Alice said primly.

' "Alice". How interesting. And how did you come to be trespassing on my land?'

While the frogs had been washing her she had prepared her story. She could see no advantage in the Duchess learning how Topper and the others had conspired to conceal Alice from her, and it might make things worse for herself as well if she was revealed to be an escaped slave.

'I do beg you pardon for that, Your Ladyship,' Alice began, hoping she sounded suitably contrite and respectful, 'but I was lost and your lake looked so beautiful and I felt so dirty after the time I'd spent wandering round the woods, I just had to swim in it. Which is why I've got no clothes.'

The Duchess looked unimpressed. 'Really, and didn't you see the signs indicating it was private property?'

'Well, yes,' Alice admitted. 'But I didn't understand them.'

'That does not say much for your education, child,' the Duchess said. 'Was their meaning not perfectly clear?'

'In a way, but only afterwards.'

'So you did understand them?'

'I suppose so.'

'Then why did you say you did not?'

This was not going the way Alice had hoped. She said quickly, 'Because I was still confused by finding myself here. You see, I was walking in some woods near my home when I fell down a hole which seemed to go on forever and then I landed here. This is Wonderland, isn't it?' she asked innocently. 'Only I heard them call it Underland. Anyway, I wandered around and got hungry and dirty until I found your lake. Please, Your Ladyship, can you help me?'

The Duchess smiled. 'So you would like food and a place to stay and proper clothing, would you, Alice?'

'Yes, please, Your Ladyship.'

The Duchess's smile broadened. 'I think I can promise you that, my dear. All those in my service are appropriately fed, clothed and sheltered.'

Alice felt a warning flutter in her stomach. 'In your service? No, please, I don't want to serve you. If you could just let me go. I won't be any more trouble.'

The Duchess's smile now looked menacing. 'You do not understand, Alice. You were caught trespassing on my land so you belong to me. That is the law of Underland. Unless anybody else had a prior claim on you?'

Alice bit her lip, then shook her head dumbly. Admitting she lied now might make it worse.

'Good. Then we shall start with your lashes.'

'Lashes?' Alice exclaimed in horror. 'But I haven't done anything wrong!'

'But you have, Alice. Let me see now, shall we say ten strokes for trespassing, five for foolishness and two for speaking out of turn?'

'But I didn't –'

'Now it is five for speaking out of turn!'

Alice clamped her lips tight. She was just making it worse for herself.

'All on that pretty rounded bottom of yours, I think,' the Duchess said. 'Prepare her!'

In a daze Alice let the footmen hustle her over to one of the columns that stood beside the fireplace. They drew her arms round the pillar as though she was embracing it and she felt metal cuffs snap tight about her wrists. Temp pulled on a chain linking the cuffs and her arms were dragged upwards, pulling her flat against the column, squashing her breasts against its cold hardness. Meanwhile Esc had drawn out a long leather strap from behind the pillar which he wrapped round Alice's waist and buckled tight, pinching in her waist and accentuating the upper slope of her buttocks. The frogs pulled her ankles round to the sides of the pillar and strapped them firmly against it. Two more straps went around her knees and thighs just below the lower curve of her buttocks so that she clasped the column between her legs and her mound of Venus kissed the smooth marble. This left her bottom utterly immobile and pouting slightly under the pressure of the straps that framed it.

How many other girlings had been secured as she was now, Alice wondered, her plans and hopes melting away as the futile fancies they were and always had been. How had she imagined she could ever escape from Underland? This was where she belonged.

Twisting her head round she saw the Duchess rise from her chair, her girling footstool crawling quickly to one side, and come over to the fireplace. For a long moment she simply looked Alice's tightly bound body up and down, savouring its soft contours. Alice's heart was racing, her breathing ragged with fear as she anticipated what was to come. Perverse excitement coursed through her as she surrendered to her bonds, the masterful confidence of the Duchess, the magnified awareness of every part of her exposed body and the tumbling, scooping sensation in her stomach.

The Duchess stroked her hair then ran her fingers down the smooth hollow of her spine, making Alice shiver. Her big hands cupped the fleshy globes of Alice's buttocks and squeezed and kneaded them with the close attention of a connoisseur sampling a fine wine. The Duchess slipped a finger into the deep-cleft valley between the mounds, briefly teased the tight pucker of her anus, then slid further to fondle the slit of her pubic pouch where it pressed against the column, bringing forth a helpless groan from Alice.

'What a pretty creature you are,' the Duchess said. 'I'm sure you will make an excellent pet. But first we must drive out any foolish belief in your own independence. All in this house obey only my will. Whatever rights or freedoms you used to enjoy are gone. You are what is known in Underland as a "girling"; a slave creature lower than these animals that serve me. Your only purpose is to give pleasure through your service by way of absolute obedience, do you understand?'

Unthinkingly, Alice nodded. It was the simple truth, after all.

'Good, then we shall begin.'

Esc was standing beside the column with a long polished wooden box which he opened for the Duchess's inspection. Inside, nestling in grooves lined with red silk, were half a dozen assorted canes and lashes. After a moment's deliberation the Duchess selected a springy length of bamboo and swished it experimentally through the air.

'Now I'm going to give you those lashes you so richly deserve, Alice,' she said, waving the footmen out. 'Think of this as both a punishment and a lesson. The marks will linger for a few days as a reminder of what you are and to whom you now belong. Don't try to hold back your screams. I won't count them as speaking out of turn. In future your silence may be enforced by gags or other means, but this being your first punishment, I want to hear your unhindered response to what is being done to you. One must be strict with your kind, you see.'

As the Duchess took up her stance to one side of the column and carefully laid the bamboo across the fleshy undercurve of Alice's buttocks to measure her swing, she began to chant a perverse little lullaby:

'Speak firmly to your girling slave,
And punish if she displeases:
Beat the slut and she'll soon behave,
No mind her cries and wheezes.'

As a sort of chorus she landed three quick blows: *Swish . . . crack, crack, crack*!

Three horizontal stripes of scarlet about a thumb-width apart appeared across the lower curve of both hemispheres, bridging the cleft between them. Alice threw back her head and gasped aloud as the narrow rod scored her flesh. Nodding in satisfaction the Duchess laid on further strokes exactly parallel with the first, working her way methodically up and over the curve of Alice's buttocks. Her yelps merged into continuous shuddering sobs.

How could she survive twenty such lashes? She could feel her pliant flesh jump and tremble under each blow but could not pull away to ride the impact because of the unyielding column to which she was so tightly bound. The shockwaves seemed to reverberate through her whole body as ripples of pure pain, radiating out from her tortured and immobile bottom which had become a virgin parchment, faithfully recording each precise stroke in shades of pink and red.

Through a haze of pain and confusion she found herself longing for the garden of Topper's house. At least there punishment had allowed for stimulation. When she had been whipped on the impaling post she had the wooden peg inside her to work herself on for pleasure. There was nothing sexual about the crimson grid the Duchess was laying out stroke by stoke on her bottom.

So why were her nipples hard, her thighs clenching the column as though it was some huge phallus, her vagina wet and pulsing, her clitoris swollen and pushing out of its hood? How could she be aroused by a beating after being used by the frogs only an hour earlier?

The Duchess rested her arm for a moment, sniffed curiously, then reached between Alice's legs and probed her pubes. She withdrew slick and glistening fingers which she held to her nose and inhaled deeply.

'Ah, so that excited you, did it?'

When Alice did not respond the Duchess clasped a handful of her hair and wrenched her head round so she could look into her tear-streaked face. 'I asked you a question, girl!'

Wretchedly, Alice nodded. 'Yes . . . Mistress.'

'Good.' The Duchess let Alice's head drop, took up a fresh stance and began to imprint an up-swinging series of vertical stripes on Alice's shivering and abused buttock cheeks. As she did so she sang:

'Bind tight a pretty girling toy,
And flog her soundly for good measure:

Submissives give the greatest joy,
For in pain they find their pleasure.'
(*Swish . . . crack, crack, crack!*)
'Is it cruel to tan pretty bottom cheeks,
So bringing tears to maiden eyes?
Not when her cunny so lustfully weeps,
And you know which orifice lies.'
(*Swish . . . crack, crack, crack . . .*)

And with every blow Alice yelped anew, but now in helpless bewilderment as well as pain.

No, it couldn't be true! Except deep down she feared it was. Pain alone was enough to arouse her now. She had been conditioned like one of Pavlov's dogs. Underland had turned her into a true masochist, or was that what she always had been?

After what seemed an eternity the Duchess rested her arm. 'Twenty. All done. That wasn't so bad, was it, Alice?'

Alice shook her head. 'No, Mistress . . .' It wasn't bad, it was terrible. Or did she mean wonderful?

The Duchess inspected the results of her attentions. Alice's normally pale bottom was a blazing pink, overlain with a regular web of scarlet slashes: eight parallel horizontal stripes spanning both cheeks, four vertical cuts evenly spaced and two pairs of diagonal welts crossing in the exact middle of each soft hemisphere. 'A neat job if I do say so myself,' the Duchess commented, patting the inflamed flesh and causing Alice to groan again. 'You won't be able to sit down for a day or so, but no matter. The cook will put some butter on those rosy cheeks if you ask her politely. You have a taste for the rod, girl. I think I'm going to have a lot of fun with you.' And she gave Alice's nipples a playful tweak.

Shamefully, Alice felt herself smiling shyly back,

knowing that helpless frisson of joy a freshly whipped dog experiences when it has just earned an unexpected pat on the head from its master.

The Duchess left Alice strapped to the column while she returned to her reading, as though she had ceased to exist. Perhaps it was a further lesson in subjugation: to demonstrate that she was no more than a room decoration like the girlings in the alcoves. The reason did not matter. It was not for Alice to know why, only to accept that it was what the Duchess, her new mistress, desired. But her body was conditioned to expected sex with or after punishment and this time there was none. She had been aroused without opportunity for release, and that was almost as bad as the caning itself. Yet if she was a true slave then she should expect nothing less. She screwed up her eyes and rested her head against the cool column. Was this going to be the pattern for the rest of her life?

An hour passed before the Duchess put down her book and came over to Alice again. She inspected her sore bottom, fondled her pubic cleft, stroked her hair, cupped her breasts as they swelled against the column and looked thoughtfully into her fearful, confused eyes.

'A little more tenderising, I think,' the Duchess said, half to herself. Then sharply she called out, 'Bell!'

One of the girlings in the alcoves immediately began to bend her knees, bobbing up and down while keeping her upper body upright. As she did so her breasts were dragged upwards by their tips, to form stretched cones. Cords ran from pulleys set in the back of the alcove that ran over the girl's shoulders to nipple rings. Somewhere in the depths of the house a bell could be heard chiming faintly.

In a few seconds Temp entered, bowing obsequiously. 'You rang, Your Ladyship?' he croaked.

'Put our new girling in harness and tell the cook to work her about the house and gardens,' the Duchess ordered. 'In a few days, when any remnant of self-will has been driven from her, she may be fit to serve me in my chamber.'

'Very good, Your Ladyship.'

So it was that half an hour later, her bottom glistening with a soothing coating of butter, Alice was on her hands and knees scrubbing the kitchen floor. Metal links clinked as she worked. She was harnessed like the other house girlings, with chains running from the back of a tight little corset to wrist and ankle cuffs. All these were secured with pins that Temp and Esc had hammered into place, so they were smoothly finished without buckles or locks.

A broad black collar encircled her neck, forcing her to keep her chin up. The Duchess evidently liked her girlings to stand straight with heads high and not to slouch. A broad strap-gag also covered her lips with an attached rubber ball projecting from its inner face filling her mouth. The frogs had shown Alice what was inscribed on her collar before it was fitted. It read: PROPERTY OF THE DUCHESS OF MARGRAVIA. Using a hammer and a set of punches they had stamped Alice's name onto a blank metal disk and now it hung from the front ring of her collar like a dog's nametag.

Alice had felt a last shiver of panic and resentment as the collar had closed about her throat, flinching at the hammer blows by her ear as the locking pin had been driven into place. Then a curious sense of lightheaded relief had flooded through her when it was done. At last she could stop fighting the inevitable. There were no more choices now: her only goal was learning the routine of the house and her place within it. Ahead of her was a cycle of menial work, discipline and punishment that she supposed would last as long as her new mistress found her pleasing. Her only hope was that she could occasionally enjoy the proper consummation of her arousal. If she was allowed that then she could survive anything.

Suddenly she was seized by sharp regret. She had been thinking only of herself, but what about Valerie? If only she was here with her to share the pain and pleasure that lay ahead, then she would almost be happy. But what chance was there now of ever seeing Valerie again?

A mansion like the Duchess's should by rights have had a butler, but in the distorted Underland fashion there was none. Mrs Braising seemed to organise the running of the house, and directed the animal servants almost as imperiously as her employer.

There were no other human staff. In addition to the two frog footmen, a housemouse called Mus served in the capacity of a boots. The gardens were tended by Niv and Erm, respectively a weasel and a stoat. All the other work – the hardest and most menial tasks – was of course performed by girling slaves. Alice's arrival brought the number up to nine. The girlings helped in the kitchen, cleaned the house, toiled in the gardens, served Her Ladyship, and waited on everybody else. They were the lowest of the low, muted by the gags they wore, constrained by their harnesses, subject to punishment for the slightest fault and teasing and humiliation for no reason at all.

That night Alice rested with the other girlings in the empty kitchen. Niv and Erm lived in the village and Mrs Braising, Mus and the frogs had retired to their own quarters in the house.

The girlings lay on mats on the floor arranged in a semi-circle about the softly glowing kitchen range, their feet warmed by its steady heat. Their wrists and ankles were cuffed together and a long heavy chain had been passed through their collar rings and its ends padlocked to eyebolts set in the walls.

It was Alice's first opportunity to talk to her fellow slaves. So far their gags had only been removed at mealtimes, and there had been little chance to gossip. Free at last they huddled together, conversing in eager whispers, plying Alice with questions about events back home, how she had arrived in Underland and what she had seen of the place before she had been captured. Isolated from the village and far from home, any new arrival was a subject of great excitement, Alice realised.

She managed to answer most of their questions, repeating her own vague explanation for her arrival. Perhaps it would not have hurt to tell them the truth, but she thought it wise not to risk the Duchess discovering she had lied to her.

According to their name tags her sisters in slavery were Tanya, Margi, Yasmin, Barbara, Brigit and Keli. Fiona and Danielle were not present, having been selected that night to serve in the Duchess's bedroom. Tanya and Brigit were blonde, Barbara and Margi brunette, Yasmin was olive-skinned and Keli coffee-dark. They were all young and attractive women, causing Alice to wonder if Underland attracted any other sort. Or was this just chance or the result of careful selection? Once their initial curiosity had been satisfied, Alice asked how they had come here.

'Most of us met a White Rabbit,' Tanya said with a giggle, and went on to relate a story very like Alice's own: restless, feeling out of place, not comfortable at home and a yearning for adventure. They had been captured the same way she had, trained and eventually sold by Topper and Lepus. Margi, Yasmin and Brigit had similar experiences. With Keli and Barbara the story was slightly different. They had made the transition to Underland by themselves under circumstances that made Alice realise how lucky she had been.

'. . . wasn't really my stepdad, 'cos he and Mum never married,' said Keli, her teeth flashing very white between her full sensuous lips. 'He was OK when he didn't drink. But one night Mum was out he got pissed out of his mind and tried to put his hand in my shirt, and I knew what he wanted and I just ran out the door. I hid in a skip round the back of the flats. I could hear him calling for me, saying he was sorry and please come back, but I knew I couldn't take no more of that sort of shit! I was all scrunched up in the stinking rubbish thinking: I've got to get away! Anyplace but this! And then I must've fallen asleep, 'cos when I woke up I was in the woods here.

'For a few days I just wandered around living on berries and things. Never known a place as quiet as this, y'know? I was scared at first, but I got used to it. Then I tried some mushrooms, but I didn't know they were the sort they give you to make you horny. Jezus! I was frigging myself like crazy. That was when some of the animals found me. They didn't seem so strange the way I was feeling right then. They screwed me and it was amazing! Afterwards they took me to the Duchess. She hadn't had a black girl before, so I was worth something to her. First time my skin's got me in somewhere special . . .'

Barbara had been living in a squat when she made the transition.

'. . . I was stoned, right, but not enough to forget where I was. I looked around at the shithole where I

165

was crashed and wondered if that was as good as it would ever get? But there was nowhere I could go back to. Then amongst the crap on the floor I saw the Alice book. Dunno who left it, but there it was. And I read it and cried and cried. Fell asleep thinking about what a wonderful place it was. Next morning I woke up in the woods here. First off I thought I was still off my head. I know they say this place is mad, but they should've lived like I did the last few years. Took me a couple of days to realise it was all real, and by that time they'd got a collar on me . . .'

Alice listened to their stories and wondered how many other people from her world ended up here. But did everybody come to the same place? How many other alternate worlds were there? More importantly, if it was possible to go one way without the aid of the Rabbit's trick watch, perhaps it was possible to get back as well. But she must not think of that, she told herself quickly, frightened that last shred of hope would melt away if she dwelt on it too long. She must surrender herself to her immediate fate. This was her new home and she must accept it like the other girls.

A naive but obvious question came to her. It was one that a supposed newcomer such as herself would be bound to raise in the circumstances: 'What do you feel about being slaves?'

'I don't get treated no worse here than I did back home,' Keli said with a shrug. 'The Duchess is all right, once you get to know her. At least when she beats you she knows when to stop. She's in control and you know it.'

'Actually, that's sort of exciting,' Brigit admitted.

'The food is better here, and you don't worry about somebody stealing your things because you got nothing to take,' Barbara said with a grin.

166

'The rules are simple. It's honest in a way. You get used without any guilt. You know where you stand,' Tanya said.

'I wasn't much good at school,' Margi admitted. 'Here you don't have to worry about money or finding a job.'

'At first I thought I would go mad, being made to have sex with this lot,' Yasmin admitted almost shyly. 'But then I found they were nicer than some men back home. I think they were the real animals!'

'Admit it – the sex here's great!' Keli said, and the rest nodded and grinned.

As Alice fell asleep comforted by the warm naked bodies on either side of her, she wondered at how the other girls had found contentment with their strange new lot in life. Yet there was sense and reason to their acceptance because, despite the demands made upon them by their bondage, they were happier, safer or more fulfilled than ever before.

Yet for all that she now knew herself to be very like them, Alice could not submit totally as they had. She sensed her own particular destiny in Underland was still to be determined.

Eight

The next day they set Alice to work in the gardens under the direction of Niv and Erm. The weasel and stoat inspected her critically as she knelt before them. They wore stained waistcoats and flat caps and had working boots on their feet.

'Bit top heavy, this one,' Niv observed.

'Her Ladyship likes them that way,' Erm said.

'Fine for her, maybe, but we've got to get some work out of the slut.' Niv poked his snout almost into Alice's face. 'Are you strong, girling?'

Alice nodded quickly, blinking over her gag.

'Only we're worried about these udders of yours. They might be a problem for garden work. Shake them about, girling, so we can see how much they move.'

Obediently Alice sat back on her heels and wiggled her shoulders, setting her breasts bobbing and swaying. The two gardeners looked at the display thoughtfully.

'Could be trouble there,' Niv said, catching hold of Alice's bouncing right breast by the nipple and lifting it to judge the weight. 'You mind you don't let them get in the way, girl.'

Alice squeaked and shook her head.

'Nasty things can happen to titties that get in the way in gardens,' Erm said, taking hold of her left breast in the same way, stretching the nipple taut. 'Shall we show her?'

'Maybe we'd better,' said Niv.

From behind his back, Erm produced a hand fork and prodded the captive globes sharply with its prongs, indenting the pliant flesh. Alice yelped and flinched.

'See, there are all sorts of tools that can give you some nasty pokes,' he said, jabbing her breasts vigorously as though he was pricking sausages and bringing tears to her eyes.

In a gloved hand Niv produced a posy of stinging nettles.

'Then there are thorns and stingers you've got to watch out for. Those big tits of yours might easily brush against them like this . . .'

He slapped the posy across her breasts from side to side, driving the tiny barbs into her skin so that they stung and burned. Alice whined and whimpered as the bumps and blotches spread across her abused mammaries.

'So you will be careful while you work, won't you, girling,' the gardeners said with a laugh.

And Alice nodded miserably, even as she felt the perverse glow of humiliation course through her.

They fastened her wrist cuffs to rings set in the handles of a large wooden wheelbarrow. While Niv and Erm dug over a flower bed she knelt on the grass between the shafts as clods of earth and weeds were tossed into the barrow. She tried not to move her stinging, smarting breasts and hoped the air would cool them quickly.

When the barrow was full Alice stood up and wheeled it away. As she did so, Margi, harnessed to a similar barrow and glistening with sweat, quickly took her place by the gardeners.

169

Alice trudged through the garden to the compost heap by the big greenhouse, wincing as her tender breasts rubbed against each other. And yet, despite the weight of the barrow Alice knew it made sense that she should be used like this. Girlings were bigger than the gardeners and could carry heavier loads in the barrows. In Underland they were natural working animals. Besides, the setting was delightful and the day, as always, was perfect.

On her way she passed other girls hard at work.

Keli was on her hands and knees lifting dandelions from a section of lawn. Her gag had been removed so she could hold a weeding tool which was strapped into her mouth. This comprised a set of long spring-loaded metal jaws with forward angled teeth that she pushed deep into the grass and closed over the weed's root. With a twist of her head she pulled it free and dropped it into a bucket. As she finished each section she would hook the jaws of the weeder under the handle of the bucket and shuffle forwards with it.

Alice's gaze lingered on the smooth lines of Keli's slim body under her glossy black skin, noting the slight jiggle of her neatly tapered breasts as they hung beneath her. Her naked public cleft pouted ripely from between taut rounded bottom cheeks, exposed for all to see. Caught up in the perfection of the scene Alice thought how beautiful she was and how very right she should be displayed in that way.

A little further on, Danielle and Tanya were harnessed to the garden roller, their arms cuffed behind their backs to its handle, sweat sheening their bodies as they strained to keep it moving. Alice smiled behind her strap-gag as she saw their thighs swelling and sweat glistening in the small of their backs as it was gathered by the round hills of their buttocks into the valley between them.

170

She reached the compost heap and with a heave dumped her load. Barbara was walking up to the heap along the path from the kitchen. She had a yoke about her neck with her arms extended and wrists fastened to its ends, from which hung two buckets full of kitchen peelings. These she tipped onto the mound of compost, then turning round with a toss of her head to Alice, spread her legs wide and let loose a stream of urine onto the lower slope of the heap. The gardeners said it was good for the compost and so the girls were ordered to pee on it at every opportunity.

Alice watched Barbara relieve herself, as she herself expected to be watched in her turn later, not just because she had come to know it as a pretty act to witness. With ordinary rights of privacy denied to them it was the sharing of such intimate moments that bound the girlings together. It was a test of trust and a reminder that inhibitions no longer existed in their lives.

Alice hung upside-down from her ankles as she was lowered through the upper branches of a big apple tree.

Most people would use long ladders or poles with scoops on the end to pick apples, but in the Duchess's orchard tall posts were mounted against the walls with pulley blocks at the tips. Ropes slung between them could be manoeuvred over the tops of the trees as required. Along these ran little pulley trains from which girlings could be dangled from lines tied about their ankles.

With the strange sensation of her breasts hanging inverted and bobbing almost under her chin, Alice reached the next bunch of ripe red apples. As she picked each one she thrust it between her thighs through a small metal hoop that held open the mouth of a long net that passed between her legs and hung down her back. The hoop was secured by a handle lodged in her vagina. It was a typically Underland solution to a simple task and one that Alice found, despite the scratches and blood pounding in her ears, both ridiculous fun and pleasurable.

As the weight of apples in the net grew she could feel the handle pressing harder against the front of her passage. With a little wiggle and clenching of her buttocks she could work it against what she suspected was her G spot. Glistening lubrication was soon welling up around the handle of the net and running up through her pubic bush. Picking apples had never been so stimulating.

When her net was full she grunted plaintively through her gag and the gardeners lowered her to the ground. She braced her hands on the grass as they emptied the net.

Niv sniffed the handle of the net, which was glistening with her secretions.

'Have you been enjoying yourself up there, girl?' he asked suspiciously. 'If this hole gets too slippery to hold it, I'll shove it up your arse, understand?'

Alice was nodding vigorously. Erm slapped her bottom. 'And you mind you don't drop any apples or you'll get worse than this.'

Alice nodded again, but the threats did nothing to diminish her sense of joy, and the slap only sharpened her arousal. As she was hoisted aloft once more she looked happily round the orchard. There seemed to be no seasons in Underland, and some of the trees were bare while others were in blossom or heavy with fruit as the one she was attending. It was strange and perfect and she felt perfectly content for that moment to be who and what she was.

* * *

172

It was a little later, as she was working her way through the thickest foliage that she heard a greeting from below.

'Good day to you, Mr Corone,' Niv said.

Through a gap in the leaves Alice saw a crow had joined Erm and Niv as they held the rope that supported her. The bird was looking about him with what seemed more than normal avian caution, then bent his head forward.

'Is it safe to speak?' he asked.

'Yes,' Erm said. 'They're all in the house.'

Alice continued to pick apples mechanically while straining her ears. She supposed they thought she couldn't hear them from where she was, or else thought girlings didn't count, which was more or less correct, of course.

'The word from the coast is that plans are well advanced,' the crow said.

'That's good to hear. We'll tell the others,' Erm replied.

'You know whom you may trust?' Corone asked anxiously.

'We know,' Niv assured him. 'And who we can't.'

'When the day comes we'll take care of the gentry's lackeys,' Erm said ominously.

'I have other calls to make. To the glorious day!' the crow said, and scurried off.

'To the glorious day!' the others called softly after him.

Now what was that all about? Alice wondered.

That night, as she was huddled up with the other girlings in the kitchen, Alice asked: 'Do you think the animals here mind serving the gentry who are all human?'

That drew some puzzled looks. Margi said: 'Well, it's the way things are here.'

'The gentry are bigger and stronger than the animals,' Yasmin said. 'I suppose it's natural.'

Fiona spoke up. She had pale freckled skin, red curls, bright blue eyes and an educated accent. 'If this world, or whatever it is, is shaped by the Alice books, especially the first one, then they can't help the positions they're in. It was told to entertain a little girl, so it had eccentrics and talking animals dressed up as people, but it was shaped by Victorian standards and morals and there was no doubt who was on top. The animals here represent the working and middle classes, but like the real England of the time, they were ruled by royalty and tradition, and those roles had to be filled by real people.'

'You don't suppose they'd ever try to change things?' Alice said carelessly.

'They moan about the royals sometimes when they're sure Cook can't hear them,' Margi said, 'but they never do anything about it.'

'One thing's for sure,' Tanya put in. 'Whoever's in charge, we'll be at the bottom doing the real work and getting screwed for the privilege!'

All the others laughed and giggled.

Alice went to sleep thinking what Fiona had said was probably true. But there was nothing to say things couldn't change.

Alice, Brigit and Tanya were taking their turn cleaning and polishing in the main hall.

Brigit was feather-dusting the banisters of the big staircase. Since her hands were cuffed behind her back the duster was socketed onto a ball-gag in her mouth. A second feather duster had been pushed up her rear, and it waggled about impudently as she ducked her head to get at the gaps between the posts. Every so often Brigit would turn round, spread her legs and stick out her bottom and swipe the reserve duster up and down the banister rail with a swing of her hips. The grin about her gag told of the pleasurable flexing the stick made in her tightest orifice.

The expression on Tanya's face was harder to read since she still wore her full strap-gag, but a certain distant look in her eyes suggested she too was enjoying her work. Her task was sweeping the hall carpet with an old-fashioned manual sweeper, whose brushes turned only when the whole device was rolled backwards and forwards. The handle of the sweeper ran up to a flaring flange at the base of a rubber dildo that curved up between Tanya's pink-flushed pubic lips. The device worked to and fro inside her with every push of her hips, making an audible sucking noise even above the burr of the sweeper brushes. But she dared not let herself come in the middle of her task. Every so often she shuddered and her eyes grew hollow as she struggled to suppress her natural instincts.

Alice was polishing the dark wooden floorboards where they were exposed around the sides of the hall. She was working on her hands and knees with large fluffy dusting pads strapped to her hands and shins. Alice also had an intimate attachment: a woolly mop on a short handle the end of which was sunk deep into her vulva. Her chains were drawn in short to prevent her from standing up, and the mop handle made it impossible even to straighten her aching back. But it was good to have a rod inside her as a constant reminder that this was no ordinary house and no ordinary domestic task.

There were no spray cans in the Duchess's house and the soft, lavender scented polish was in a large flat open tin beside her. Of course, with the cloths fastened to her hands she could not transfer the polish to the floor to start the process. But being Underland that was no problem.

Alice shuffled over to the tin and, dipping her torso, pushed her right breast firmly into the scented wax. Her mammary plumped out fatly as she worked it sensuously round and round, gathering a coating of wax as her hard nipple ploughed its own furrow. When she had enough she shuffled back and wiped her heavy globe across the floor in front of her, wincing as her erect nipple grated across the cracks between the boards. When she was done she set to work buffing the wax into a high shine, wiggling her hips as she did so to mop away any smudges she might leave as she progressed, or tell-tale drips of excitement from her plugged orifice.

When they were done Mrs Braising inspected their work personally, while the girls knelt trembling in the middle of the hall. The cook sniffed as she ran her fingers along ledges and inspected every corner, but eventually she nodded.

'It'll do. Tanya and Brigit, you start on the library. Alice, come with me.'

With her cleaning accessories removed and chains loosened, Alice stepped quickly after Mrs Braising as she led the way back to the kitchen. It was mid morning and the kitchen was empty. Pots bubbled on the range but the big table was clear except for a couple of pots and a bunch of carrots.

'Up there,' Mrs Braising said, and Alice climbed nervously onto the table top, crouching on her hands and knees.

Mrs Braising drew her wrists together in front of her and linked her cuffs, pushing Alice forward so that her face and breasts lay flat against the scarred wood, while her arms rested between her legs. She

176

bent Alice's knees still further, pulling apart her ankles as she did so until her hips were thrust out and back. Then she drew in the slack of her ankle chains linking them to the back of Alice's corset, running them over the outside of her calves and thighs until they were tight, forcing Alice's belly to dip closer to the table top.

Now Alice huddled face down with her bottom high and her buttock cleft and pubis stretched and exposed. Mrs Braising examined the intimate valley of flesh carefully, pulling apart the soft pink lips to reveal the dark, crinkle-edged tunnel beyond, pushing a big finger up her anus to judge its tightness and heat. Finally she nodded.

'First time I saw you I thought you could take a good stuffing,' she said. 'Now we'll see how you take to my special recipe.'

Mrs Braising poured some olive oil onto her fingers and thrust them up Alice's cleft, working them deep into her vagina until she was thoroughly lubricated. Then she took a lump of some firm doughy mixture from one of the basins, rolled it into a thick sausage and fed it into the ready-oiled passage until it was lodged well up inside her. Alice squirmed at the strange sensation of the heavy yet malleable mass filling her passage. What was the cook doing?

'Now we stoke your oven, girl,' Mrs Braising said.

She selected a large thick carrot from the bunch on the table and, holding it by it's feathery leaves, dipped it into the second basin, which was full of some crimson sauce that exuded a spicy aroma. The carrot came out richly coated in the sauce. Spreading Alice's bottom cheeks, Mrs Braising pushed the end of the carrot into her rectum. Alice gasped as she was stretched wider by the reverse taper of the vegetable, then sighed with relief as her anal ring closed over its fattest end, leaving the fronds hanging out of her like a green feathery tail.

For a moment she felt well plugged but nothing more, and wondered if this was all Mrs Braising planned for her. Of course she made a humiliating spectacle set out on the table bound and stuffed like this, but it was not so different from many regularly inflicted upon the Duchess's girlings. Then it began.

She became aware of an itching, burning sensation in her rear, as though the carrot filling her was turning into a glowing ember. It warmed and teased, then seared and tormented. Alice wriggled her bottom desperately, but of course there was no escape.

'Beginning to feel the pepper now, are you, girl?' Mrs Braising said with a smile.

A heat such as she'd never known before spread through Alice's loins. It seeped through from her burning innards into the channel of her vagina and the thick plug of dough within. In a minute yeast was beginning to ferment at a furious, unnatural pace. What kind of dough was this? It hissed and bubbled inside her and Alice groaned and writhed and squirmed. Mrs Braising pushed a kitchen tray between her splayed legs and patted her taut bottom already beading with sweat.

'I'll leave you to cook,' she said, and returned to her preparations for lunch, leaving Alice whimpering and helpless on the table.

Now she understood. It was a lesson in subjugation, intended to teach her that there was no use to which she could not be put, no experience that she could not be made to endure in mad Underland. The dough was rising inside the oven of her vagina, stretching her wide, pushing slowly, sensuously, oozingly out of her. It was as though she was giving birth to a French stick – a phallic loaf, its soft crust bearing ripples indented upon it by the ridges of her vaginal wall. It extruded grotesquely from between her thighs, growing ever longer.

Dimly she was aware of Temp and Esc entering the kitchen, and later Mus and some of the girlings. Now her pain and arousal was on show for all to see. She received grins and ribald comments from the animals, and looks of commiseration from the girls. Had they all been through the same torment? It was horrible and perverse and frightening and deeply exciting all in one.

It was not until the others had dined and left and the girlings were hard at work washing up that the stick of bread finally dropped from her lovemouth onto the tray, leaving Alice empty, weak and trembling. The heat from the sauced carrot faded and blessed coolness returned.

Mrs Braising sniffed at the new loaf approvingly. 'A nice piece of girl-baked bread, this. Her Ladyship'll have it with her tea.' She pulled the gag from Alice's mouth and examined her flushed features. 'Now, tell me what you are, girl.'

'I ... I'm a girling slave, Mrs Braising,' Alice choked out.

'What's your purpose?'

'To serve, to give pleasure ... to suffer.'

'Who do you serve?'

'The Duchess ... Her Ladyship.'

'Do you beg to serve her, no matter what she demands of you?'

'I beg to serve her ... no matter what.'

Mrs Braising nodded. 'I think you're fit for bed-chamber duty now. But heaven help you if you don't please her!'

* * *

So it was that night that Alice, Barbara and Margi, all freshly washed, brushed and chained, were led along to the Duchess's bedroom by Esc. Alice's heart thudded. She had hardly seen the Duchess since the first day, except glimpses as she swept grandly along a corridor or sat out in the garden. Now Alice trembled with both apprehension and curiosity, wondering what would be required of her.

Esc paused as he reached the door of the Duchess's bedroom, giving their nipples a quick pinch and tweak to keep them perked up alertly. Then he opened the door and led them in

Her first impression was of a rosy glow. Pink-tinted lamps shone on red and gold wallpaper. Heavy scarlet drapes shrouded the windows and formed the canopy of the great four-poster bed. In an alcove Keli, who had been attending the Duchess's bath, stood motionless and attentive. The Duchess herself was resplendent in a vast red and gold silk gown. She waved Esc away and smiled down at the three girls who knelt before her: wrists clipped to the back of their corsets, a chain linking their collars. They were not gagged. They needed their mouths and tongues free that night.

'Ah, yes. It is Alice's first time in my bedroom. Still keeping your nipples up, I see, girl. That's good. Do you understand what is required of you?'

'Whatever you wish, Mistress,' Alice replied humbly.

'That's quite correct. I think you will be low girl tonight. Keli, prepare them.'

Keli stepped forward quickly, unclipped Barbara and Margi's collar chains and led them round to the sides of the bed, leaving Alice kneeling at its foot. Meanwhile the Duchess slipped off her own robe. Underneath she was completely naked.

Alice gaped at her. She was gloriously voluptuous rather than fat. Pendulous breasts like pink beach balls capped by large red nipples thrust out over a fleshy belly that would have seemed potlike except that it was put in proportion by the fullness of her hips and plump thighs. Chubby buttocks hung in heavy moon-curves that shivered as she moved.

The Duchess climbed onto the bed and lay back on the mound of pink silk pillows piled against the headboard, looking like a reclining goddess as portrayed by some classical artist. Unconcerned, she spread her legs to reveal a thick triangle of dark pubic hair.

Keli positioned Barbara and Margi on either side of the Duchess, who raised her arms to let the two girls lie against her. Immediately they began kissing and licking her huge breasts. The Duchess smiled indulgently and lowered her arms, enclosing each in her embrace. Her big plump hands cupped and squeezed their bottoms. Keli clipped their leash chains to the headboard, then came back for Alice.

'She shall use the cushion,' the Duchess said to Keli. 'And you will wear a number three rod to keep her in time.'

'Yes, Mistress.'

From the bottom of a vast wardrobe, Keli brought out a thick triangular red cushion that had a pattern of small silvery checks on one side. She placed the cushion carefully between the Duchess's thighs, then, taking hold of Alice's leash, guided her up onto the bed and had her kneel down facing her mistress.

Alice gaped at the thick pink lips pouting and glistening from the luxuriant tangle of pubic hair that filled the delta between the Duchess's thighs. It was like a miniature forest cut through by a gorgelike pubic cleft. And she was supposed to pleasure it.

Keli eased her forward so that her chest would rest on the red pillow. As Alice's breasts touched it she gave a little yelp. The checks were not a pattern, but small metal pyramids with sharp points stitched into the fabric, that pricked her soft flesh. She bit her lip. Did she expect pleasure without pain? Her pain and the Duchess's pleasure, of course. It was not her place to resist, only to obey; to suffer for her Mistress. She let the weight of her upper torso rest fully on the pillow, flattening her breasts into fat pancakes against the grid of pyramids, the points digging into her hard nipples.

Now her nose was brushing the Duchess's sex and her nostrils filled with its musky aroma. Behind her, Keli was strapping on a large rubber phallus that wagged impudently from between her dark satin thighs. Margi and Barbara were kissing the huge pale mounds before them with steadily increasing vigour, causing the nipples to rise like organ stops. The Duchess's fingers had slipped between their thighs as she played with their pubic pouches.

Keli knelt between Alice's knees and fed the tip of the phallus into her slit. Leaning forward, Keli braced her hands on the bed and then drove all the way into Alice. The thrust rocked her forward, rolling her breasts over the metal-studded cushion and grinding her face into the hot wet cleft of the Duchess's lovemouth that muffled her gasp of pain.

Keli pulled back slightly, allowing Alice to breathe, then thrust again, establishing a slow, steady rhythm, using Alice's face as a sex toy to pleasure the Duchess. Each time she was rammed into her mistress's cunt, Alice eagerly licked and nuzzled its slippery depths, loving the soft lips that unfolded and clung like a mask. She worked her tongue into a gaping vaginal tunnel that could have swallowed her

182

whole hand. Even Topper would have been hard put to fill such a cavity. Lovingly she kissed and sucked an erect clitoris the size of her little finger.

Her mistress's hips were rolling from side to side and twitching with pre-orgasm tremors. Her huge thighs were clenching about Alice's head, making her fearful of being crushed between them. Margi and Barbara redoubled their efforts, suckling greedily at the great pulsing nipples as their mistress's fingers worked their way into their bottom holes.

With a braying grunt and moan of pleasure the Duchess came, slapping Margi and Barbara's bottoms as she clamped Alice's head between her thighs and deluged her face with her sweet exudation. Keli gave an extra hard thrust and Alice found her own joyful release.

Half-smothered with her breasts feeling like pincushions, Alice lay placidly under the body of her fellow slave and between her mistress's thighs. She knew she had given pleasure, and that was all that mattered.

From that time on Alice regularly served in the bedchamber, pleasuring the Duchess directly or coupling with the other girlings in endless combination for her amusement. She attended on her mistress during the day, standing patiently in alcoves, alert for a word of command, or else knelt to be used as a convenient footstool or table. She served diligently with the others when the Duchess entertained guests – human never animal. These were local titled or professional people appropriate to the Underland setting, such as a baron, doctor or clergyman. Alice didn't recall them from the original story. Might they have come from her world? Perhaps they had simply appeared as Underland had developed to populate the background of an increasingly complex society.

Alice's punishments for minor faults were few, though her bottom and breasts often wore the blush of the strap, cane or spike. But as long as such things displayed her mistress's pleasure in seeing her suffer, she bore them happily, finding her own strange delight as each mark was laid upon her. She had become a completely pliant creature, totally subservient to the Duchess and dedicated to her house.

Her life in the real world seemed a very distant memory now. Apart for wistful thoughts of Valerie and a vague feeling that she had not yet reached her rightful place, she was happy enough in the company of her fellow girlings, who had become intimate friends and lovers. Days merged into weeks in the timeless Underland way.

Then one day Alice was unexpectedly summoned to the Morning Room. As she knelt before the Duchess, who was reading a letter, she saw an open parcel on the table containing a small blue-glass bottle.

'It seems the Queen is holding a competition,' the Duchess said half to herself, much as one might speak before a pet. 'The Royal Alchemist has created a new milking potion and wishes it tested on as many girlings as possible. The results will be judged at the Palace and a prize, as yet unspecified, will be awarded.' The Duchess raised a sceptical eyebrow. 'How uncommonly generous of her.' She smiled at Alice. 'No matter, it will be amusing to see how it works on a sweet, full-breasted girling such as yourself. Give her the dose.'

Yasmin stepped out of an alcove. She removed Alice's gag, then poured a measure of pink liquid from the bottle into a saucer and placed it on the floor. For the briefest of moments Alice hesitated, wondering what the potion would do to her, then the instinct of obedience overcame her qualms and she lapped the mixture up, licking the saucer clean. It tasted faintly of strawberries.

A wave of dizziness came over Alice, her stomach churned and her breasts tingled. She tried to sit up but seemed unable to get off her hands and knees. The idea suddenly seemed alien to her, almost as bad as standing on two feet. Her fingers clenched together, as though robbed of their natural dexterity. Her breasts hung hot and heavy under her, seeming fuller than they had been only moments before. Then her panic faded as quickly as it had come, to be replaced by a strange sense of calm.

She was aware that the Duchess was speaking, but though she heard the words it took an effort to work out what they meant.

'Take her out to the field . . .'

Still on her hands and knees, Temp led her out of the Morning Room and through the house. In the scullery he hung a bell on her collar, then took her out into the garden, past the greenhouse and through a gate to a small field. In one corner was a water trough and low shed, while the rest was a carpet of lush grass. Its fresh clean smell filled Alice's nostrils and her stomach suddenly ached emptily. Without thinking, as though it was the most natural thing in the world, she dipped her head and bit off a mouthful. It was fine grass with a little clover for sweetness. She chewed and swallowed, then took another bite.

After a while she shuffled over to the trough and drank some water. There was a pit beside the shed which she squatted over to relieve herself, then she returned to cropping the grass.

Alice felt the warm skylight on her back and fuzzy contentment filled her mind. Time drifted but it didn't matter. All was right with the world.

By evening her breasts felt taut and incredibly heavy. Niv appeared and led her into the kitchen, her bell clonking slowly. She tried to take in the familiar surroundings, but they all seemed very complicated and she longed for the simplicity of her field. They made her climb onto the kitchen table where she rested placidly on her hands and knees facing Mrs Braising. The cook put a small bucket under her, took Alice's thick plump teats in her hands and began to tug and squeeze downwards, left then right.

The milk spurted thickly from her udders, splashing musically into the bucket. A new glow of satisfaction filled Alice as she was relieved of her burden, knowing her breasts now functioned as nature intended.

When Alice was drained, Mrs Braising dipped her finger in the still warm milk and tasted. 'Golden and creamy. A good couple of pints as well. A fine little cowling you make.'

That night Alice slept locked in the small shed in the field. She found herself vaguely missing her friends, whose names she had to struggle to recall. She remembered they had talked together at night, not that she had felt any urge to talk now.

That disturbed her for some reason, but it was hard to think clearly. Of course she was a cowling and she was meant to produce milk, not talk. Cowlings didn't talk.

No, that wasn't right. She was a girling, a girl . . . a person! This wasn't right! What had they done to her?

* * *

She tried to hold onto that sense of resentment all through the following day and the next, but it kept slipping away from her. She knew who she was and everything that had happened, but the potion slowed her mind and made it easier not to care. How much simpler just to eat grass, make milk and let the time pass by. No worries, no challenge, no choices to make. It was a terribly seductive lifestyle.

She shook her head. But it was not for her! She remembered the girl-cows she had seen back in the village. Had they taken the same potion, or did they still have a choice? The Duchess had said this was new. Was the 'improvement' a higher milk yield, or a more placid girling?

It was the insidious loss of control and awareness that was wrong. Ordinary bonds, punishments, forced sex, that was all honest and, she admitted, enjoyable. But that was an understanding she had come to with a clear mind. Maybe they could mess with her breasts, but not with her thoughts, not like this. The uninhibited cakes had just made her loosen up and the effects had been temporary. This was different. And her worst fear was that she would gradually surrender to its lure.

At some point Alice became aware that somebody was looking at her. The Cheshire Cat sat primly on the grass regarding her with curious eyes.

'What have we here?' he said. 'Alice chewing the cud like a cowling in the Duchess's field. And do my eyes deceive me, or are your mammaries even fuller than I recall?'

Alice forced her tongue to move and her lips to shape the words: 'It was a new potion from the Palace. Stay here. Talk to me. Please.'

'I might, for as you know I am a famous raconteur. But what can you offer me in return besides words?

You are a little large now to have sex with properly, though I suppose it might be managed with a little ingenuity.'

At that moment Alice would gladly have had sex with him, which seemed by comparison with her present condition the most natural thing in the world. What else did cats like? Of course.

She spread her arms a little wider, letting her distended breasts sway enticingly. 'They say my milk is very creamy . . .'

Alice bit her lip as he sucked at her engorged nipples. His teeth were sharp and kept nipping her engorged teats. Oh God, I'm suckling a cat, she thought! But at least he's enjoying it . . . and he's talking to me.

Finally the Cat had his fill and sat licking his lips. 'I must congratulate you,' he said. 'That was quite the finest milk I have tasted for many years. I said when we first met that I would like to have you at my mercy for a week for carnal use. I now amend that wish to include your breasts in their current state. What a feast to plunder your cleft and sup from your titties!'

'You could have me . . . if you can get me out of here,' Alice said miserably.

'But don't you belong to the Duchess now?'

'Not like this. Not with my mind screwed up!'

'True, there is no sport in mastering a dumb animal,' the Cat agreed. 'Cows are such dull creatures. But is this all the Duchess's doing? You said the potion that changed you came from the Palace.'

'Yes. The Royal Alchemist wanted it tested. The Queen's judging the competition at the Palace to find the best cowling.'

'Then your condition is beyond my ability to counter,' the Cat said. 'The Royal Alchemist, or Joker as he is commonly known, is a most talented

potioner, and the Queen a most capricious ruler. I
will provide company, in return for your milk, until
you depart for the judging. But then beware, my
fulsome Alice. In all mad Underland there is no place
madder than the Palace of Hearts!'

Nine

The carriage rattled along the winding road through the woods towards the Palace. Temp and Esc sat up on the box seat at the front. Inside the closed compartment the Duchess rode with Tanya and Keli, who would act as her maids. On top of the trunks, strapped to the baggage rack over the rear wheels, was Alice's cage.

It was just big enough to hold her on all fours, a position she had been in ever since she had taken the potion. Amazingly, the posture didn't feel uncomfortable, even though her back and neck should have been in agony and her knees raw by now. Presumably her tolerance was also due to the cowling transformation.

A short chain from the back of her collar to the top of the cage kept her upright, while two more chains from her corset to the cage sides prevented her from chafing against it with the motion of the carriage. A sheaf of grass hung in front of her face and there was a pot strapped between her thighs in which to relieve herself. What else did a cowling need?

Everything! she kept telling herself, as she continued her struggle to think clearly. Companionship, conversation, the love of her fellows. Talking with the Cat had helped, but she was on her own now. I'm not

190

a cow, I'm a slave! she shouted inside her head, aware that it lacked something as a protest slogan. All that sustained her was the hope that, after this competition was over, the Duchess would have her turned back to normal. After ten sexless, punishment-free days, Alice longed to be used in the way her nature demanded.

The Palace of Hearts appeared ahead of them as the woodland opened out into fields and the road curved round towards an imposing gatehouse. From out of a checkerwork of paths, fountains and ornate gardens, rose a gothic confection of courtyards, towers and turrets. Flags flew, tall windows arched and battlements were crenellated.

Was this the maddest place in Underland, as the Cat had warned her? She would soon find out.

Their carriage drew up in an inner courtyard before a broad flight of steps leading up to iron-bound double doors. As bewigged attendants assisted the Duchess out of the carriage, a flustered figure ran down the steps to meet her, bowing and talking at once. He wore medieval doublet and hose trimmed with lace and gold incorporating a diamond pattern.

'The Chamberlain of House Redheart welcomes Your Ladyship,' he said breathlessly. 'We feared you might not arrive in time.'

'In time for what?' the Duchess demanded haughtily.

'The judging of the girling competition, Your Ladyship.'

'I understood that was to be tomorrow,' said the Duchess.

The Chamberlain looked embarrassed. 'Oh, it was, Your Ladyship. However, Her Majesty decided it should be brought forward. She said it was a virtue to show willing, therefore her will was a virtue, and if she willed this, nobody possessing any virtue could possibly complain.' He coughed delicately. 'One of her little whims.'

'How like her!' the Duchess exclaimed. 'And how much time do we have to prepare?'

'An hour, perhaps less, Your Ladyship.'

'An hour or less!' The Duchess's voice rose dangerously. She turned to Temp and Esc and pointed at Alice. 'Get her unloaded at once!'

Alice's cage had wheels on the bottom and, once on the ground, Temp and Esc pushed her along in the wake of the apologetic Chamberlain, who led their party rapidly along lengthy corridors, passing scuttling girlings and palace staff, who seemed to be moving at an equally frantic pace. They were mostly dressed in simple white tabards marked with spades, clubs or diamonds. Of course, Alice recalled, they represented the spot cards from the story, though they were obviously real people and not flat cards as they had been portrayed in the illustrations. She forced herself to remember the system. Yes, the diamonds were courtiers, the clubs soldiers, and the spades (naturally) gardeners.

There seemed to be more of them than a single pack of cards could supply. Well, the Palace was a big place and obviously needed more than one of each card. If Underland had grown over the years then presumably their numbers had increased in proportion.

In the apartment reserved for them, the Duchess changed while Tanya and Keli hastily washed and groomed Alice, polished her harness and put a bow in her hair. When they were done they made for the Rose Garden where the competition was to be judged.

A row of small podia had been set up in the garden, with a card on each bearing the entrant's name. They found their allotted stand and Alice was installed upon it, like some prize dog at a show. On either side were more heavy-breasted girlings, their owners fussing over them. Most looked as flushed and angry as the Duchess, presumably because of the Queen's change of plan. Yet there was also an unmistakable sense of apprehension, even fear about the gathering.

A fanfare of trumpets sounded. The Chamberlain stepped out before them and announced grandly, 'My Lords, Ladies and Gentlemen: The King and Queen of the House of Redheart!'

Out of the Palace doors came the royal retinue. Even at a distance Alice could see that they were dressed in period costume, heavily embroidered and trimmed with lace and fur, much as the court cards in a standard card pack. Attendants flitted about them, while a few were leading girlings on leashes like dogs.

As they got closer Alice saw the King and Queen more clearly. As massive as all the other humans in Underland, the Queen appeared haughty and imperious, moving like a galleon under full sail, while the King was beaming about him with vague amiability. At the Queen's side was a man in a multi-coloured tunic and flamboyant hat. As they proceeded he was peering at the row of girlings with minute interest.

'The Joker inspecting the results of his potions,' she heard the Duchess mutter half to herself.

A tall young man walked a little behind the Royal couple, looking slightly bored. The Knave of Hearts, of course. He had similar strong features to Topper, and in his way looked quite handsome. Did he ever get into trouble like his namesake, Alice wondered? A muzzled, dark-haired girling was padding along at his heels.

Alice's stomach flipped and the garden and the chatter of the company about her seemed to dim and mute.

It was Valerie!

Distantly Alice was aware that the royal party was making its way along the line of cowlings, examining each in turn and sampling their milk. But she could not take her eyes off Valerie. How had she got here? Perhaps the Knave had simply bought her from Topper.

'That's right, hold still, girl,' the Duchess was saying. 'Head up proudly . . .'

The Royal party had reached them. The Duchess bowed stiffly; the Queen nodded absently back, her eyes flashing over Alice. Behind her the King ogled Alice amiably while the Joker regarded her with more clinical interest. His nose was hooked, his face running to a pointed chin and his mouth wore a perpetual grin. After a moment he nodded, apparently satisfied with Alice's external appearance.

'I say. Pretty young cowling, isn't she, my dear,' the King said.

With experienced hands the Queen pulled open Alice's jaws to examine her teeth, ruffled her hair to check the colour of her roots, squeezed her breasts to sample their plumpness, prodded and pinched her buttocks, cupped and fondled her pubic pouch and finally pushed a hard finger up her bottom. As she wiped her hands on a moistened towel, an attendant placed a silver cup under Alice's breasts and carefully drew on her teats until it was half full. The cup was handed to the Queen who sniffed and then sipped the warm fluid, rolling it round her tongue with the concentration of a wine taster.

'Might I try some?' the King asked hopefully.

The Queen ignored him, spat on the grass, rinsed out her mouth with water and muttered something to the Chamberlain, who made a note on a clipboard.

Alice hardly noticed any of this. As she was being examined Valerie's eyes had widened between the straps of her muzzle. Now their gaze was locked even as they each held their places beside their owners. Alice saw amazement turn to sadness and longing on Valerie's face. As the royal party moved on to the next in line and Valerie had to scuttle after her master, Alice watched her go with tears welling up in her eyes. Was that it? Would that be the last she ever saw of her?

The Duchess patted her rump. 'Good poise, Alice. I think you impressed Her Majesty.'

Alice almost laughed. She had earned a compliment from the Duchess while she had been at her least attentive.

Finally the judging was done. After a few more words with the Queen, the Chamberlain stepped forward.

'Your Royal Highnesses, My Lords, Ladies and Gentlemen. I have the privilege of announcing the winner:

'Our gracious Queen is pleased (hurrah, hooray!),
at seeing so many gathered here today.
You have travelled from every corner of Underland,
to put your girlings on these stands.
And that all display such copious lactation,
is a tribute to our glorious nation.
With udders most plumptious and gracefully swaying,
finding a winner takes some weighing.

195

Diligently has Her Majesty judged the contest,
supping milk fresh from every breast.
Creamy sweet and golden the precious fluid flowed,
but which is the best we beg to know?
Well the cowling who has achieved supreme success –
belongs to Margravia's only Duchess!'

Alice blinked as the Duchess rubbed her hands in
satisfaction. She had hardly been paying attention to
the announcement, but was staring at Valerie as she
knelt beside the Knave. So she had won the contest.
She supposed she would get a rosette and they would
go home and she would never see Valerie again. And
did it mean now she was a champion cowling the
Duchess would keep her like this? No, please no . . .

The rest of the competitors were clapping politely
as the Duchess bowed before the Queen. Then the
Chamberlain waved his hand for silence.

'I regret that, due to a clerical error, details of the
prize were not included with the invitations. I can now
announce that the grand prize is no less than . . . the
privilege of giving the winning cowling to the Queen!'

The Duchess gasped audibly and looked as though
she was going to protest, then seemed to think better
of it as the Queen smile wickedly. There were a few
stifled chuckles from the crowd. Alice found her own
heart skip a beat. Her world was being turned upside
down once again.

The Duchess's party left the Palace that same day
with the barest minimum of formality. Meanwhile,
Alice's collar was changed for one bearing the royal
crest. She would be in the Palace close to Valerie, but
as the property of a malicious tyrant. The Cat had
been correct. It was the maddest of places.

Ten

Alice's duties turned out to be very simple. At mealtimes she stood beside the Queen's chair serving as her personal drinking fountain. The Queen had taken a fancy to girling milk and wanted it fresh from the breast. How long the passion would last nobody could tell.

An upright rectangular metal frame mounted on a small wheeled platform held Alice rigidly erect. Straps and cuffs bolted to the inside of the frame secured her collar, stomach, wrists, knees and ankles. The frame was hinged at waist height. A pull on the loop of Alice's dangling collar chain bent her forward so that her heavy breasts hung free for Her Majesty to grasp. A slight squeeze of her big hand was enough to eject milk in lusty spurts into a cup. When it was filled, springs at the back of the frame pulled Alice straight again.

The restraints were not in themselves irksome, the problem was that Alice ached for sex. She wanted to feel a rod of flesh pushed into any orifice, or have a girling's tongue lick her out. It was weeks since she had known release, and all she could do was suffer in silence behind her gag. What made it worse was that she saw Valerie about the court almost every day, but they had been unable even to pass a single word, far less make love. From the penetrating stares the Knave directed at her and his occasional aside to Valerie, Alice guessed she had told him of their previous relationship. From the worshipful glances Valerie bestowed upon him in return, Alice suspected she had found her true master. She was happy for her, but so wished they could also be together. For the moment all Alice could do was observe the peculiarities of Underland court life and its anxious and fragile undertones.

The court was composed of a shifting assembly of royal relations and lesser dignitaries, plus a few carefully selected and obsequious animals. All fawned and flattered and yet feared the Queen, and for good reason. The original Queen of Hearts in the story had, Alice recalled, been fond of ordering the execution of anybody who earned her displeasure. Her counterpart in Underland would occasionally, as an 'amusement', order the Royal Executioner to give a public demonstration of his wood-cutting skills. The logs were always laid horizontally and were about the diameter of the average neck. His axe was sharp and never failed to cut each cleanly in two with a single blow. Apparently no execution had yet been carried out, but the whispers suggested it was only a matter of time.

There was talk of revolution in the air.

Alice also enjoyed the dubious privilege of sleeping in the royal bedchamber. Or at least, sleeping as well as she could while being ready to provide the Queen with warm milk at any time of the night. The King himself occasionally got a sip if the Queen was feeling generous. He was as mild and downtrodden as his fictional counterpart.

A couple of girlings were bound across the foot of the bed under the covers as foot-warmers, while others took a more active role. Whatever their other differences, Queen Redheart's tastes in sex appeared similar to those of the Duchess, preferring the skilled tongue of one of her girlings to her husband's penis. If he was lucky the King could exercise his passion in the girling's rear as long as he did not disturb her rhythm.

One night, not long after Alice's arrival, just such a threesome was unexpectedly interrupted by a nervous girling maid, bearing the message that the Queen was required by her senior courtiers to attend to urgent affairs of state. With a visible effort the Queen controlled her natural response, merely going red in the face and thundering, 'It had better be important or I'll have their heads!'

Kicking aside the King and the girling who had been pleasuring her, she heaved her bulk out of the bed, pulled on a gown the maid held out, cuffed the unfortunate girl aside, and made for the door. Apparently determined that if she was not enjoying herself then nobody else would either, she called back over her shoulder, 'And don't you dare come in her until I return!'

The door slammed behind her, leaving the King sprawled on his side with his shaft still buried deep in the girling's rear and an agonised expression on his face that suggested he was very close to the point of no return. Alice saw him looking about desperately, weighing up his position. Then his eyes fastened upon her. She could see his mind working. The Queen had said he was not to come in the girl they were sharing, but nothing about Alice.

With a sucking pop, he pulled out of the girling's rear and almost ran round the bed to Alice, his huge glistening erection bobbing desperately in front of him. He dragged her frame away from the wall, twisted it round and bent her over as though she was making a stiff bow, so she presented her bottom to him. Grasping the uprights of the frame he rammed into her. Alice shrieked behind her gag as his thick cock stretched her neglected bottom painfully wide, then almost fainted with relief to feel hard flesh pistoning inside her once more.

The King was in a frantic hurry, both from need and to be done before his wife returned, but Alice was on such a hair trigger that she came twice before he finally emptied himself into her bowels. He seemed to take her exuberant response as a compliment to his prowess, and patted her with vague affection.

'Lively little thing, aren't you.'

Alice herself felt blissful relief. If her mouth had been free she would have thanked him profusely.

Both she and her stand were back in their proper place and the King was lying in bed looking the picture of innocence, when the Queen finally stomped back into the room. Alice hoped she would not notice the sperm slowly seeping out of her anus and down the back of her thighs. Fortunately the King distracted her by asking quickly, 'Anything wrong, my dear? Nothing serious, I trust?'

The Queen scowled. 'Fresh reports on sightings of the principle ringleaders, and some news of the enemy over the water. The spies think they're moving closer. I ordered the patrols increased.'

'I always thought those two seemed such inoffensive animals,' the King mused. 'Used to sing that amusing song, I recall.'

'They were unnatural creatures, and that song was banned as subversive,' the Queen snapped. 'I don't want to hear of it again.'

'No, my dear. Sorry, my dear. Shall we continue where we were? It might take your mind off things.'

The Queen sprawled back on the bed and the girling was positioned once more between her legs so she could resume tonguing the Queen's great plump mound of Venus. Tentatively, the King returned to his station behind the girl and slid his noticeably less rampant cock into her.

'And don't you come until I'm done,' the Queen reminded him.

'Oh, I won't hurry, my dear, I promise.'

And so, unknown to his wife, the King was doubly satisfied that night.

But such occasions were rare, Alice soon realised. The Queen utterly dominated the King, as she did all her subjects by fear, sheer force of will and the almost hypnotic control extreme personalities could exert over those around them. This had happened time and again back in her world, Alice knew, and it seemed even more natural in Underland. Such an owner Alice might have learned to live with, along with the humiliations, restraints and punishments that she had come to think of as a normal part of her life. She would even welcome them if they also allowed her a regular release for her passions. But now there was a new fear of being changed in both mind and body. The effects of the cowling potion were hard enough to live with, but she soon discovered that the Royal Alchemist had accomplished far more radical transformations.

When she was not serving, Alice was let out to graze in a field next to the Palace stable block. There, besides the quite ordinary and apparently non-sentient horses, were housed several girlmares. The first time she saw them being exercised she could hardly believe her eyes.

They were tall and elegant girlings with stiff manes of hair, that ran rather like a Mohican cut across their crowns then turned into a cascade down their backs. These they tossed about as their ears, which were long, horselike and mobile, twitched nervously from side to side. Their breasts were high, small and pointed. Full tails of hair arched out from the small of their backs to hang clear of their firmly rounded buttocks and sturdy thighs. As they were led about the paddock by their grooms, their heads bound in bridles, they strutted elegantly on long legs which were slightly bent at the knees. This was because their calves ended not in feet, but in fetlocks, pasterns and delicate pink hooves, that clip-clopped crisply. At first Alice thought they were wearing some sort of elaborate shoes, but gradually she realised they were genuine.

It was a dramatic example of the Joker's craft, and one that filled her with fear. She supposed that altering a body like that was not as incredible or apparently contrary to the laws of nature as the shrinking she had undergone, but somehow it seemed more shocking. Still, it put her own change into perspective. Tits full of milk and a taste for grass did not seem so bad by comparison.

As Alice ruminated on these matters the reason for the Rabbit's secretiveness about the growth/shrinking potion dawned on her. Its possession was probably against the law. The Queen was worried about civil unrest amongst the animal population, and would obviously not permit widespread distribution of the Alchemist's creations until she was sure they could not be used against her in any way. Even the cowling competition had really been a limited test of the new formula before making it generally available. Alice could not imagine how the ability to turn a girling into a more docile cow posed a threat to law and order, but she could think of several ways the size-changing potion could be.

Then the secretive conversation between Niv, Erm and the crow in the Duchess's orchard came back to her. Were the animals really planning a revolt against the human gentry who ruled Underland? Could the White Rabbit be part of the conspiracy?

This disturbing line of thought faded as her concentration slipped once more. She groaned miserably. All she wanted was to be normal again.

A couple of the girlmares were casting her curious glances across the paddock fence. They turned away tossing their heads proudly, as if to show off their manes. Evidently they thought showing interest in a cowling was beneath them. Perhaps they were content with their new bodies and even flattered by the attentions of their grooms. Alice could think of a few pony-obsessed girls she had known at school who would have made very good girlmares. Were they the sort who would end in the Queen's stables?

Did Underland have the right niche waiting for everyone who found their way there? If so, what was hers?

Alice's chance to speak to Valerie finally came beside the Palace croquet lawn.

There were no hedgehogs or flamingoes in evidence, but instead the Joker's art had been employed to give the game a uniquely Underland twist. The hoops were formed by girlings bent over backwards, making their ribs stand out, until their hands and feet rested flat on the ground. They were somehow locked into these positions so that only the swivelling of their eyes and the rise and fall of their taut stomachs showed they were still living things. The croquet balls were also girlings, painted in bright colours and curled up incredibly tightly and frozen in place the same way as the living hoops. The Joker had also done something to make them lighter than normal, and a good blow from the broad mallet heads sent them bouncing across the grass as easily as beach balls. Of course, as they did not form perfect spheres they did not roll true, but this hardly mattered as the rules and order of play seemed to change as the game progressed, and there was much arguing amongst the players as the girlballs were knocked about the lawn, rebounding off each other with little grunts and yelps, and occasionally actually passing through a living hoop.

In fact only one rule seemed to be observed throughout the game: the Queen had to win each round.

Meanwhile, Alice was tethered to a tree beside the lawn. She was ungagged so that she could graze off the long grass around the tree and yet be available should her mistress require refreshment.

The game had only been under way for a short time when Alice saw the Knave appear, leading Valerie on a leash as usual. Casually he strolled round the lawn until he reached her tree, where, without sparing Alice a glance, he tethered Valerie.

He called out, 'Do you mind if I join in, Mother?'

The Queen looked up in surprise. 'I did not think croquet was your game, Atheling.'

'I thought I might give it a try. It looks amusing.'

'As you wish.'

Another player, rather gratefully it seemed, surrendered his mallet and the Knave joined the crazy game. But Alice saw none of that. She only had eyes for Valerie and saw her feeling mirrored. For some moments neither could find the right words to say.

Finally Valerie asked softly, 'Oh Alice, what have they done to you?'

'It's not so bad,' she said, trying to sound off-hand. 'I've got used to it. They do weirder things here.'

'I know.' Tears sparkled in Valerie's eyes. 'I was so worried when we heard you'd escaped from the Rabbit. What happened?'

In a few words, Alice explained about her time in the woods and unwillingly entering the Duchess's service. Valerie grimaced sympathetically when she heard about her encounter with the Cheshire Cat.

'I've seen him around here a couple of times. I think he turns up every so often to annoy the Queen. She goes completely wild but she can't stop him. Atheling, my master, secretly thinks it's rather funny.'

'How did he get to own you?'

'That was easy. When they were sure the Duchess wasn't going to call again, and they'd given up searching for you, they brought me back from the village and we went on with our training. When we were ready they held an auction and Atheling just turned up. Apparently it was his birthday and the Queen had promised he could have a girling all to himself. He wanted to buy one fresh and he chose me. And it's been perfect ever since.'

'Is he the one, then?' Alice asked.

Valerie smiled dreamily. 'Yes, I think so. He's clever and kind, not like his mother at all, though he can also be very strict at times.' She grinned. 'But you know I rather like that. I told him who you were and he's been trying to get us together without his mother suspecting. Isn't that wonderful of him?' Suddenly she looked concerned. 'I still love you. I always will, believe me. But he's my master now, which is different. Do you understand?'

'Yes,' Alice said gently. 'And I still love you.'

There were tears on Valerie's cheek. 'I wish he could own you, then we'd be together and everything would be perfect.'

'Is there any chance of that?'

'Everything here depends on the mood the Queen's in. She suddenly gets bored with things. It could happen with you and she might just give you away. Atheling said he would be ready to ask for you if that happened, but he can't rush things.'

'I understand. And tell him thank you from me for letting us talk like this.'

There were cheers and groans from the lawn as a red girling ball rolled between the straining limbs of a hoop and bounced off another rigidly upright girling buried knee-deep in the ground. The Queen was congratulated and mallets were shouldered. The game was coming to an end.

Valerie said quickly, 'Whatever you do, be careful not to make her angry.'

'I won't,' Alice promised.

It was nothing Alice did that caused her sudden fall from the Queen's favour. That happened without warning, and was quite beyond Alice's control.

One day at dinner, the Queen suddenly peered suspiciously at the cup she had just filled from Alice's breast.

'Why do I always drink milk?' she asked aloud.

There was an awkward silence, then the King said tactfully, 'Because you said you liked the taste, my dear.'

The Queen scowled at him and then at her cup, as though ready to dispute his explanation. Then with a shrug she threw the cup aside. 'Well, I would like some wine instead.'

'Certainly, my dear. Bring wine for the Queen!'

For the rest of the meal she drank wine. Alice was trembling with apprehension and hope. She saw Atheling looking from her to his mother intently, awaiting his moment.

As they rose from the table the Queen glanced round at Alice.

'Take her away!' she commanded. 'She smells of milk.'

'She is rather pretty,' the King said timidly. 'Perhaps we can keep her for the bedroom. She would make a nice ornament.'

'No, I'm tired of her,' the Queen snapped petulantly.

'If you don't want her, I'm sure I can make good use of her, Mother,' Atheling said lightly.

'You already have a new girling of your own,' the Queen said. 'Give her to the Joker. Perhaps he can do something more amusing with her.'

Helpless in her restraining frame, Alice shivered in horror.

The laboratory was situated in one of the high round towers of the Palace. Its main chamber occupied an entire floor, lit by a ring of high narrow barred windows. The centre of the room was cluttered with workbenches, many filled with complex arrangements of tubes and flasks and bubbling retorts. Around the walls were tottering stacks of shelves holding rows of jars filled with dried plants and herbs. Beside these were bookshelves sagging under the weight of ancient leather-bound volumes. In a block to themselves were piled a dozen or more cages containing the Joker's guinea pigs.

It was in one of these cells that Alice awoke the next morning. For a moment she could not remember where she was. Then it came back to her. Anxiously she felt herself all over. She could use her hands properly again! Her breasts had returned to their normal size, which seemed small by comparison with the udders she had been carrying around for the last month or more. She could stand up, as far as the cage allowed, her mind was clear and she had no craving for grass.

She was normal again, but for how long?

Not long after she woke, the Joker appeared. He was bare-headed and had an apron tied over his many-coloured tunic. Humming cheerfully, he made the rounds of the cages, dispensing food and water to the girlings. His grin was wider than ever. When he came to her cage, Alice found herself smiling hopefully back.

'Ah, yes,' he said, reaching through the bars to take hold of her chin and turn her head from side to side. 'The Queen wants me to make you more amusing. I must try to find something suitable.'

He set to work. Herbs were crushed and ground, measured and mixed. Many-coloured bubbling fluids were heated and purified, filling the air with strange scents. Eventually he had a measure of pinkish liquid in a test tube. From the cages he selected a freckled, redheaded girling. She wore a look of resigned acceptance as the Joker strapped her to a heavy wooden bench tilted at a convenient angle on its stand. Its boards had been polished dark by the bodies of many girls who had lain on it before her.

The Joker pinched the girl's nose, forcing her to open her mouth, and tipped the potion down her throat. She swallowed reluctantly. For a few seconds nothing happened, then she moaned, arched her back and tugged against her straps. Two red spots appeared on her chest under her pale rounded breasts, spreading and darkening. The skin about them swelled and filled even as the spots popped up to become the nipples of a second pair of breasts.

In moments the transformation was complete. The Joker prodded the girl's new mammaries, which were slightly smaller than her first pair but otherwise perfect replicas, tweaking and pinching the nipples to see if they erected properly. He carefully recorded the results in his notebook, then released the girl from the test bench and put her back in her cage, where she curiously explored her altered body.

The Joker began to mix another batch of potion.

During the next few hours Alice saw a girling grow wings, another sprout a prehensile tail, and a third have her hair turn silver while her skin became gold. Alice watched it all in a state of helpless fascination that made it impossible to look away, even though she feared it would be her turn next.

It was not exactly a chamber of horrors, she decided, because the Joker did not go out of his way to torture the girlings that served as his experimental animals. Nothing he did caused them undue pain, and they received no more punishment at his hands than the usual cuffs and slaps a girling expected as a matter of course. It was more as though he was an artist and they were living clay for him to shape into new and wonderful forms. But the idea of undergoing another transformation filled her with queasy apprehension. Taking the shrinking potion had been special and wonderful in its way, but it had been her decision to try it, and she had remained herself, just differently scaled in relation to the rest of the world. The changes she had witnessed were something else.

Then she thought of the visitor's declaration she had signed in Topper's garden, which seemed an age ago now, and the lines about agreeing to the administration of 'diverse' potions for any purpose. She supposed this fell under the same category, so she could hardly complain. Surely, if she got turned on by being caned and screwed by a dozen different creatures, she could also find pleasure in this. Was that common sense or madness? Which was most appropriate to Underland?

It was late afternoon when inspiration seemed to strike the Joker. A new animation seized him and he rushed about checking his references and then selecting ingredients. At the end of an hour he had produced a tube of softly luminous green fluid and a waxy lollipop of some duller material coated on a stick. Then his eyes turned to Alice.

She felt numb as the Joker led her over to the test bench and laid her against its hard boards. The straps binding her to the bench helped a little. Firm leather bands and heavy buckles constraining her limbs, the enforced immobility a reminder of her proper place. A slave, a girling, an experimental animal, there to be shaped by another's will. The lowliest creature in Underland, and yet paradoxically at that moment the focus of its master alchemist's complete attention, so perhaps also the most important. Helpless and excited, Alice felt her whole body coming alive as anticipation coursed through her.

The Joker saw the look in her eyes and smiled.

'Frightened, girling? Don't be. I shall make something special of you.'

She did not resist as he held the tube to her lips and swallowed down the minty-tasting fluid. She felt it warm her stomach and then kindle a pricking tingle in her breasts. No, not her breasts again, she thought, struggling against her collar strap to look down at them. Her nipples were stiff but outwardly nothing else had changed.

Meanwhile the Joker had gone to the wall and was turning a crank handle. Cords rattled over pulleys and blinds closed across the high windows, casting the laboratory into gloom. He came back to the test bench and picked up the waxed-coated stick. Reaching between her thighs he pushed it up her rear. As soon as it was lodged inside her, with the stick protruding from her anus, she felt its surface begin to dissolve away. That intimate intrusion brought Alice both distraction and relief. It was good to have something up her rear that was comfortably warm and did not sting like Mrs Braising's carrot. But what was it supposed to do?

Then she realised the Joker's face, as he looked down at her, was getting lighter. But what was illuminating it? Oh, no . . .

Her breasts were glowing, growing steadily brighter moment by moment as though they had light bulbs inside them. Her nipples were red as traffic lights while the fleshy hemispheres shone with a pinker radiance. In panic she wriggled and tugged at her straps, but that only set the shadows her luminous globes cast about the chamber dancing and jigging.

The Joker slapped her cheek by way of a warning. 'Calm yourself, girl. There's nothing to fear.'

Alice fought down her panicky breathing. Her breasts felt a little warmer than normal, but the light they gave off was without real heat. Each was about as bright as a forty-watt bulb. Nature created luminous plants and animals even in her world, she told herself, so maybe this is not so far out. Alice the human firefly; the girl with the glowing tits.

The Joker probed her breasts and satisfied himself that their luminance was constant. Then he pulled the stick out of her rear. The glow slowly faded and in a few seconds she was outwardly back to normal.

He has even fitted me with an on/off switch! she thought. But at least my mind is still my own.

'Good,' said the Joker. 'I'm sure the Queen will find you both amusing and practical.'

The Queen was greatly amused by Alice's transformation, as the light she gave was clearer than either candles or oil lamps. She ordered three more girls transformed in the same way. They were mounted on pedestals to light the dining table in the Great Hall, where everybody agreed they were a great success. A few of the Queen's most favoured supporters were given the potion to use on their own girlings.

For Alice it was hardly better than being a milk fountain. She was still the Queen's special possession and could only gaze longingly at Valerie from afar. Little more than a utility item, she spent much of the day bound to a post; untouched and frustrated, comforted only by her rod switch when it was inserted. The King cast covetous eyes on her, but she was less accessible to him than before.

Her training had prepared her for constant handling, physical exertion and regular sex. Even the dark pleasure of the whip was denied to her.

This was real torment.

Then came the day when the Palace awoke to greater confusion that usual.

From what she overheard from harried staff bustling past, Alice gathered that the Queen had decided the court would go for a picnic on the beach. The shore ran along one side of the Palace estate, but the preparations were still considerable. Because the party might last into the evening, Alice and the other girling lamps were hastily bundled onto one of a string of carts carrying all the necessary materials for a few dozen people and their servants to spend a day outdoors.

The carts clattered along a twisting drive, through a cutting in a ridge of trees and down a path onto a broad crescent of beach. The golden sands were bounded by rocky outcrops at either end and looked out over an expanse of rolling ocean, merging in the far distance with the pearly bright sky. Alice wondered if there was anything beyond that hazy horizon. Was Underland a proper world or was it no bigger than had been described in the books?

The girlings were unchained and set to work under the direction of the servants unloading chairs, tents and hampers. Everything had to be ready in time for the arrival of the court. After her relative immobility as a cowling and now a lamp, Alice enjoyed fetching and carrying and hauling on guy ropes. It was good to stretch her muscles and work up a sweat. She could rub against the bodies of the other girls as they worked, and they laughed and giggled together.

Despite the hasty preparations, the day started well. The Queen seemed to enjoy the change of scene and was as amiable as her manner allowed. Nobody actually bathed, but some, led in boyish fashion by the King, paddled about the water's edge. A few girlings were allowed to splash in the surf and run after sticks thrown by their masters or mistresses.

Alice was set helping to serve lunch, and was able to get close enough to Valerie to exchange secret glances and quick smiles. The Knave fed Valerie scraps from his own plate and she took them from his hand. When dinner was done and they were clearing away, Alice watched Valerie curl up at her master's feet like a faithful dog. She looked very happy.

After a siesta, the King hesitantly suggested they might hold girling races along the beach. The idea seemed to amuse the Queen and so everybody joined in enthusiastically. Tracks were marked out in the sand. All restraints but collars were removed from the competing girlings so they should be unencumbered. The Queen personally suggested Alice should run, which immediately made her the royal favourite. Alice felt uncomfortable, wondering if the others would let her win. Perhaps to even the balance, the Knave entered Valerie.

As there were more girls than tracks, they decided to form them into teams and run relay races. Alice and Valerie automatically became the captains of each team. Up and down the sands the girlings pounded, buttocks twinkling and breasts bouncing prettily, until Alice's team was declared the winner. Alice suspected the others had been holding back, but enjoyed the simple pleasure of running naked. It reminded her of pulling the White Rabbit along on the hobby horse. If she had known what was going to happen to her, would she ever have tried to escape?

Alice and Valerie had clearly been the best runners in their teams, but who was the fastest between them, somebody wondered? They would hold a novelty race to determine the answer. A dozen smooth round pebbles of approximately equal size were gathered. The two girls would have to transport six pebbles each, one at a time, from one end of the track to the other, carrying them in their vaginas. At the far end they would have to drop the pebbles into buckets and return. The first back after having deposited her last pebble would win. The Knave himself prepared to insert the pebbles into Valerie, while the Chamberlain performed the same function for Alice.

Alice didn't think for a moment of the spectacle she made as she doubled over with her hands on the ground and legs spread, exposing her pubic pouch so the Chamberlain could push the first pebble into her. Nor did she consider the use her body was being put to as degrading or humiliating. Such concepts were probably meaningless to her now, anyway. All she was conscious of was the pleasant feeling of the stone being worked into her already wet passage, excitement at being the centre of attention and having Valerie near her. If court life could be more like this she would be happy.

As they lined up side by side, Valerie whispered, 'I'll make it look good, but you know you've got to win to keep the Queen happy.'

'OK. Save it for the last lap.'

They were sent racing down the sand, limbs pumping, breasts jigging and bouncing. Alice suspected Valerie was faster if for no other reason than she was less top heavy, but she was making it look like a serious contest.

Yet it was also fun. The weight of the pebble was arousing in her under-used vagina. It seemed to jump inside her with every step, and she had to clench it with the muscles of her sheath to avoid expelling it too early. They reached the buckets together and squatted over them, squeezing hard. The glistening pebbles shot out of their pouches and rattled into the receptacles, and they sprinted back to the start for the next ones.

Alice was soon in a lather of sweat and arousal. Her vagina was leaking fluid down her thighs, and she was having to work harder to hold each one in place as she ran. She read the same barely contained excitement on Valerie's face. It would be hilarious if they both came before they finished the race. But would the Queen see the joke?

The last pebbles plopped into the buckets and Valerie started back up the course a few paces ahead. The court was cheering wildly, caught up in the excitement of the race. The King was shouting delightedly and even the Queen was smiling. Alice saw Valerie wobble as though at the end of her strength and lengthened her stride for the last moment comeback. Panting hard she pulled level, then surged ahead by a breast. There was just a few more paces to go –

And then her foot turned in a softer spot of sand and she fell flat on her face!

Valerie tried to pull back, but it was too late. Sheer momentum carried her over the line.

The cries of the onlookers faltered and died. The Queen's choice had been beaten. How would she take it?

All eyes turned to her. Alice looked up, spitting out sand, to see the Queen's face darken.

The Queen pointed a sausage of a finger at Alice. 'Beat her until she learns not to be so clumsy again!' she commanded.

Valerie, kneeling by the Knave, hung her head in dismay.

And at that moment the tremendous unfairness of it all struck Alice. She had accepted everything that had been done to her, every perversion and humiliation, even down to having her body altered for the Queen's amusement. But now the Queen was going to punish her for not being perfect, for a single unlucky step. Filled with righteous indignation, Alice forgot common sense or who she was talking to.

She scrambled to her feet. 'That's not fair! I tried my best. I was just unlucky, that's all. It was just an accident . . .'

She trailed off, realising that there was no sound on the beach but the rush of the waves. The entire court was staring at her in open-mouthed disbelief. Her stomach suddenly flipped. What had she said?

The Queen was shaking with rage. 'How dare you speak to me so, miserable girling! Lash her until her back is raw! Leave her where the waves will wash her and salt her wounds. She is not to be released until she begs for forgiveness!'

Guards ran up and grabbed Alice by the arms. The King shook his head sadly. The Knave turned to the Queen.

'Perhaps the girl is still shaken from her fall, Mother. And it was an accident. If she apologises . . .'

'She shall be punished as I decreed, as a warning to all who do not know their place!' She pointed at a white-faced Valerie. 'And I'll have her for myself. At least she can run without falling.'

Valerie looked horror-struck. The Knave took a deep breath. 'No, Mother. She is my private property, bought with my own money. You cannot have her.'

For a moment the Queen was rendered speechless in the face of her son's defiance. The King fluttered about them making vague pacifying bleats, then shrank back at the sight of his wife's apoplectic expression. 'Return to the Palace immediately,' she commanded. She turned to glare at the guards still holding Alice. 'Why is she not already screaming in pain?'

In a desperate rush the guards dragged Alice down to the water's edge. Tent pegs and cords were brought and hammered into the sand. Face down, Alice was stretched out wide between them and her wrists and ankles hastily bound. Then with crops and canes the guards set about her back, buttocks and thighs, and the crack of leather on skin rang out across the water.

Alice yelped and screamed and sobbed under the blows, but she did not beg for mercy. She would not give the Queen the satisfaction.

This time there was no pleasure to be found in her beating because it was for nobody's enjoyment. It was not a prelude to sex, nor a proper lesson in obedience, or even a test of her submission. It was just a pointless and disproportionate punishment for an accidental error.

In a part of her mind untouched by the pain Alice knew that she would never satisfy the Queen. She would always be at the mercy of her uncertain temper and fickle whims, as was the rest of the court. This life was not safe. If she could never be with Valerie, then she had to escape.

Only when Alice lay limp and half conscious on the sand, her back criss-crossed with red and purple weals, did the Queen signal the guards to stop. It was very quiet and the onlookers were subdued. A few drifted away up the beach. Servants began to clear up after them. The picnic was over.

Alice was left alone. After a while a wave rushed up the sand, funnelled into the open 'V' of her legs and burst in her groin, sending a shower of salty water over her raw flesh. The stinging pain brought her back to her senses. With a groan she realised the tide was coming in. Did Underland have a moon to drive the tides she wondered, lightheadedly? Another stinging shower of spray washed over her, and she bit her lip to stop herself crying out. Her back and bottom felt as though they were on fire. How long would the Queen leave her here? Nobody amongst the tents seemed to be paying her any attention. There was not even a guard watching over her.

She realised the pearly skylight was dimming. It must be getting on towards evening.

Another wave broke over her, bringing new pain and rolling well over her buttocks. Where was the high tide mark? Surely the Queen would not leave her to drown? Was that the idea, to frighten her into calling out for all to hear, begging for forgiveness?

She set her teeth and tensed herself to resist until the last moment but she felt the rope securing her right arm give a little.

Hardly daring to breath she pulled on it a little harder. Yes, the stake was loose. It had not been driven in deep enough!

As it loosened she had a little more freedom of movement to employ, surreptitiously tugging on the other stakes. Slowly the one holding her right leg began to give as well. If she pulled hard now she could free half of her body. But then the guards would be bound to see her. Could she wait until it got a little darker? She saw lights come into being around the tents. Three sets of pale globes. Her fellow girling lamps had been turned on. Evidently the Queen was going to wait until the last moment.

Water rushed up the beach, swirling about her chest. She had little time left.

As the next wave almost covered her she tugged the two right-hand stakes free and then lay flat again. No time to untie any of the ropes. She would only have one chance.

With the next wave she twisted about, ignoring the agony of her back, and wrenched with all her strength at the cord securing her left arm. The stake came free with a jerk and she sat upright.

She heard a shout from the tents but she ignored it, grabbing hold of the last stake and desperately working it back and forwards to free it from the suction of the wet sands. Footsteps pounded towards her. The stake came free and she scrambled to her feet. There was only one direction she could go now.

With the stakes dancing and jerking about her, she ran into the sea and dove under the next wave.

Breaking the surface again she kept swimming as well as she could encumbered by the tethers. At least the water was warm. The guards splashed into the shallows but did not try to swim after her. She kept heading away from the shore, wanting to get well clear in case they had boats.

After a few minutes she could only see the beach at intervals between the wave caps. From the shore in the fading light she should be almost impossible to spot. She stopped swimming and trod water, concentrating on untying the ropes. The wet knots took some time to pry open, and she had to duck under to free her ankles. When she was finally free and looked back to land, she found the party beach had vanished. There must be a strong current running along the shoreline. The twilit night of Underland was falling fast now and the land was fading into a dark silhouette, making it hard to judge how fast she was moving.

She began to swim back towards the land, only to find she was fighting to cross the current carrying her parallel to the coast. The sky had dimmed to a deep electric blue. The land was a dark smudge that kept vanishing as she slipped into the troughs of the waves.

Exhaustion began to set in now. Her back was stiffening and the water seemed colder. Surely she must strike land soon. She thought she could hear waves breaking on a beach. Was it ahead of her? Her foot touched something solid. Land? She struggled desperately forward. The swell picked her up and sent her tumbling over and over with a breaking wave, pounding the breath from her. Then everything went black.

Eleven

Alice awoke to the sound of raised voices.

At first she thought it was the sea washing across the shingle. Then she realised it was two people having an urgent conversation. Who were they, and where was she?

It was daylight. She was sprawled in the middle of a jumbled outcrop of rocks half covered by seaweed. Her back stung and ached, she was stiff and salt-crusted. But she was alive, and free of the Queen.

Painfully slowly she sat up and untangled herself from the clinging weed. Her lips were dry and her throat raw. She had to find fresh water. Perhaps the unseen talkers could help her. But she should learn who they were before revealing herself.

Cautiously she peered out from between the rocks.

Pacing up and down the sand by the water's edge, heads together in urgent conference, were two creatures bizarre even by Underland standards. One was an upright turtle with a calf's head, hind feet and tail. The other had the head and wings of an eagle, with the lower body and tail of a lion. Of course: the Mock Turtle and Gryphon. Her namesake had met them by the sea in the original story. Perhaps they lived around here. At least it made sense for the Turtle, as much as

221

anything did where such a ridiculous creature was concerned. Perhaps Gryphons nested on the seashore.

Alice shook her head, trying to clear the last of the confusion from her mind. What was she doing trying to make sense of it? This was Underland.

Then she took notice of what the pair were saying.

'But will they be ready in time?' the Gryphon asked.

'They say they will,' said the Turtle. 'They are strongly motivated –' a tear trickled down from one eye, which he wiped away clumsily with his foreflipper '– the gentry have certainly dined off enough of their kind in the past to make them so.'

'Yes; very sad, but you must control yourself,' the Gryphon snapped. 'Are there going to be enough of them to overcome the Palace guards?'

What? Alice thought.

'They are assembling by the quadrille out there,' the Turtle said, pointing out to sea. 'They just await the signal.'

Alice's head was spinning. She recalled the secretive crow in the Duchess's orchard bringing '. . . the word from the coast. . .'; then there was the Queen coming back to her bedroom from that urgent conference with her advisors talking of, '. . . the enemy over the water . . .' and '. . . sightings of the principal ringleaders . . .'; and the King's words: '. . . those two seemed such inoffensive animals . . .'

The Turtle and Gryphon were the ones leading the revolution!

For a moment she did not know what to do. Should she show herself to them? They were against the Queen, which was fine by her right now, but getting mixed up in a revolution could be dangerous. Perhaps it would be smart to hear a little more of their plans first.

The odd pair were pacing back in her direction again. As she shifted her position to crouch lower, her foot slid on some weed. She scrabbled to find a new foothold but everything was treacherously slippery. With a despairing cry she tumbled down a cleft between the rocks and onto the sand.

The Turtle and Gryphon spun round in alarm at her dramatic appearance. The Turtle wailed, 'A spy. We are undone!'

With surprising agility, the Gryphon bounded over to Alice before she had a chance to run and caught her by the hair with one of his large clawed hands. Up close he suddenly seemed less comical. That beak could rip her to pieces.

'No, a girling,' he said. 'But look, she has a royal crest on her collar!'

The Turtle began to sob in despair. 'She has found us! I said we were too close to the Palace.'

Alice said quickly, 'No, I'm not a spy. I hate the Queen. Look at my back. That's what she did to me. I've just escaped from her.'

The Gryphon turned her round and examined the weals on her back and buttocks. 'Hmm, she does seem to have been punished recently. But how did you escape, girl?'

'I'll tell you everything. But please, can I have a drink first? I've been in the sea for hours.'

'Don't trust her,' said the Turtle.

'It can do no harm to listen,' the Gryphon said. He gave Alice a warning shake. 'But mind you don't try to trick us.'

With the Gryphon still holding her firmly by the hair, they led her up a steep path that cut through the tumbled rocks of the low cliff that bordered the beach and into the wood of pine, scrub beach and juniper that covered the hill beyond. Here a clear stream tumbled down to the sea through several pools. As the Gryphon stood guard over her, Alice drank deeply from one of these and washed the salt and grime from her body. Then, sitting by the bank under the suspicious gaze of the two conspirators, she told her story, starting with the Queen's devious acquisition of her from the Duchess, and emphasising every example of her misuse at the Queen's hands. She did all she could to portray herself as an innocent slave who had finally rebelled at her unjust treatment. Before she finished, the sensitive Turtle was nodding in sympathy at her suffering.

'Well, your tale seems plausible,' the Gryphon said when she was done. 'But the fact remains you have discovered our hiding place and overheard our plans. For the sake of the revolution, you cannot be allowed to return to the Queen.'

'But I don't want to go back to her!' Alice protested. 'I just want to get home. Can you tell me the best way to get to the village of Margrave? I could find my own way back from there.'

'And you might also report to your former mistress the Duchess, another of the gentry.'

'No, of course not. I mean she wasn't as bad as the Queen, but I don't want to belong to her again either.'

'All gentry are as bad as each other and the rest of the humans,' the Turtle said. 'That is why they cannot be allowed to rule over us any longer.'

The Gryphon was shaking his head. 'We cannot risk letting you go.'

'Look, I'll tell you all I know about the situation in the Palace,' Alice suggested quickly. 'Wouldn't up-to-date intelligence be useful? That'll prove I'm telling the truth.'

'Perhaps, but nonetheless, you must remain our

prisoner until the revolution comes. Either that or you must be silenced for good.'

'Hey, now wait a minute!' Alice exclaimed.

'It would be a sad necessity,' the Turtle said, beginning to snivel again. 'We hope you would understand.'

'There's a cave not far from here,' the Gryphon said. 'Perhaps we can seal you in there. After the revolution you have our word we will free you.'

'And if the revolution doesn't quite go to plan?'

'We shall not contemplate defeat!' the Gryphon said stoutly.

Alice wondered how far she could run before the agile Gryphon grabbed her again. If he could really fly as well she had no chance. As she eyed the two creatures uncertainly, she realised there was another possibility.

'I don't want to be shut up in a cave,' she said. 'Why not let me be your slave instead? I can be useful. Fetch, carry, cook, anything you want. I've been well trained. Try me out . . . masters.'

She knelt down submissively before them. It was preferable to the alternatives and it might just buy her time until something better turned up.

The animals seemed taken aback by her unexpected offer. The Gryphon recovered first. 'The institution of slavery is a product of human ruling class decadence,' he said with distaste.

'But you're not human or of the gentry, so why should that bother you?' Alice replied innocently. Maybe I can get them confused over their ideology, she thought.

'The status of girlings after the glorious day is as yet undecided,' the Turtle said. 'You are of the same original species as the gentry, after all. It may be necessary to return all girlings to the Overworld.

'By force?' Alice wondered.

'If need be.'

'I think a lot of girlings would like to stay here,' she said. 'If they're happy to serve animals, would it hurt? For that matter, a lot of animals seem to like keeping girling slaves.'

'They will have to give them up if they are judged ideologically incompatible,' the Gryphon said.

This was beginning to sound familiar, Alice thought. 'For their own good?'

'Naturally. The continued presence of girlings might perpetuate the concept of master and servant. Public displays of servility would be incompatible with the state of freedom and equality that would be enforced throughout Underland.'

'Enforced freedom? Isn't that a bit, well, contradictory?'

The Turtle hesitated while the Gryphon glowered irritably. 'We do not have time for any further discussion, girl. You must be dealt with one way or another.'

'What about my being your slave? I can be useful in lots of ways.' She lowered her voice suggestively. 'I mean, you must get lonely, plotting away out here without any company. How long has it been?'

She was getting good at reading the expressions on animal faces, and recognised the looks of acute embarrassment that suddenly filled them.

'Haven't either of you ever had a girling?' she asked.

'In fact –' the Gryphon began. 'That is to say . . . never.'

'And there really aren't any female animals in Underland?' She was aware that she might be treading on dangerous ground, but she had to play to her only strength.

The pair of conspirators looked subdued. The Turtle said sadly: 'Not sentient ones, it is true. There were a few, long ago. But as things in Underland changed they . . . went away.'

Alice didn't ask how it happened. That would have to wait for another time. She tried to sound as sympathetic as possible. 'I'm sorry. It must be very frustrating for you. But then wouldn't having some girlings around after the revolution help?'

'A society of equals working for a common purpose can rise above such things,' the Gryphon said stiffly. 'Life will continue.'

Does nobody age here? Alice wondered. Aloud she said: 'Yes, but why should it be boring or harder than necessary? Just because the gentry use girlings doesn't mean you can't as well. Maybe you can show there's a better way to keep slaves. That would prove you were the rightful leaders of Underland. And you two can start right now with me. Think of it as a social experiment. Then you can speak from personal experience when you're in charge of everything.' As they hesitated, she added, 'You will be in charge after the revolution, won't you?'

'At first it may be necessary to assume the roles of provisional leaders,' the Gryphon admitted, 'while we deal with those who supported the gentry and institute the new order.'

'Oh, I love orders,' Alice said, deliberately misunderstanding. 'I get excited at being told what to do by powerful people.' She glanced down at herself. 'Look, my nipples are already standing up at the thought. Don't you think they're pretty?'

Both the Turtle and Gryphon were looking at her with a new interest. Of course she'd been unclothed all the time they'd been talking, which had become such a normal state for her she was hardly aware of it. But now she began to feel truly naked and exposed under their gaze, and to respond in turn.

She smiled up at them, trying to look innocent and hopeful at the same time. It was not hard after so long without proper sex, and she was not about to get particular now. Her nipples were blatantly erect and her vagina wet and pulsing as her hidden passage opened. She just hoped the pair had the right equipment to fill it. (Where did turtles keep their cocks?) Now, what else could she do to encourage them? Oh, yes . . .

'Of course, you'll want to tie me down, then you won't have to worry about me trying to get away while I serve you,' she said brightly, holding out her crossed wrists. 'I'm quite used to it, as long as it's done properly, of course.'

The Turtle and Gryphon exchanged awkward glances.

'I suppose she would be no threat to the revolution if we kept her suitably restrained,' the Turtle said.

'Since she has suggested it herself, we are not acting as oppressors, unlike the gentry,' the Gryphon pointed out.

'Far from it. We would be conducting a valuable social experiment.'

'It might settle the girling question. Saving time later for more weighty matters.'

'We have been working long and hard to achieve the final victory,' the Turtle mused. 'Perhaps the cause can spare us for a little while to, er, ease our private concerns.'

'Then we will return to the struggle refreshed and rejuvenated,' said the Gryphon.

'More alert and capable,' agreed the Turtle.

'Just so.'

'In fact you might even say we are doing this to aid success.'

'It is almost our duty!' said the Gryphon.

'Then let us have her!'

They advanced eagerly on Alice, who held out her crossed wrists expectantly. They paused.

'Do we actually have any rope to bind her with?' the Turtle asked.

'Er . . .' said the Gryphon.

'There's some ivy over there, masters,' Alice suggested helpfully.

They tore strands of ivy off the tree, then dithered about, unsure of where best to secure her. They are planning a revolution, but they cannot tie up one girling properly, Alice thought to herself in disbelief. Aloud she said, 'Maybe you could use that fallen tree over there, masters?'

It was the remains of an old pine that had toppled long ago. The lower portion of its thick straight trunk now lay at an angle of about thirty degrees to the ground with a space beneath. The Gryphon and Turtle dragged her across it, pulling her arms down and back and tying her wrists behind the trunk. Alice winced as her sore back touched the rough bark but said only, 'That's right, masters. Bind me tightly so I may serve the revolution!'

They pulled her legs apart, clumsily coiling strands of ivy about her ankles. As she had hoped, neither had the right hands for tying effective knots. It would not be hard to wriggle free later, but for now it was exciting to feel the coarse strands biting into her flesh, to be at their mercy knowing what was to come. Alice saw the glistening tip of a thick shaft emerging from the base of the Gryphon's belly, while hairy testes swayed between his legs. He really was hung like a lion. But what about the Turtle? Something long and pink had popped out of the orifice between plastron and shell under the root of his cow-tail which looked serviceable.

Now the need had taken over Alice arched her back, pushing out her hips and gaping wet cunt-cleft towards them. 'I'm here to serve you. Take me, masters, please!'

'I must admit, it is quite . . . er, pleasant to see a girling offering herself like that,' the Turtle said, his cow-eyes wide and covetous, licking his lips with a long tongue.

The Gryphon was pawing at the ground, his erection standing out like a rod. 'Perhaps we should have done this earlier. I think I had better go first . . .'

'I think my need is greater than yours,' the Turtle said, his voice trembling as he put a restraining flipper on the other's shoulder. ' "To each according to their need," remember?'

'No!' the Gryphon snapped, temporarily abandoning his revolutionary principles and shouldering the Turtle aside.

Springing onto the trunk between Alice's legs he clasped her breasts with his talons, making her yelp as the sharp tips sank into her tender flesh. Beak gaping, growling and cawing in fierce delight, he drove into her with all the strength of his powerful hindquarters. Alice screamed in pain and delight as he filled her. This was real animal sex.

Resentful fire burned in the Turtle's normally mild eyes. Coming up behind the wildly thrusting Gryphon he grasped him round the waist with his flippers and, taking advantage of his greater weight, heaved him aside.

Alice moaned in dismay as the Gryphon's pizzle was pulled out of her, leaving a terrible emptiness.

The unnaturally wild calf-face of the Turtle replaced the Gryphon's avian visage. His plastron ground against her belly as his pulsing member re-filled her gaping hole.

But he had only time for a few thrusts before the Gryphon tore him away and took his place between her legs. With a snort of rage, the Turtle grappled with him once again.

Turn and turn about the two chimerical beasts penetrated Alice, each for no more than a few seconds at a time, struggling and shouting in their desperation. Under them Alice writhed in her bonds, her lovemouth sucking hungrily at whatever prick was inside her without favour. She came as the Turtle was ejecting his own seed, and she was still jerking and shuddering in delight when the Gryphon supplanted him for the last time and finally spent himself in her well-ravaged passage.

It was a while before Alice took notice of her surroundings once more. When she did it was to see the two creatures carefully avoiding each other's eyes, while conversing in abashed tones.

'That was, ah, a most interesting experience,' the Turtle said.

'Interesting, yes, exactly,' the Gryphon said, embracing the word with relief.

'Evidently we need more than one girling to avoid any potential future, shall we say, disagreements,' the Turtle said.

'Disagreements must be avoided at all costs,' the Gryphon agreed. 'Yet we have learned that girlings have their uses,'

'Undeniably.'

'With the proper re-education they might be successfully integrated into the new order.'

'We could make it a revolutionary promise,' the Turtle suggested. 'One girling for every animal.'

'An excellent idea. Meanwhile, until we can obtain another, may I suggest we share this one according to a roster?'

'Of course, my dear Gryphon.'

'Each according to their needs, my dear Turtle.'

Despite her sore passage, aching back and scratched breasts, Alice relaxed in her bonds, knowing there was no chance of her being shut away in any cave now. And as soon as the opportunity came she would slip quietly away.

For the next two days Alice played the part of a perfect slave. She prepared meals from the conspirators' frugal stores, sat attentively at their feet while they propounded their revolutionary doctrine and generally fawned over them. At regular intervals, in accordance with the roster they had drawn up, she obediently bent herself over the tree stump so they could relieve the tension such arduous plotting generated.

During that time several birds visited the wood, swooping in low over the trees, bringing urgent messages to the conspirators and leaving with new instructions. Presumably this was how the revolution was being co-ordinated, using agents like Mr Corone. As the activity intensified Alice began to wonder how near they were to making their move. It was the only thing that made her hesitant about escaping. Would it help or hinder to have the country in the throes of revolution? And if the Queen was overthrown, would she need to escape?

As they paced up and down discussing their plans, the Turtle and Gryphon occasionally paused to pet and fondle Alice. They had taken to leading her about like a dog on a leash of twisted vines. Obviously, having a girling to themselves was a new experience and they were painfully naive, playing with her almost like children. Had they ever been children, she wondered, or did they just come into existence with the rest of the place? She concentrated on appearing docile, pretty and anxious to please, while flattering them with plenty of, 'Oh, I like that, masters,' or 'Thank you, masters.'

Then a bird brought a message which sent the pair into an excited dance.

'They did it!' the Gryphon exclaimed.

'Success is within our grasp!' said the Turtle joyfully.

'Is it good news, masters?' Alice asked, trying to show interest.

'Our agents are in place within the Royal Palace itself,' the Gryphon explained. 'Your tyrannical former mistress and her entire family will soon be dead, marking the start of the glorious revolution!'

Alice went cold. 'What! I thought you were just going to overthrow her. Send her into exile, or something?'

'She has to die,' the Turtle said gravely. 'Whether now or after a trial before a revolutionary court, it must be done. She is too dangerous to allow to live.'

'But not her whole family as well!' Alice protested. 'The King's harmless and the Knave actually seems quite nice. You can't blame them for the way she acts.'

'The Redheart line must end,' the Gryphon said. 'They have no place in the new order, just as there is no place for royalist sympathisers and apologists!'

They were looking down at her with cold eyes, and Alice realised she had let her tongue run away with her once again. 'I just meant you could show her family a little mercy,' she said lamely.

'Have you been deceiving us?' the Turtle demanded.

'No!' Alice said.

'Using your soft girling body to worm your way into our affections?' the Gryphon asked with a sneer.

'No!'

'Spying on our plans?' said the Turtle. 'We cannot allow such actions to go unpunished. The people's army will decide your fate.'

'No, please –'

But they were taking no notice.

They dragged her down the path to the beach, hustling her so fast that she tripped over and slithered painfully part of the way. While the Gryphon held her leash, the Turtle dived into the waves and vanished. He was only gone a minute when he broke the surface again and waddled back up the sand.

'They're coming,' he said simply.

'Who?' Alice demanded, tugging futilely at her leash. 'Look, I'm not a spy, I'm just against killing people. I think you could be kinder. Show you're better than the gentry.'

'If you are not with us, you are against us,' the Gryphon said with flat finality.

'Here they are,' said the Turtle.

The water heaved and half a dozen articulated forms emerged from the waves. They were lobsters; dark and red and as big as people. Their whiplike antennae bobbed in the air ahead of them, their eyes dead and cold. Huge fore-claws were held out as though ready to give an embrace. Alice gave a shudder as the crustaceans came to rest in front of them, waiting silently.

'This girling has spoken against the revolution,' the Gryphon said. 'She may be a spy. Put her to the test.'

He gave Alice a shove that sent her stumbling into the semi-circle of lobsters, which closed about her. She struggled to her feet, looking for a gap to slip past them. But they were closing the circle about her, their huge claws clicking and snapping. She shrieked as pairs of long antennae brushed sensuously over her naked flesh.

They looked like something out of a nightmare rather than a children's story. If this is all a dream then this is the time to wake up, she thought desperately. But the creatures continued to advance; cold and hard and deadly.

'Tell us who you really are,' the Turtle said.

'I've told you the truth!' Alice shouted. 'I'm not a spy, I'm a runaway slave.'

The lobsters edged closer. Claws snapped about her legs and she was jerked off her feet onto her back. Her ankles were wrenched apart. More claws fastened about her bound wrists, holding her down. She was struggling in the middle of a circle of twitching mouthparts, and curious, probing antennae.

'I'm not a spy!' she shouted desperately. 'Please believe me!'

'Tell us what you believe,' the Turtle said.

A claw was fitting itself round her throat, others about her breasts, opening and closing in a terrible teasing motion, pumping them up and down as though testing their resilience. A claw tip slid into her vagina, beginning to force her open wider and wider, threatening unknown pain and pleasure.

'Long live the revolution!' Alice shouted. 'Down with the Redhearts!'

There was a commotion on the beach about her but she didn't hear it. She had her eyes screwed shut and was screaming at the top of her voice, 'I don't care – kill the Queen!'

Then she realised the imprisoning claws were gone and she was lying limp on the sand. Cautiously she opened her eyes.

The lobsters and the Turtle were no more than spreading ripples on the sea. The Gryphon was just a dark speck in the sky, beating the air with his powerful wings. In their place was a circle of mounted soldiers, looking down at her menacingly.

'It seems we've found a traitor,' said their Captain.

Twelve

It seemed to Alice that she was floating in a fuzzy cloud. A small part of her knew she was actually strapped to the Joker's test bench in the Palace, but the cloud was a nicer place to be. It was warm and there were no cares, no limits. She could do anything in the cloud.

Occasionally she was aware of distant voices, but she paid little attention to them.

'This will loosen her tongue, Your Majesty. It will subvert her natural tendencies and so negate any attempt at concealment.'

'If it fails there are simpler methods. One way or another she will tell us all their plans. Record everything she says. I will have their heads for this!'

At some point Alice became aware of fingers probing her lovemouth, parting its fleshy petals and tickling her clitoris. Then a nice fat ribbed dildo was slid up into her willing channel. She giggled happily. It was so nice to be properly plugged again. The fingers began toying and teasing with her nipples, occasionally pinching their hardness and sending little shivers of pain through her to throw her pleasure into starker relief. These were all the things she liked best. Aroused, she squirmed ecstatically in her bonds. This was lovely; this was perfect. Soon she was flushed with sexual heat, panting and groaning, a love sweat beading up her. The familiar knot of tension was tightening in her loins, winding itself up to an orgasm. And winding, and winding . . .

She wanted to come, but for some reason she could not. It was agony. Now she began to moan and tug helplessly at her bonds in frustration. 'Please, help me . . .' she called out.

'You will know release, but only after you tell me certain things,' said the Joker soothingly.

'What things?' Alice asked.

'Nothing very complicated. Let us start with the simplest. What is your name?'

'Alice Brown.'

'And how did you come to Underland, Alice?'

'I was in Shifley Woods. I'd just come out of school. It was a hot day.'

She told the story of her adventures from beginning to end. And as she spoke she felt relief seeping into her. The more she spoke the better she felt. It was a joy to answer any question put to her. Of course, it was perfectly logical. Her cunt was plugged so she could not talk through that. Therefore her mouth had become her sexual organ, gushing out an orgasm of words.

Again that small isolated part of her knew what she was doing, that she had been fed some drug to make her speak, but it was impossible to stop. She tried not to talk of Valerie or say how she escaped from the Rabbit's house, but had no idea if she succeeded. And the words flowed on and on . . .

Then she was wide awake and coldly aware of her surroundings. She was still strapped to the test bench, but now she felt empty – drained in mind and body. A gag filled her mouth. She had said all they wanted to hear.

The Joker was tidying away his vials of potion while the Chamberlain, seated beside the bench, was just finishing his notes. He closed his book with a snap and then signalled to guards who had been waiting to one side. He pointed to Alice.

'Take her to the dungeons. She is to be confined in isolation under maximum security until the trial.'

The trial took place in the Great Hall of the Palace.

Tiers of seats had been erected along its sides to hold the spectators. Other benches were set aside for witnesses: Topper and Lepus, the White Rabbit, the Duchess, Mrs Braising, the Knave and Valerie. At the far end of the room on a high dais sat the King and Queen. The King wore a judge's wig while the Queen scowled about her impatiently. Below them were birds in shorter wigs and black legal robes, and a railed stand for the witnesses. On the other side sat the jury, all nervous-seeming animals.

Alice took in the scene with dazed disbelief, unsure whether to laugh or cry. It was a parody of the trial from the end of the original book.

Could it just be chance? Or was her adventure, perhaps the adventure of any Alice who found herself transported here, always destined to end this way? Would it have come to this whatever she had done, because that was the way the story finished and she was trapped in its resonances which shaped the foundations of Underland? But this was not quite the same, she reminded herself. In the story the Knave of Hearts had been on trial for a ridiculous crime, and the nonsense had ended when Alice woke up.

This did not feel like nonsense.

She shifted her knees on the wooden floor, trying to ease the weight of her chains. They felt all too real, as did the heavy yoke that lay across her shoulders, holding her arms bent in an attitude of surrender. Double leash chains ran from her collar to the fists of the guards standing on either side of her, while more ran down to her ankles, themselves linked by a short hobble chain. She had escaped from the Queen once and was not being allowed a second chance. A sort of scold's bridle encased her head, sprung metal jaws reaching in from its gag band to clamp firmly around her tongue. When it was time she would be permitted to speak and not before.

She might have enjoyed this extreme bondage if she had not been so sick with uncertainty.

The Queen was putting on the trial as warning to anybody else who might plot her downfall. She had to make an example of somebody, and Alice seemed to be the most likely candidate.

The King called the court to order.

'We shall hear a report,' he announced, 'on the progress of the investigation into the evil and mis-guided attempt by fanatical revolutionaries to over-throw our glorious kingdom.'

The Chamberlain stepped forward. 'Working on information obtained from a suspected revolution-ary –'

Alice gave a plaintive squeak of protest only to be cuffed across the back of her head by one of her guards.

'– loyal forces were sent to various locations to arrest suspects and detain witnesses for questioning. Certain animals have gone into hiding and are still being pursued, namely the weasel Mustela nivalis and the stoat Mustela erminea, both formerly in the service of the Duchess of Margravia in the capacity of gardeners. A special watch is also being kept for a crow going by the name of "Mr Corone". The Cheshire Cat is being sought as a matter of routine, though with little hope of apprehension.'

'And what of the ringleaders?' the Queen demanded.

'Yes, what of them?' the King added as brusquely as he could manage.

'I regret to say that the creatures known as the Mock Turtle and the Gryphon cannot be found, though the search is continuing. A precautionary watch is also being kept on the coast for the appearance of lobsters in any large numbers or organised groups.'

'Have any of the revolutionaries been caught?' the Queen asked.

'Er, none I regret so far, Your Majesty. The only suspect in custody is the girling Alice Brown.'

'Then we shall try her,' the King said. 'Bring her forward!' Alice was dragged into the centre of the room and made to kneel before the assembly. 'What is she charged with?'

'Various heinous crimes, Your Majesty. Deception, escaping from lawful slavery, collaborating in revolutionary activity and publicly voicing inciting, insulting and anti-royalist slogans.'

'These are serious charges, girl,' said the King. 'How do you plead?'

'We have no time for this,' interrupted the Queen. 'Off with her head!'

'Later, my dear,' the King said. 'We must follow the proper procedures first. Then you can have her head cut off. Now, girl, how do you plead?'

Alice shrugged and threw up her hands as well as she was able, pointing to her bridle.

'Oh, I see,' said the King. 'Remove that thing.'

When Alice could speak, she said, 'I'm not guilty!'

'We shall be the judge of that, girl,' said the King. 'First the prosecution must make its case, then the defence.'

A wigged and gowned Parrot stood up and bowed to the royal couple and the court. 'I will conduct the case for the prosecution,' he announced grandly. 'I shall prove beyond a shadow of doubt that this girling is guilty of all charges.'

A Canary barrister rose. 'And I shall prove that the defendant is innocent, and that all the alleged crimes were in fact committed –' he paused for dramatic effect '– by her identical twin sister!'

'I haven't got a twin sister,' Alice said, unable to stop herself.

'In that case the defence begs leave for time to re-consider its case,' the Canary said, looking crestfallen.

'We've no time for that!' said the Queen dangerously.

'Then we shall start the prosecution case and you must catch up,' the King said.

The Prosecutor stood up. 'Ignorance of the law excuses no man, not that all men know the law (that's my profession, after all) but because it is an excuse every man (or I suppose woman, in this case, or girling to be exact. Well, let's say anyone who knows that excuse) will plead, and no man (or woman) can tell how to confute him (or indeed, her). The point I am endeavouring to make is –'

'How long will this take?' the Queen interrupted.

'I have a mere five hours of opening statements prepared, Your Majesty, and then –'

'Too long!' the Queen thundered. 'If we do not finish this today, hers will not be the only head to roll!'

There was an ominous silence in the courtroom.

'Let us question the witnesses for both the prosecution and the defence at the same time,' the King suggested quickly.

'But that will confuse everybody,' Alice protested.

'Only on average,' the King replied. 'Taken separately each will make perfect sense.'

The White Rabbit was called to the stand. He was fiddling with his watchchain and looking incredibly nervous. Alice could guess why. Had she incriminated him in her confession?

'You were responsible for bringing Alice Brown to Underland?' the Prosecutor asked.

'I meant no harm,' he snivelled. 'She was a sweet, tender young thing. Such fine ripe breasts, such a curvaceous posterior –'

'Is it true she later escaped from your care?'

'Yes, but I don't know how,' he said quickly.

Alice tensed. Did they know he kept size-changing potion?

'And you had no idea she was a potential revolutionary?'

Before the Rabbit could answer her Defence council said, 'I object! It is not yet proven that Alice is a revolutionary.'

'On the contrary,' said his colleague, 'it can be demonstrated that she is revolutionary, since she can certainly be turned round and round.'

'Objection overruled,' the King said.

'What! That's nonsense,' Alice exclaimed.

'Silence in court!' said the King. 'Gag her if she speaks out of turn again.'

Alice bit her lip. It was all mad! But the Prosecutor seemed to have finished with the Rabbit. He stepped down, flashing her a grateful smile, and Topper and Lepus took the stand.

'You trained this girl, I believe?' the Prosecutor asked.

'That's right,' said Topper. 'A natural submissive. Very passionate.'

'A fine tight rear,' Lepus added.

'We've got the declaration she signed, so legally she still belongs to us,' Topper said. 'She's a valuable girling.'

'In fact, you valued her so highly you concealed her from the Duchess of Margravia when she toured your establishment,' the Prosecutor said.

The partners looked uncomfortable, while the Duchess glowered at them.

'Is this relevant?' the King wondered.

'I am endeavouring to show that this girl has been subjected to an atmosphere of deceit and evasion since coming to Underland, which has influenced her later actions and making her easy prey to revolutionary indoctrination,' he explained.

'Well then get on with it!' the Queen commanded.

The Duchess took the stand.

'When the accused came into your possession, you had no idea she had been in training with Topper and Lepus?' the Prosecutor asked.

'No, she said she was new to Underland and I believed her.'

'You see, Alice Brown was already lying about her past,' the Prosecutor told the court.

'The jury must make a note of that,' the King said. 'Proceed, proceed.'

'Why did you choose her to test the new cowling potion, so generously supplied by Her Majesty?' the Prosecutor continued.

'Because she was the plumpest and fullest breasted of all my girlings, and I expected the best results from her.'

'You had no ulterior motive?'

'Of what are you accusing me?' the Duchess roared indignantly. 'She was the best choice, ask my cook!'

Mrs Braising was hurried onto the stand.

'Oh, yes, a fine, creamy milker she was,' the cook confirmed. 'And such a hot little box inside her, as well.'

'Faster, faster,' said the Queen impatiently.

'I call the girling slave known as Valerie,' said the Prosecutor.

'What can a slave tell us?' the King asked.

'She knew the accused from their time with Topper and Lepus, and I believe she has formed a close attachment to her. Yet she did not reveal any of this even after Prince Atheling obtained her from the same emporium.'

'That may be significant,' the King agreed. 'Put her in the box.'

'I will stand with my slave,' Atheling said, leading Valerie into the witness box. 'If she has committed any offence, then I take responsibility for it.'

A surprised murmur ran through the court.

Alice looked at Valerie standing trembling but defiant, and thought how lovely she was. Valerie flashed her a brave smile and she felt a lump grow in her throat.

'Is it true, girl?' the Prosecutor demanded. 'Did you conceal what you knew about Alice Brown?'

'All I know about Alice is that she is kind and pretty and I love her,' Valerie said simply. 'And I can't believe she'd hurt anybody, or meant anything she's supposed to have said.'

Alice's eyes misted with tears. She mouthed, 'I love you,' back.

'Even though she came into the Queen's service under false pretences,' he challenged.

'I knew she'd gone missing. I didn't know how she came to belong to the Duchess.'

'But you learned later when you talked to the accused.'

'Well, yes . . . but it didn't seem important.'

'We'll be the judge of that,' said the King.

'And was it equally unimportant that you deliberately beat her in the race on the beach to spite me?' the Queen snapped petulantly.

Valerie stood firm against the display of royal rage. 'I didn't beat Alice deliberately, it was an accident. We always lose to your favourites. Nobody dares beat you at anything, Your Majesty!'

The court gasped. 'Impertinence!' the Queen roared. 'Off with her head!'

'That is a little extreme, my dear,' the King pointed out, 'otherwise how should we punish more serous crimes? Perhaps a few lashes to teach her to mind her tongue in future.'

'Very well,' the Queen agreed grumpily. 'But do it here and now so they can all see her suffer.' And her gaze flashed menacingly about the courtroom.

'Ten lashes for the slave Valerie,' the King declared. 'To be administered immediately.'

'I said I would take responsibility for her actions, therefore shall administer the punishment myself,' the Knave said. 'Let the marks I place upon her show beyond doubt that I can maintain discipline, and that she does nothing without my leave.'

The court buzzed at this unexpected declaration. For a moment Alice was just as surprised, then understanding dawned.

Hardly daring to breath, she watched as Valerie calmly stepped out into the middle of the court just a few paces from her. Giving Alice a quick, reassuring smile, Valerie went down onto her knees, spreading them wide, and bent forward, pillowing her head on her crossed forearms. Her slender waist was dipped, her hips were pushed out and back, her bottom wide open and taut, displaying her lovely delicate pubic

245

mound. It was a posture which meant exposing herself to the maximum degree possible. But then this was to be a master's beating, and she had nothing to hide from her master. Yes, Alice understood now.

The Knave had obtained a short whip from one of the guards, and now he took up position behind Valerie.

He did not hold back his arm. The leather cracked solidly across the pale twin hills of his slave's buttocks and left a searing red blaze across the smooth skin. Alice saw Valerie's face screw up and her fists clench, but she did not attempt to draw away from the whip. The second blow fell. This time it licked around the curves of her thighs and kissed her most intimate cleft. Valerie stifled a yelp of pain, but held steady for the next stroke, which was administered with equal strength. Her master's only concession to her suffering was that the lashes were delivered quickly to reduce the agony of waiting, and so to complete the punishment as soon as possible. And Alice thought she had never seen anything so terrible yet at the same time loving in her life.

The echoes of the tenth stroke faded from the courtroom and the Knave tossed aside the whip. Valerie's trembling bottom was red-raw and crossed with scarlet and purple weals. Yet she was still hunched over in the same position, stifling sobs of pain, apparently ready to suffer further if it was asked of her.

'There, it is done as all can see,' the Knave said. He glanced at his mother meaningfully. 'Now let that be an end to any question of loyalty ... or of whose slave she is. Come with me, Valerie.'

Swaying slightly, her face red and tear-streaked, Valerie rose to her hands and knees, shuffled painfully about, then bent and kissed the boots of her master, who smiled and reached down and stroked her hair tenderly. He returned to his seat and she followed, still on all fours. She curled up by his feet and rested her head against his legs, her bottom raw, sobbing quietly, yet not it seemed from sadness.

That is true slave love, Alice thought, and now everybody knows it. Valerie really had found her perfect master and Alice did not begrudge her happiness. Yet the strange scene just played out had also served to defuse the Queen's anger towards Valerie and her master. It may have saved them both from a worse fate.

Alice realised the barristers and King were conferring under the Queen's impatient gaze. Then the King said, 'Alice Brown will take the stand!'

Alice was dragged into the witness box and her leashes tied to rails.

'You have pleaded not guilty to the grave charges brought against you,' said the Prosecutor. 'Yet this court has heard that you are in fact an escaped slave, who lied about her past to the Duchess of Margravia, and so entered the Queen's service by false pretences.'

'Look, I'm sorry I lied to the Duchess. I just thought telling the truth might get Topper and Lepus into trouble. After all, it didn't make any difference to her where I came from.'

'And were you happy serving the Duchess?'

'It was all right most of the time.'

'But according to your own confession, extracted by the ingenuity of the Royal Alchemist, you resented being transformed into a cowling by the Duchess.'

'I didn't enjoy it much, if that's what you mean.'

'Even though it was not your place to question the decisions of your lawful owners.'

'It doesn't stop me thinking about it,' Alice said.

'And do you bear the same animosity for all the gentry?'

'How can I? I haven't met them all.'

'Answer the question properly!' the King said.

'No.'

'Were you happy or unhappy to enter Her Majesty's service?' the Prosecutor asked.

'It wasn't my choice. She took me from the Duchess with that stupid competition.'

'And she then kept you for some time as a cowling?'

'Yes.'

'So you bear a grudge against Her Majesty as well?'

'Yes ... no. I mean, I don't like her, but that doesn't make me a revolutionary.'

'Ah!' said the Prosecutor with satisfaction. 'Now we come to the crux of the case. It is a fact that the soldiers who found you in the company not only of the principal revolutionary ringleaders themselves, but some of their so-called "People's Army", have sworn that you were shouting revolutionary slogans and calling for the Queen's death. Do you deny that?'

'No, but I didn't mean it!'

'So you were lying, a thing that seems to come naturally to you. Are you telling the truth about lying now, or lying about telling the truth? In either case I put it to the court that you are a most untrustworthy girling, who repays the Queen's gracious interest in you by plotting against her!'

'That's not true.'

'Your Majesty, this entire case hinges on whether this girl says what she means, or means what she says. Either way she condemns herself.'

'Very well put,' the King said. 'The Jury should make a note of that.' And there was a murmur of agreement round the courtroom.

'No, I just said what I did to save myself,' Alice protested. 'In that position I would have said anything.'

'Then why didn't you?' asked the Prosecutor.

'What do you mean?'

'Say "anything". Do you deny that you know the word: "anything"?'

'What? No of course not, but –'

'Yet you chose to utter those monstrous phrases calling for the death of our beloved Queen. By your own admission you could have said "anything", but you did not. This girling is condemned from her own mouth! I rest my case.'

There was a roar from the court. Topper, Lepus and the Rabbit were silent, staring at their feet, the Duchess was shaking her head and shrugging, Valerie was looking at her white-faced with dismay.

Alice tried to speak but she was drowned out. Then she realised there was no point. The Queen needed to make an example of somebody and she was the only possible choice. Crazy Underland logic was only the tool.

'Consider your verdict!' the King told the Jury, who bowed their heads in urgent discussion.

Using animals to condemn her was very clever, Alice thought. It looked impartial, but they really had no choice, since their loyalty was obviously being tested. And what did the fate of a girling matter to them? Better her than one of their own.

The foreman of the Jury stood. 'We find the accused, Alice Brown, guilty as charged!'

'And about time,' the Queen said grumpily. 'Off with her head!'

'Perhaps a show of clemency, my dear?' the King suggested.

The Queen turned her ferocious gaze upon him. 'Are you volunteering to take her place?' she asked ominously.

'Alice Brown, you will be executed tomorrow at dawn,' the King said quickly. 'No reprieve. Sorry.'

The words numbed Alice's brain. The whole place might function according to its own mad logic, but that did not mean axes here were not as real as the chains that bound her.

She was going to die.

The most sycophantic of the court cheered as Alice was led away. As she gave one last glance back she saw something that re-kindled a faint glimmer of hope within her.

Valerie was surreptitiously giving her a thumbs-up sign.

The cell was small and very solid, dimly lit by a couple of candles. The door was iron-banded oak, and tightly fitting. Outside were guards with strict orders to let nobody enter or leave until morning.

There was only one item of furniture in the cell: a massive frame formed of thick baulks of timber, shaped into a horizontal 'X'. Alice was stretched out on this frame and firmly secured. Solid hinged metal hoops bolted to its top were closed and padlocked over her neck, upper arms, wrists, midriff, knees and ankles. She was as completely confined as she ever had been since coming to Underland.

A bucket was a suspended at the apex of the lower cleft of the 'X' beneath her bottom for the purpose of catching her wastes. Currently it was receiving the sperm that dripped from her still flushed and engorged vagina. It had been a parting gift from the guards who had secured her and then taken advantage of her helpless posture before putting the bucket in place, knowing nothing they might do to her would be worse than what was to come.

The strange thing was she did not resent their action.

She thought of that and many other things into the small hours of the night. Sleep evaded her. The threat of imminent death was obviously an insomniac. Her mind wandered. One curious metaphor she concocted to explain her current situation was that of a cake. A cake may be wrapped in ribbon and covered with fancy pink icing but it can still have poison in the middle. She knew it lacked a certain something, but it did seem appropriate. She had bitten too deep into the improbable, sweet, ridiculous nonsense that was Underland, and now she was going to pay the price.

At about two o'clock she started to cry softly.

At ten to three, the Cheshire Cat sprang out of nowhere and landed on her stomach.

'Quiet!' he hissed, cutting short her gasp of alarm. 'I did not mean to frighten you, but I do not care to waste the effort I have spent on your behalf this night. The door is thick but we must not risk the guards overhearing us.'

Alice recovered herself enough to ask softly, 'What are you doing here?'

'I am a cat, and a superior sort of one at that,' he replied haughtily. 'I do not need a reason to be anywhere, as you should know. But in this instance, I bring a gift from your friends Valerie and Prince Atheling.'

For the first time Alice realised the normally collarless Cat had a string tied round his neck. From it, on lengths of cotton, dangled two waxy-looking ampules, one red the other yellow.

'These will aid your escape, if all goes well,' he continued. 'But understand that if you do evade execution the Queen's wrath will be terrible. You must leave Underland, and there is only one way to do that. But it will require careful timing, and there is a certain degree of danger.'

'What have I got to lose? Are those things part of it?'

'They are indeed. Your friends obtained them from the Joker's chamber. They were debating how they might pass them on to you when I dropped in. I had heard you had got yourself into the most extraordinary trouble and was curious to see what would happen next. I must say the Prince has developed quite an independent spirit recently, defying his mother, no less! I was quite impressed. Anyway, I agreed to help them. The results should be highly amusing.'

'Was that the only reason?'

The Cat tried to sound offhand. 'I admit it would be a waste to see such a lively and pleasantly scented girling such as yourself die on the whim of a mad Queen.'

'Thank you,' Alice said simply.

'Yes, well, enough of sentiment,' the Cat said briskly. 'You must learn the plan and how to use these potions. You will have to help free them from this ridiculous collar. It is the only time I regret having paws. Still, the assistance of one of your hands will be sufficient. When they are suitably secreted about your person, this is what you must do . . .'

He described the plan and hope grew within Alice. Yes, it could work. When she had everything fixed in her mind, she asked, 'So, you'll wait until they come for me?'

'Until just before. They must not suspect you have had a visitor.'

'I'm glad. I . . . didn't want to be alone.'

The Cat looked about him. 'However this dismal place offers little in the way of comfort.'

'Rest on me,' Alice said. 'I think I'm the softest thing in here.'

'By far. But you don't mind?'

Alice smiled ruefully and tugged at the metal bands that held her down. 'I'm in no position to object.

Anyway, after what you're doing for me it's the least I can offer. Sorry my tits aren't pumping out milk anymore.' She suddenly grinned. 'Of course, there is one other thing I can offer, if you want it. I'll do my best, though it won't be much of a chase, and maybe I'm too big for you now.'

The Cat arched an eyebrow. 'Really, even in your current situation? You are a remarkable girl.'

'I think fear makes me horny.'

'Then perhaps this puss should inspect your puss.'

He turned delicately around on her stomach and bent over her wide open groin. Observing her matted pubic hairs he sniffed curiously. 'You have been used recently.'

'That was the guards who put me in here.'

The Cat looked round at her thoughtfully. 'I saw tears when I arrived. Was that the reason?'

'Oh, no. That was just fear getting to me at last. What the guards did was nothing. In fact I –' She sought for the right words. 'You see, I've learned something while I've been in Underland. Things I used to worry about aren't so important. What matters is not to give up hope and having good friends. I know that sounds horribly syrupy when I say it out loud, but it's true. Back home, just before the White Rabbit found me, I was wishing for an adventure.' She grinned. 'And I got one, all right. But on the way I found out more about the real me than I expected.'

'Those sort of adventures can be the most danger- ous,' the Cat said. 'What did you discover?'

'That I like sex more than I ever imagined, but in a complicated way. I'm a masochist and submissive, but I can't just ask for it. I need to be in situations where it's forced on me, so I can enjoy being taken against my will, when the right person, or animal, proves they can master me. It's perverse but it's how I am and I won't fight it anymore. I came when the guards had me earlier, even when I thought I was going to die tomorrow. I suppose it's like taking part in a weird sort of game, except it would be too dangerous back home. But I can, could, play it safely here where people know how to treat types like me. The Rabbit must have sensed that when he sniffed me out.'

'He does have a nose for such things,' the Cat agreed.

'But I can also use what I am to keep on going, to keep playing the game. It's a sort of power, and that's given me self-confidence, which I was a bit short of. A confident submissive sounds like a contradiction, but I think that's what I am. And the real adventure is to keep testing myself against whatever comes up.' She paused. 'Except, if I have to go home now, it all has to end.'

'We shall see,' said the Cat. 'Meanwhile, I seem to be standing on the securely bound body of a self-confessed submissive masochist with time on my paws. Now, how should I spend it?'

Alice shivered with helpless delight. 'Any way you wish . . . Master.'

He padded up to her chest and sniffed at the valley between her breasts. 'I might bed myself between these for warmth, but are they soft enough? The tips seem to be going hard.' He prodded and patted the resilient flesh with his paws, his claws pricking and teasing as he did so.

Alice gasped and strained at the unyielding metal bands that encased her. 'Yes, make a bed of my tits, Master!'

'Maybe I shall. But first, I will avail myself of your pussy hole.'

He hooked his front claws over the metal band that crossed her stomach and lowered his hindquarters between her legs, bracing his rear paws on the edge of the frame. His groin pressed against her mound, his tumescent erection sliding between the folds of her labia, rubbing against her swelling clitoris, working downwards, forcing its way into the depths of her cleft. She tightened herself to embrace the small hard rod of flesh that was so perfectly defiling her.

'Use me, Master!' she whispered. 'Like I'm cat litter.'

'Never that,' said the Cat as he ground against her. 'You will always be uniquely yourself, Alice Brown!'

Thirteen

It was another perfect Underland morning. The sky was bright and the mild air, fresh from an overnight shower of rain, wafted delicate flower scents across the Palace courtyard.

It was a ridiculously beautiful day to die, Alice thought.

A large crowd had gathered, by order, in the courtyard to witness her execution. The Queen wanted everybody to see first hand the fate of revolutionaries.

As she was led out into the yard, still heavily manacled and surrounded by guards, Alice's eyes passed over the crowd. They were all there, those she had known during these last months. Those who had trained, used, or befriended her, and one small figure to whom she had to pay special attention.

Two thrones had been carried out into the yard for the occasion, and the King and Queen were already seated. The Queen looked as impatient as ever. There was no trace of compassion in her eyes as they met Alice's. Mad and tyrannical, she was no longer restrained by the storybook conventions from which she had grown. No doubt the plotters would get her one day. The King for his part looked genuinely sorrowful. Alice held no grudge against him. In his feeble way he had tried to avoid this moment.

Her eyes fixed onto the black-hooded executioner, leaning on the haft of a gleaming axe by a massive wooden block. Her stomach churned. This was it.

The Chamberlain stepped forward.

'By royal decree and warrant: this day the girling Alice Brown shall be executed for the crimes of high treason and sedition.' He turned to the executioner. 'Carry out your duty.'

The guards led Alice to the block and forced her down on her knees. Her collar and manacles were removed, and her arms stretched out to be secured by metal hoops screwed into the ends of the block, while her neck rested in a scalloped groove cut out of its edge. She found herself staring down into the wicker basket resting against the side of the block ready to receive her head. In a spasm of panic her bladder cut loose and her pee hissed and splattered over the gravel. She heard the executioner chuckle, and murmur: 'Don't worry, girl. Soon be over . . .'

He stepped back and hefted his axe.

There was a scream from somewhere in the crowd.

Alice twisted her head round to see hands waving and pointing. Floating over the courtyard, swollen to the size of some bizarre carnival balloon, was the Cheshire Cat's disembodied head.

Panic ensued. The Queen was on her feet purple with rage shouting, 'Catch it, catch it!', soldiers were running about and even the executioner had taken a few uncertain steps towards the grotesque apparition.

From being the focus of every eye, suddenly nobody was looking at Alice. She bit down on the red capsule which she had been holding in the back of her mouth, and swallowed the oily fluid contained within it.

'I am the ghost of a poor innocent cat, unfairly beheaded by cruel Queen Redheart,' the Cat moaned as he drifted lower. 'Now I have come to take my revenge!' And with a theatrical 'Whoo-oo!' he dived at the crowd.

Alice felt the air rush from her lungs as she began to shrink. For a moment her hands jammed against her wrist cuffs, then they slipped through and she was free. She scrambled to her feet and began to run unsteadily towards her target, stumbling as her size-change stabilised, leaving her about as tall as a child. Now her skin was pricking as feathers began to sprout from her arms.

The Queen was shouting, 'Kill that thing!' and guards were ineffectually throwing spears at the bobbing, weaving, mocking head of the Cat.

Alice dodged through the milling crowd, fighting waves of sickness as golden feathers replaced her hair, her arms lengthened into wings and a tail sprouted from her spine. Then her target was in front of her. She sprang forward, knocked the White Rabbit to the ground and snatched at his watch. But her hands had been lost somewhere in her new wings. She could not pick it up!

'Please!' she said to his face.

For a moment the Rabbit hesitated. Then with a smile he pulled out his watch and thrust its chain between her teeth.

She bounded clear of the crowd and across the courtyard, gathering speed, feeling talons where her toes had been scraping at the gravel. She hoped the actual flying bit came naturally, because she had no idea what came next. Beating her wings as hard as she could she sprang into the air.

She soared upwards, leaving the limits of solid ground beneath her. Another wing beat and another. Up past the turrets and flagpoles she flew, feeling the wind in her feathers as a new world unfolded around her.

It was amazing!

A flick of her tail and Alice turned her ascent into a lazy spiral. Below her the Cat's head seemed to have vanished and the Queen was now pointing up at her and screaming new orders. But it was too late now. She was beyond her reach. She was free!

The last thing she saw as she passed over the Palace walls was Valerie blowing her a kiss.

For some moments Alice exalted in her newfound freedom, weaving and soaring and diving through the air. This surpassed everything she had done before. She never dreamed it would feel so good.

Then, reluctantly, she forced herself to concentrate. It could not last, she knew. This was just a means to an end. Mixing the two potions had been risky, the Cat had explained, and the transformation might not be stable. She had to find her way home as soon as possible.

Underland rolled away level in all directions into the pearly haze. Even beyond the ragged coastline that cut a great bite out of the landscape there was no sign of curvature to the horizon. Perhaps the place really was flat.

Scanning the ground below with eyes that now seemed sharper than normal, Alice picked out the road she had taken to the Palace on the back of the Duchess's carriage. She swooped along it, flying hard, driving the air behind her, tracing its winding way back through the woods, covering in minutes what had taken hours. Over fields and past isolated houses, skirting other villages whose names she would now never know, holding who knew what adventures. Then ahead she saw the grand outline of the Duchess's mansion. A little beyond that was the village of Margrave. She circled round the straggling cottages.

Where was Topper's house? There along the lane, standing taller than the rest. She glided down, spiralling earthwards, reluctantly leaving the open air behind. The grass came up and she landed on springy feet in the back garden beside the party table. She could find her way to the great oak tree from here.

Now she must reverse the transformation before she lost her nerve. She carefully laid the Rabbit's watch on the grass and then squatted down and pushed. The yellow potion ampule popped out of her vagina where the Cat, with much pleasurable fumbling, had concealed it an hour before.

She crouched down and nipped the ampule awkwardly between her teeth, wishing she had grown wings from her back like an angel, rather than her arms. The capsule split as she worked it between her lips and a few drops fell to the grass. She sucked and swallowed the rest down hastily, licking her lips to catch it all.

The nausea struck her almost immediately and she flopped onto her back. Her skin crawled as her feathers shrunk back into her body, bones re-articulated, muscles adjusted and her hands emerged once more. Then she was growing and fighting for breath, her body mass returning from wherever it had been stored.

In a few moments she was herself again, lying on the cool grass and mourning the loss of that freedom she had so briefly known. It was hard but she had to let it go, she told herself. She had to return to reality, to her world.

For the first time in who knew how long, she thought of Wellstone, of her home, her parents. They would have given her up for dead by now. How could she have thought only of herself all this time!

Scrambling to her feet she snatched up Rabbit's watch and examined the strangely marked face with its three hands and curious concentric rings of nameless symbols. *Reset to twelve o'clock*, the Cat had told her, if you want to get back to where you began.

Alice started for the garden gate only to hesitate. She could not return to Wellstone and all its inhibitions naked! Then she thought of the trophy room in the house. Her clothes would be there, and Topper, Lepus and Rabbit were back at the Palace.

At a run she burst through the side gate, heading for the back door.

Half a dozen girls were in the yard fastened to the training frames. Limbs were bending, muscles stretching, naked breasts swaying, orifices penetrated. Fresh young bodies being shaped on the very pieces of apparatus that she and Valerie had once shared. The smell of flesh being tempered filled the yard, mingled with the lingering scent of helpless arousal and a hundred ecstatic orgasms.

The girlings looked at her with curious eyes, and she wanted to tell them: It's all right, I know it feels strange now, but you'll get used to it. I'd join you, but I've got to go back home.

Alice raced into the house, up the stairs, along the high corridor and into the trophy room. She searched the pigeon holes until she found a bundle with a dangling label that read: ALICE BROWN. Tucking it under her arm with the watch, she ran down and out through the back door again.

Something cracked against her ankles, sending her tumbling down the steps on the grass. She looked up dizzy with surprise to see the Dormouse's face leering at her, yard broom in his hands. Of course – they left him behind to look after the girls.

He jabbed the head of the broom at her, the stiff bristles scratching her skin, keeping her on the ground.

'So, Melon Tits has returned,' he said with a chuckle. 'Wondered who it was. I heard you'd been a bad girl. Escaped again, have you? I'll probably pick up a reward for this when the others get back. But right now there's just me and you, and you're going to get what I should have given you months ago.'

He jabbed the bristles into her again. 'Now, on your hands and knees and show me that nice tight bumhole of yours.'

Alice felt the tug of the invisible strings of obedience. Slowly she rolled over onto all fours and spread her knees.

'That's right,' the Dormouse said, stepping up between her legs. 'Good, Melon Tits. Show how much you want to please me.'

His small hard hands clasped and spread her buttocks. The tip of his fast rising pizzle probed between them into her humid cleft with its secret treasures.

Time seemed to stand still.

Alice looked at the helpless girlings in the yard. She knew the lure of their happy torment, the joy of surrender and the bitter-sweet depths of submission. Like them she was a natural slave. But was just anybody worthy of being her master? No, that privilege had to be earned.

'You could have had me if you'd been nicer,' she said aloud to the Dormouse. 'But I'm not Melon Tits, I'm Alice Brown . . . and I'm going home!'

And she kicked backwards as hard as she could.

As the Dormouse tumbled to the ground cursing, she snatched up her bundle and ran.

Out of the side gate then through the garden. Bare feet pounding over the grass, Alice sprinted into the wood and along the winding path, past the perfect glades and groves with their carpets of improbable flowers. She heard the Dormouse's voice through the trees. He was not giving up. Then ahead was the great oak with the dark mouth opening between its roots. She plunged into its musty coolness and looked up. There was nothing to see but blackness, yet that was the way back home.

She adjusted the hands of the Rabbit's watch until they all pointed to twelve and thought she felt it tingle. There was no time to dress, so stuffing the watch into the bundle of clothes and clasping the string in her teeth, she began to climb.

Roots and vines lined the interior of the shaft, forming a rough sort of ladder up which she scrambled. Up and up.

The light from below faded. Faintly she thought she heard an angry echo, but ignored it. How far was there still to go? Surely she had already climbed the height of the tree. Then a point of light appeared above her, as though an eye had opened.

Panting, she scrambled on. That was it. Home. She could see it was a ragged disk of sunlight now. She was almost there.

Then the trailing watch chain hooked about the end of a root. Before she could stop it, the watch was jerked from the bundle and spun away into the darkness.

Immediately the circle of light above her began to contract. No! Not when she was so close!

With a desperate heave, Alice reached the edge of the disk and hauled herself through –

– and tumbled out of a rabbit hole into Shifley Woods.

Fourteen

For some moments Alice lay still on the ground, adjusting to a different reality.

There was a windblown crisp packet on the scrubby grass, she could hear the distant rumble of motor traffic, and the tang of exhaust fumes assailed her nostrils. The beauty of mad Underland was no more. She was home.

She became guiltily conscious of her nakedness as she had not done for . . . how long? Wearily she sat up, undid the bundle of clothes and began to dress.

The fabric felt strange and scratchy next to her skin and her shoes seemed uncomfortably confining. She would just have to get used to them again. Where was her bra? Of course, she had left it here. Well that was long gone by now. She pulled her shirt tight about her, and, with one last backward glance at the innocent seeming rabbit hole, set off towards the main path.

What would she tell her parents? How could she explain where she had been all this time? If only she still had the Rabbit's watch. That would have been some sort of proof. Without it who would believe her?

There was something white and straggling lying on the grass before her. Curiously she picked it up. It was a bra. It had her name written on the label.

For a moment she could not make sense of it. How had her bra lain here all this time undisturbed? There must have been a search for her. The woods were an obvious place. Somebody would have found it by now. Unless . . .

Alice broke into a run, back along the way she had come when she had followed the Rabbit . . . how long ago?

She reached the edge of Shifley Woods. There was the line of the bypass in the distance. Here was the straggling oak under which she had sat down on that hot afternoon. And in its shade . . .

Her bag and blazer were exactly as she had left them. This was the same afternoon. No time had passed here. She was back exactly where she had started.

Alice walked home in a daze.

Dust and petrol fumes made her nose itch. She flinched at the cars as they roared past. Everywhere seemed dirty. The people were all the same size as she was. There were no animals walking and talking with them, except for a dog which was just . . . a dog.

She ran for the door of her house and fumbled with her keys until she managed to get it open.

It was blessedly still and quiet inside. She checked the hall clock. Her parents would not be back for another hour at least.

The Rabbit's watch had brought her back to the same time as well as the same place. Or perhaps time passed in a different direction in Underland, and she would always have come back to the same moment she left.

Or had it all been a dream?

The daily paper on the kitchen table held the same headlines she had seen that morning. This morning?

Surely months could not have passed between then and now.

The weight of familiar reality pressed in on her, insisting that there was no such place as Underland. She began to doubt herself. If only she had even a scrap of proof. Wait! The label written by Topper that had been tied about her clothes. That would be something. Frantically she searched through her pockets and bag, but it was not there. Had it come off in the oak tree shaft . . . or had it never existed?

Suddenly she felt cheated.

If Underland had been a dream then it had been too good. Real life could not match up. What was worse, everything she thought she had learned about herself had gone with it. Now she would have to start again.

Her clothes suddenly seemed binding, sweaty and unnecessary. Up in her bedroom she tore them off with relief. She felt dirty with town dust and grime. Her hair was dull and lank. She had rarely needed to wash it in Underland.

Or had she never been to Underland?

Was she going mad?

She went through to the bathroom and turned on the shower. Under its hot jet she soaped and shampooed herself vigorously. That felt better. But was she washing away false memories or unpleasant reality?

Her fingers slid down to wipe the soap from her pubes and then she choked in dismay and joy.

Where her pubic hair had been, she now had fine golden feathers.

NEXUS NEW BOOKS

To be published in September

NATURAL DESIRE, STRANGE DESIGN
Aishling Morgan

Natural Desire follows the efforts of the pagan Nich Mordaunt and the unprincipled lothario Anderson Croom to locate the legacy of notorious cultist Julian Blackman. Each has his own agenda, and their search takes them through a series of ritualistic and outright perverse erotic encounters towards the climax. Mothers, their daughters, and sadistic mind games feature in this novel of erotic ritual.

£6.99   ISBN 0 352 33844 X

PUNISHING IMOGEN
Yvonne Marshall

Charlotte and Imogen, the young debutantes who featured in *Teasing Charlotte*, were childhood friends whose fascination with the mysterious society beauty known as Kayla led them into a bizarre vortex of submission and domination. Now Charlotte herself is 'Kayla' – never a real name at all but the moniker for a *very* particular, very kinky high-class courtesan. Imogen, however, thinks there's room for a rival, and Charlotte must take stern measures against her old friend if her dominance is to be assured.

£6.99   ISBN 0 352 33845 8

SUSIE IN SERVITUDE
Arabella Knight

Under the stern tutelage of Madame Seraphim Savage, Susie is in training to be a *corsetière*. A keen student of fashion, Susie soon discovers that at the Rookery – madame's private establishment – discipline, correction and other special services are always in vogue. Madame's clients, it seems, appreciate the bite of the cane as much as they do the cut of their clothes. That's just as well, as madame's cardinal rule – that the customer always comes first – is strictly enforced.

£6.99   ISBN 0 352 33846 6

To be published in October

VAMP
Wendy Swanscombe

A beautiful dark-haired lesbian lawyer from central Europe travels across the sea to the legend-haunted realm of Transmarynia, where she is to help a mysterious blonde stranger prepare for residence in Bucharest. What she discovers is beyond her most erotic nightmares and may mean the end of the world as she and her sisters know it. Bram Stoker's tale of obsession and desire is turned on its head and comes up dripping with something quite other than blood. Read it and stiffen with much more than fright.

£6.99   ISBN 0 352 33848 2

GIRL GOVERNESS
Yolanda Celbridge

Sloaney blonde ice maiden Tamara Rhydden, nineteeen, thrills to her own exhibitionism and teasing. Working for a London escort agency, her aptitudes fit the job description, but Tamara doesn't 'go with' clients; she finds that some men – and women too – prefer to be spanked for their insolence. A rich slave gets her appointed as governess of Swinburne's, a bizarre academy for grown-up schoolgirls in the earthy West Country, where maids come to study 'etiquette'. The etiquette, she uneasily discovers, is that of discipline. The maids practise a role-playing, spanking cult of Arthurian chivalry ... Tamara tries to put her past behind her, but the cheeky minxes compel her to exercise her caning arm, despite the governess's new-found tastes for being governed. How will Tamara make sure her *real* needs are taken care of?

£6.99   ISBN 0 352 33849 0

THE MISTRESS OF STERNWOOD GRANGE
Arabella Knight

Amanda Silk suspects that she is being cheated out of her late aunt's legacy. Determined to discover the true value of Sternwood Grange, she enters its private world disguised as a maid. Menial tasks are soon replaced by more delicious duties – drawing Amanda deep into the dark delights of dominance and discipline.

£6.99   ISBN 0 352 33850 4

If you would like more information about Nexus titles, please visit our website at www.nexus-books.co.uk, or send a stamped addressed envelope to:
  Nexus, Thames Wharf Studios,
  Rainville Road, London W6 9HA